A Cry of Innocence

A novel of the Pendle Witches

by

Kate Mulholland

Cover and illustrations by Roy Hubbard

Hendon Publishing: Nelson.

First published in Great Britain, 1990
by Hendon Publishing Co. Ltd.,
Hendon Mill, Nelson, Lancashire.

ISBN 0 86067 129 1

Printed and bound in Great Britain for Richard Netherwood Limited,
Huddersfield by Biddles Ltd., Guildford and King's Lynn.

List of Illustrations

This story is based on fact. The people mentioned were all living in the period in which the novel is set. This is my interpretation of what happened so many years ago.

It is my intention to evoke the flavour of those times in the mind of the reader, and therefore the reader is asked not to criticise historically the contents of this book, but generally to enjoy its authentic realism.

Dedicated to the memory of
my mother
who first showed me
Roughlee Hall

Introduction

In the preparation of this book I have read many varied books and manuscripts relating to the social history and religious persecution of the years covered by my story, which are too numerous to mention.

I would, however, like to thank the Revd. F. J. Turner, Archivist of Stonyhurst College, near Whalley, for his introduction to the Catholic Martyrs, Bl. John Nutter, seminary priest, and Ven. Robert Nutter, seminary priest, of Reedley, near Burnley. Perhaps I have helped in a small way to record their lives, which were taken from them so cruelly. I would also like to mention all the authors in the bibliography, to all of whom I give my grateful thanks. Not least, my husband, for his patience on our many trips, from museums, to Lancaster Castle, to trudging over wind-swept moors in driving rain to find Firber House – now derelict.

Rose Bay Willow Herb grow now on the spot where Alice Nutter said good-bye to her son Miles, and the rutted track down which they rode is a narrow country lane, covered in tarmacadam, and used mainly as an access road to country houses, whose occupants care little, or nothing, for the fate of those poor unfortunates of a time of ignorance, the so-called Pendle Witches.

Kate Mulholland, 1990

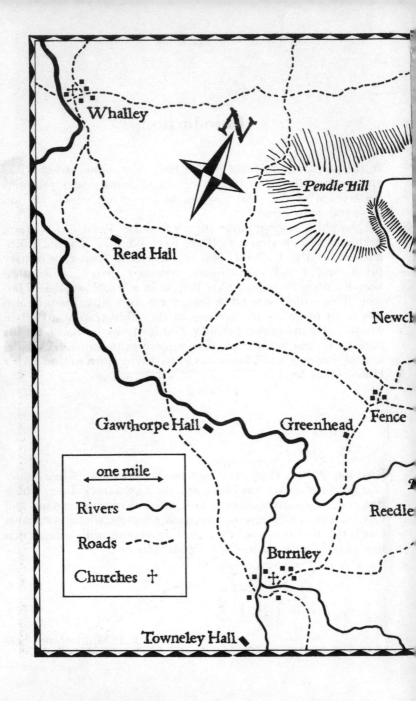

PENDLE,
1583~1612

A List of Principal Characters and Their Homes

ROUGHLEE HALL
Miles Nutter, Senior
His son, Richard (Dick) (married to Alice Nutter of Reedley)
Their children:
Miles, Junior, who became a farmer
Margaret
Charles, who became a priest
Christopher, who became a sailor
Servants:
Anne Redfern, née Whittle (married to Tom Redfern)
Their daughter Maria who married Christopher Baldwin of Wheathead
James Wilsey
Henry Mitton
Other characters at Roughlee: James Bulcock, James Hargreaves a constable, Christopher Howgate, Old Demdike's son and half-brother to Elizabeth Device.
GREENHEAD
Christopher Nutter and his wife
Their children: Robert, John and Anne
Living in a cottage on their land Mistress Whittle, known as Chattox (Anne Redfern's mother)
REEDLEY
Mistress Nutter, a widow, her children
John, Robert and Christopher (all priests)
Alice, (married Dick Nutter of Roughlee)
Servants: John and Martha Moore and Jim Lacy
BAWLE HOUSE
William and Sybil Bannister
Their children: Ruth, Joseph (who married Isobel) and others
Servants: Katherine Hewitt and others
MALKIN TOWER
Old Mother Demdike and her daughter Elizabeth
Elizabeth's husband, Will Device, the pedlar
Elizabeth's children: Beth, Tom, James, Alison, Jennet and others
WHEATHEAD
Richard Baldwin, the Miller
His wife and children, Christopher, Sarah and Anne

FIRBER HOUSE
Thomas and Martha Firber and family
READ HALL
Roger Nowell J.P.
His wife, Ellen and their children
Other characters mentioned in the book:
Doctor Gabriel, The Physician
Nicholas Assheton, J.P. of Downham Hall
John and Mary Towneley of Towneley Hall
Anne and Henry Towneley of Carr Hall
Sellars of White Moor
Sir John Southworth of Samlesbury Hall, his son, Christopher, a priest
John Law (the bewitched pedlar)

Book One

I

In the year 1583, a young girl aged about seventeen stood in the garden of her home. She was wearing a white-lace cap on her dark hair and matching lace ruff over a gown of grey which had a tight fitting bodice and full skirt. The house in the background was rambling and old, built first in the time of the Queen's grandfather and extended in the modern style several years ago. A profusion of climbing roses clung to the grey walls and lazy curls of smoke rose from some tall chimneys. A winding rutted road led away from the front of the house and she was looking anxiously in that direction.

'Alice,' called a shrill voice, 'Alice dear, is there any sign of Robert?'

'No, Mother,' replied the girl, 'but maybe Mistress Towneley needed him longer.'

Alice turned towards the middle-aged lady who, leaning heavily on a stick, now came slowly out of the front door. She was dressed in a sober black gown, relieved only by the white-neck ruff of lace and her grey hair showed briefly on her forehead. Her back hair was concealed, as was the fashion in those days, by a caul. Her face, once beautiful, was lined with pain and the fingers which clutched the stick were swollen.

'Mother,' said Alice, 'you should be resting. Let me help you back indoors.'

But even as she spoke the sound of horses' hooves could be heard in the distance, and looking quickly back towards the road, mother and daughter waited quietly as two horsemen galloped towards them. They were young men, clad in leather jerkins encircled by narrow belts. Undershirts showed briefly with loose-winged sleeves. Their breeches were gathered at the waist and they wore high-leather soft boots; on their heads were tall-crowned hats which they raised in greeting as they approached.

'Why, Robert, how worried I have been. Cousin Dick, welcome,' said the older lady.

'Mother, we were detained at Towneley,' said the first as he dismounted, and then called loudly, 'Tom, where are you?'. He

1

handed the bridle to an ungainly youth who appeared round the side of the house. 'Take Dick's horse too, quickly. Prepare another for me. I ride almost immediately.' Dick swung himself to the ground and went quickly towards Alice and took her hands in his.

'Welcome, cousin,' she said shyly. 'It has been too long.'

'Come into the house and tell us your news,' said Mistress Nutter to her son. 'Alice and Dick, do not tarry outside.'

'Bad news, Mother', said Robert Nutter as he lovingly helped his mother into the house. 'Please sit down.' They moved into an oak-panelled room where a large fire burned cheerfully in an ingle-nook fireplace. Reaching for a rope, he rang the bell and a young servant girl appeared.

'Anne, bring us refreshment, quickly.'

'Yes Sir,' she said.

Alice and Dick had now joined mother and son by the fire and Alice moved to take her mother's hand.

'It's John, isn't it?', said Mistress Nutter. 'He's been arrested?'

'Yes, Mother,' replied Robert. 'He is held at Lancaster. They were waiting as he left the boat at Warley's Creek.'

'Oh, I pleaded with him to stay in France. Why did you both come back? You know the danger. Thank God Christopher is safe in France,' and putting her hands to her eyes she tried to hold back the tears.

'Mother, I must leave as soon as I have eaten. They look for me also. I was able to escape while they were arresting John. He and I had agreed that we would not endanger both if one could escape. They will search for me here. Dick will take care of you and it is my wish that you go with him to Roughlee Hall where Uncle Miles will take care of you both'.

As Anne came in with food and wine, Robert helped himself to meat and bread, and placing more in his bag took a deep draught of wine. Holding his mother close, he whispered, 'God go with you dear, I will be back when I can. I will send you a message when I am safe again in France with Christopher.'

He turned to Alice and kissing her, he said, 'Farewell, Sister. Pray for me, and for John, who needs our prayers the most.' Then crossing himself he went quickly to the door, and calling for his horse was soon galloping away into the distance.

'Come, dear aunt,' said Dick, 'Alice and you will be safer at my home.'

'Dick, I cannot travel, my legs will not hold me. I fear I must return to my bed. Surely an old lady and a young girl are safe from arrest?'

'I will not leave mother,' said Alice.

'Then I will stay a few days until you feel stronger,' replied Dick. 'Tom shall take a message to my father.' So saying, he strode outside, and shortly, another horse was heard galloping along the same road. As the hoof beats faded into the distance, mother and daughter clung together in their distress.

'I must retire to bed, Alice,' said Mistress Nutter. 'I feel so tired, my heart pains me. Your father would have grieved if he had lived to see this day. If only one of our sons had been content to be a farmer, I should feel secure, but they were always determined to be priests.'

Anne came into the room and, putting her hand in hers, the old lady was escorted towards the staircase. They slowly mounted the stairs, and as they reached the bedroom door, Mistress Nutter asked Alice to leave her as Anne would prepare her for bed.

'Then, when I am settled, I would like to speak with Dick,' she said.

Alice went slowly down the stairs, and re-entering the warm and pleasantly furnished room, she gazed bleakly towards Dick, who coming quickly across the room, took her hands in his.

'Better days will come, Alice. Days when Roman Catholic priests will not be persecuted, when we can worship as we choose.'

'Oh, Dick, I hope so' replied Alice.

'Until then, dear, we must pay lip service to the Church of England if we are to survive. You do realise that, don't you?'

'Oh yes, Dick, I do.'

'Then, dear Alice, I will always look after you, dear companion of my childhood. You know I love you dearly.'

'I love you, Dick, and I trust you. Maybe John will escape and return to us.'

The shadows began to flicker on the walls and ceiling, and soon Anne came in to ask Dick to go and see Mistress Nutter. He mounted the stairs and walked quickly towards his aunt's room, he had stayed in the house with his cousin on so many occasions over the years. He had no brothers, and John, Robert and Christopher were his close companions, and they had chosen the priesthood. But he was content to farm with his father, who owned many acres at Roughlee in the Forest of Pendle.

Knocking on the door, a faint voice bade him enter, and he walked quickly across to the four-poster bed. The curtains were drawn back and his aunt lay against the pure white pillows. Rays of sun filtered through the mullioned windows and danced on the carpet imported from Italy. The Nutters were not simple yeomen, but educated

3

people, and their house and furnishings spoke loudly of this. Alice had been educated in France and spoke the language fluently. Mistress Nutter beckoned to Dick.

'John, Christopher, Robert and Alice were all born in this bed,' she said, 'and my dear husband died here, also, two years ago. I have known my greatest happiness in this house, and here I wish to remain until I die. These are troubled times and our religion is forbidden to us. Take Alice to Roughlee Hall. Do not betray your faith, but keep it hidden. I want Alice to have a family life.'

'I will take care of Alice,' said Dick. 'It has always been my intention to marry her and I know she cares for me also, but I will stay here awhile until you feel stronger and then, maybe, you will come to Roughlee.'

'Good boy, Dick. Now leave me to sleep. First let us pray for John, that he doesn't suffer the rack for his faith. Oh, my dear son, where is he this night?' The old lady sank into the bed, her face buried in the pillow.

Dick stood by the bed not knowing what to say, but in tune with her thoughts. Then she raised her head.

'I have asked Anne to prepare your room. Please take charge of the servants until I am able to issue orders again. Perhaps in a few days I may take the coach to Roughlee Hall.'

Dick needed no second bidding and quickly made his way downstairs. Alice was waiting, and together they walked outside, round the house to the stables. One of the farm servants, Jim Lacy, who had worked for the Nutters for many years was busy in the milking shed. He assured Dick all was well.

'I am sorry about Master John,' he said, 'but he would keep to the faith.'

'We must pray for him Jim,' replied Dick, and he and Alice retraced their steps to the house. Dick told her of his conversation with her mother.

II

Several months went by and Mistress Nutter slowly recovered. Dick divided his time between Reedley and Roughlee. Alice and her mother spent Christmas at Roughlee Hall, but the occasion was sad because of the anxiety over John's fate, and soon after the New Year celebrations Alice and her mother returned to Reedley.

Few visitors called at the isolated Reedley farmhouse which was bounded by the river at the back and approached only by a long road at the front. One day in February 1584 the clatter of hooves disturbed the silence and tranquillity of the afternoon, and horsemen were seen riding towards the house. They drew rein, and the obvious leader, a man in his early thirties, swung himself from the saddle. As Alice and Dick came out of the house, he said, 'I am Roger Nowell, Justice of the Peace at Read. These are my constables,' as he pointed to his men. 'We come with news for Mistress Nutter.' Alice stepped forward, 'I am Alice Nutter and my mother is frail. This is my cousin Richard Nutter from Roughlee. Please state your business.'

'I know Richard,' he said, and Dick nodded in agreement.

'Well, Richard, I am surprised to see you here with a family of papists who have been warned many times to embrace the new faith. You endanger yourself by being here.'

'You refer to my cousins, Roger. Their faith is their affair. I am here to care for my aunt and cousin Alice. Now please state your business and leave us in peace.'

Roger Nowell unrolled a scroll and read out the proclamation that John Nutter, Seminary Priest, of Reedley Hallows, was executed on the 12th February 1584 at Tyburn. 'I also have a warrant for the arrest of his brother Robert, also a known priest,' he said.

'Robert is not here,' said Dick as he put his arm around Alice, who had fallen, half fainting against him. At the same moment there was a cry from inside the house and Mistress Nutter, who had been descending the stairs, lost her footing and tumbled to the bottom with a cry. Alice spurred into action and rushed to her mother, crying to Roger Nowell who was following her.

'You have murdered my mother, begone immediately.' She knelt, sobbing by the still form of her mother.

Nowell turned to Dick, and speaking quietly he said, 'I am sorry, Dick. I had no intention to cause added grief. Please let me send a physician to Mistress Nutter.'

'Oh, mother has opened her eyes,' cried Alice. 'Please help me to

5

lift her and take her back to her room.' Roger and Dick came forward and gently Mistress Nutter was carried upstairs and laid in bed.

It was late evening. Roger Nowell and his men had long departed and Alice and Dick sat quietly by the fireside.

'What am I to do, Dick?' Alice asked. 'I do not even know where John's body will be laid to rest.'

'Alice dear, these are evil days. You must look to your own future with me and a life at Roughlee Hall.'

'When mother has recovered I will come,' she said.

The following morning, when Anne entered her mistress's bedroom and drew back the curtains from the four-poster bed, she leaned over. Speaking gently, she said, 'Are you awake, dear Mistress?' then, looking closer, she realised that the shock of hearing of her son's death, and the fall downstairs, had been too much for the frail lady. She had passed away in her sleep, as she had wanted, in the bed where her dear children had been born and where her husband had died.

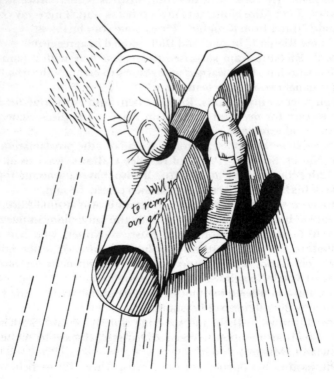

III

It was a cold spring day when Roger Nowell and his friend Nicholas Assheton urged their horses along the stony track towards the Pendle Forest.

'I have a mind to see what goes on at Reedley these days,' said Roger. 'No word has been heard of Robert Nutter, he must have left the country and joined his brother, Christopher in France. I hope they stay there. It does not please me to hound them. I studied with them at Towneley, and I grieve that religion must make us enemies.'

'Yes, it would be a difficult thing to betray our friends,' replied Nicholas. 'Personally, I will look the other way if I see one of them.'

'Well,' said Roger, 'I have not initiated any searches or investigations since Mistress Nutter's death. Young Alice's look on the day I had to call was venomous. I know she blames me for her mother's fatal accident.'

'Mistress Nutter had been ailing for years, Roger. 'Twas said she had a failing heart, and her limbs were swollen with rheumatism.'

'I know,' Roger replied, 'but the shock of John's execution was the last straw. I wish I had broken the news easier.'

'There is no easy way to break news like that,' said Nicholas.

'It is at times like that I miss my father,' said Roger. 'He was older and wiser and would have chosen his words more carefully. It irks me to realise what is lacking in me.'

'The law says you must ferret out and punish papists and recusants,' replied his friend, 'you have no choice until the law is changed.'

'I thought Queen Bess would have relaxed the laws, but maybe she is scared of the papists herself,' said Roger.

'Her father started it and she may finish it. You will never get the whole population to worship in the same way.' Nicholas spurred on his horse.

Dropping down through Goldshaw Booth, they crossed the Pendle Water riding hard. Fording the river once more they arrived at the Nutter farmhouse. A dog chained to a gate gave warning of their approach. A man-servant came towards them.

'Good day,' said Roger. 'Are you in charge here?'

'Yes, Sir,' said Tom Lacy. 'Miss Alice married her cousin Dick in February. She will not be returning here. Her home is at Roughlee.'

'She will be kindly treated there,' said Nicholas. 'Dick Nutter is a good man.'

'Let us ride to Roughlee,' said Roger.

'I doubt your welcome there,' replied Nicholas.

'I'll risk it,' Roger replied. 'Miles Nutter has no quarrel with me,' and, spurring his horse, he was off down the track.

They were soon passing through the village of Fence, then, riding hard uphill, they drew rein and gazed down into the valley below, dominated as it was by Pendle Hill, which was carpeted at this time of the year by rust-coloured bracken. Sparse trees grew from gulleys, and sheep grazed where they could find some vegetation.

'There is something brooding about Pendle,' said Nicholas. 'It holds secrets.'

'It holds poverty too,' replied Roger, 'and poverty breeds lawlessness. There is not enough employment for the people, and since the dissolution of the monasteries there are too many beggars roaming free.'

Together they picked their way downhill to the Pendle Water, and following it to the right, they galloped for perhaps a mile, passing several mean hovels with hens picking round barren earth, and mangy dogs tied outside. Shabby children played in the dirt by the stream.

Suddenly, through the trees, they saw the chimneys of a large house, low and mullioned, gable peaked, comparatively new and prosperous looking, with neat walls and a pretty garden. A dog rushed out barking and men-servants turned from their labours and stared at the two gentlemen. An elderly man dressed in homespun jerkin and leather breeches approached, hand outstretched.

'Master Roger and Master Nicholas. Welcome to Roughlee. Please come in and have refreshment. I have a good October ale for you to enjoy.'

'Thank you, Miles,' replied Roger. 'We have had a long ride. We called at Reedley to see how Mistress Alice was and were told she was here. I trust she is recovering from her bereavement?'

'Seeing you brings it all back, Master Nowell,' said Alice, coming from the house, a frown on her face. 'Do you hound me here then?'

'No, no, Mistress Alice,' said Roger. 'It gave me no pleasure to bring those bad tidings and I ask your forgiveness for the manner in which I told you. I lack the gentle touch, which I hope I will learn.'

'Now, Alice,' said Miles, 'do not blame Master Nowell for the troubled days in which we live. Please be good enough to arrange refreshment for these gentlemen.'

'I will, said Alice, 'and I accept your apology Sir.' Alice turned towards the kitchen with a glint of unfriendliness still on her face.

Dick Nutter arrived at the house and came forward, hand outstretched. 'Good day friends, please excuse Alice, she frets for her mother and her brother.'

'Understandably so,' said Roger. 'However, I wish you happiness in your marriage.'

'I too,' said Nicholas, and the three young men walked into the house.

There was comfort in Roughlee Hall. Miles Nutter was a prosperous and sensible man. He had a well organised farm, flocks of sheep, cows and poultry, and Dick had been an apt pupil, who now worked for his father. But he had been educated at Towneley Hall, so was not ill at ease with the two gentlemen he had known for many years, and with whom he had studied. Alice had spent three years in a convent in Douai, France, and also mixed well with the young squires. Their home was the most refined and sophisticated for many miles, and Roger and Nicholas were pleased to accept hospitality from the Nutters.

A fire glowed in the ingle-nook fireplace; Alice stood by a long oak refectory table and supervised as the servants brought in the ale in tankards, large platters of cheese and home-made bread. Pasties, pickles and spices accompanied the feast, and Roger and Nicholas were quick to enjoy the repast.

When, later, they were cantering homeward, Roger said to Nicholas, 'Alice Nutter is a handsome girl, and Dick is lucky if he tames her. I have a fancy for her myself.'

'For shame, Roger,' said Nicholas, 'and your wife shortly expecting your first child. But I agree, Alice is a fine young woman, educated and attractive.'

'Ellen was chosen for me,' said Roger. 'My father looked to the Newcastle coalfield her family owned and the financial benefits I would derive from the coal, and out of sheer laziness I acquiesced, but Ellen has not the education or the conversation of Alice, or you my friend. That is why I search you out so often,' and urging his horse forward, he broke into a gallop.

Back at Roughlee, Alice was standing at her window, with drooping shoulders, when Dick came and placed his arm around her. 'Roger Nowell did not execute John, my dear,' he said.

'He brought the news,' said Alice, 'and for that I find it difficult to forgive him.'

'Someone had to bring the news,' replied Dick.

Miles continued to oversee the farm at Reedley. He often asked himself why, but it was profitable, and Robert and Christopher needed the money on their various visits to England. If he was ever discovered hiding one of them, he knew that at the very least he would have to pay a massive fine. The Towneleys were constantly paying fines for recusancy, as well as spending long periods in prison.

The house was a problem. Alice consistently refused to even visit there and check it over, but Miles was a man with foresight and he felt the time may come when Alice would need a refuge such as this house could offer. He appointed John Moore and his wife Martha to run the farm, and made rooms available for them. They were to run the house as if it were inhabited. A fire was always to be blazing in the hearth, and the furniture polished. All the rushes had been cleared from the kitchen and the stone flags cleaned, while sheepskins gave warmth. Dick and Miles always called on their way back from Burnley.

John Moore and his wife, and the stable lad, Jim Lacy, were trustworthy and loyal. Reedley was a suitable venue for friends when it was possible to celebrate a mass, usually in winter when darkness came early and the moon was new.

This sixteenth century was a time of oppression and intolerance, socially and religiously, and only the strong survived. The law of the land gave great credit to those who would extirpate Roman Catholics.

On many nights a small group of horsemen would cross the Pendle Water and urge their horses towards Reedley. On one such night Roger Nowell reined in his horse on the road to Fence as Thomas Firber passed by. Roger knew where he was going, and turning for home he noted the date with a malicious expression, making a mental note to make further enquiries.

Luckily for the gathering, Roger Nowell was not a man to forsake his warm fireside without a definite reason, nor was he prepared to risk his social life by antagonising his neighbours. He was more discreet and would pass on the information rather than take action himself. He had a healthy respect for Miles Nutter and had no intention of crossing him, although he knew the Nutters were at the centre of Catholicism in the area, second only to the Towneleys.

Christmas brought news of Robert and Christopher by a pedlar passing through, one Will Device, who called at Roughlee Hall and asked for Mistress Alice Nutter. Being shown into the kitchen he began to produce samples of ribbon, and trinkets, carefully selected from the cart outside. Alice began to examine the ribbons. The pedlar lifted the edge of the tray and she saw a letter in Robert's handwriting. Carefully checking to see there were no servants in sight, only Anne Whittle her close confidante, she slipped it into the pocket of her dress, and controlling her excitement, she ordered the goods she required. Then asking Anne to prepare ale and meat for the pedlar, she went upstairs.

Will Device was a Welshman who travelled the country with his wares. He was tall and dark, welcome in the kitchens of houses great and small. He was entrusted with messages from lords and servants alike because he was totally trustworthy and a master in the art of self-preservation. He had been at Roughlee Hall the previous summer and asked Anne Whittle of news of Elizabeth Demdike, who lived in the village at Malkin Tower.

'She is well, Will,' she said, 'but it is said she is carrying your child, the third one.'

'I know, I know,' said Will, 'but I will make an honest woman of Elizabeth. I shall help her whilst I am here,' and finishing his repast he rose quickly and hurried out of the house. Making his way northwards he came to Malkin Tower, a house of stone with a roof of slabs and saplings. A curl of smoke rose from the rude chimney and several hens pecked outside.

Two children clad in ragged clothing ran towards him, and picking one up under each arm he said, 'Good day to you Beth and Tom,' and going to the door he pushed it open with his foot.

Elizabeth was standing by the fire. She was in an advanced state of pregnancy.

'Will, you have made me the object of derision again,' she said, 'Richard Baldwin, the churchwarden, had me in the stocks again. I am unable to work. My mother is nearly blind and is a cripple.' She broke down in sobs.

'Come, my dear. I have good food and money for you and we will arrange our marriage before I leave. In the meantime you must understand that I have to go. I have messages to deliver far and wide, but whenever I go, you know I always return.'

Elizabeth's sobs subsided and he tenderly put his arms around her. The children eagerly set about searching his pack for the sweets he had brought them.

Meanwhile, Alice was showing Miles and Dick the letter from her brothers. It gave news that they were both safe in France and were not planning to return for some time.

'I can look forward to Christmas now, Dick, knowing they are safe,' said Alice, 'although it will be the first without mother.'

IV

Food for Christmas was prepared in grand style. Busy in the kitchen with Anne, Alice listened to the gossip of the village.

'And Will Device, the pedlar, has married old Demdike's daughter Elizabeth at last. He was ready to murder Richard Baldwin when he heard she had been in the stocks again.'

'Richard Baldwin is a pitiless man,' said Alice, 'Maybe as he gets older he will become more kind. I feel sorry for his wife and children, he is so stern.'

'My dear Madam', said Anne, 'were it not for you, maybe I would be a beggar. My mother has only me and Beth to offer her support, and she grows stranger every time I visit her. She sees people who aren't there, and calls to animals I cannot see. I fear her sanity is leaving her, and her teeth chatter all the time I am there.'

'You must visit her this Christmas Anne,' said Alice. 'I will ask Tom Redfern to escort you. He is home from his duties at Gawthorpe Hall. I know you like him,' she said with a twinkle in her eye. Anne blushed and hurried to tend the fire.

On Christmas Day, Alice and Dick, together with Miles, rode on horseback to Newchurch for the service. It was frosty, and a pale sun peered out of a cold blue sky. The church was cold, and Alice hoped the sermon would not be too long. She studied the congregation and met the gaze of Roger Nowell, sitting with his wife, who was heavily pregnant. Alice was surprised to see Ellen there so late in pregnancy. She had heard Ellen was from Newcastle, where her father owned a coal mine. They were very rich, as coal was now widely used. Miles Nutter had extended his chimneys to take the extra smoke from the coal be burned now, in addition to the logs.

Alice felt herself tremble as she remembered the dreadful day when she heard the news of John's death and her mind went back to other Christmas days when she was young, and her father, mother, brothers and herself had sat round the table at Reedley. Her hand found Dick's and he smiled at her, pressing her fingers in his. As long as I have Dick, she thought, I can face anything.

Outside the church the congregation gathered to talk to their neighbours, and Roger Nowell made his way over to Alice and Dick.

'Allow me to present my wife, Ellen,' he said. Alice made a small curtsey and held out her hand.

'I am pleased to meet you,' said Ellen, in an accent Alice had not heard before. 'I have few acquaintances in Pendle and I would be pleased if you would visit me.'

Alice looked at the honest, open and rather plain features of the other woman, who was not much older than herself. She felt dislike for Roger Nowell but pity for his obviously lonely wife.

'I will be happy to call upon you, Mistress Nowell. I will ride to Read when the weather allows. I wish you happiness in your confinement and a speedy recovery.'

'Thank you, Mistress Nutter. I will be happy to welcome you,' replied Ellen.

Snow was falling heavily and Miles called to them that they should be returning home without delay. As Roger and Dick doffed their hats at each other, Alice turned to follow Miles. At the gate the Nowell carriage was waiting, with the arms of Nowell emblazoned on the side. Little conversation was entered into on their way home, all quiet with their own thoughts, and all eager for the warmth of Roughlee Hall.

On their return, Alice ran quickly up to her bedchamber, and unlocking a small oak box, she removed her rosary, and taking it in both hands she knelt by her bed in prayer. As she rose to her feet Dick came into the room.

'Do you feel you have really been to mass now, dear?'

'Oh, Dick, I do wish Robert or Christopher could share this Christmas Day with us,' she said.

'They will some day,' he replied, 'but for today we have each other, and maybe next year, a child of our own.'

'Oh, I hope so Dick,' said Alice. 'I pray for that also. I envy Ellen Nowell her pregnancy, but now to our Christmas meal.'

Anne Whittle, and two small maids about fourteen years old, were busy in the kitchen, and soon the table in the dining-room was filled with food. A large stuffed goose was placed in the middle of the table, and small salvers of ham, chicken and pork were arranged around it. There were dishes of beans, turnips and leeks. Herb sauces, prepared previously by Alice, were carried steaming hot to the table. There was October ale, and wine from France, and following grace, they all did justice to the food.

Talk flowed freely between the three who were close friends, as well as family bonded, and for a while their recent tragedy and bereavement were put to one side and serenity settled on the scene.

'I was surprised when you accepted Roger Nowell's invitation, Alice,' said Dick.

'Ellen is far from home, and I cannot imagine Roger Nowell as a good husband,' she replied.

'He is like his father,' said Miles, 'selfish and arrogant and covetous of what others have. His father fixed the marriage, as the girl comes from a respectable but lowly family, who gained their riches by the discovery of coal under the fields they were farming. Ellen is their only child and her parents are ailing. She is their heiress and it is said she brought a large dowry to Roger Nowell. Her family thought they had done well to marry Ellen to a country squire.' Miles gazed ruminatively into the flames leaping in the ingle-nook fireplace.

'Roger Nowell was more proficient with his sword than his lessons at Towneley,' said Dick, 'I was careful not to cross him, but Robert, John and Christopher often had disagreements with him, and he was always quick to deny any leanings towards the Faith.'

Miles smiled at him, 'John, Robert and Christopher would be sharing Christmas Day with us if they had but paid lip service to the Church of England,' he said.

'I do not like Roger Nowell,' said Alice decisively, 'but I will be friendly with his wife because I think she needs a friend.'

The following day saw Alice, warmly dressed, with breeches of fine leather, wool cloak and high hat, accompanied by Anne, distributing the remains of their Christmas Day feast to the poorer homes nearby. Children clamoured for the sweet things Alice had made, especially from recipes learned in France, sugar mice and marzipan.

Whilst they were at the door of a tumbledown cottage by Pendle Water, a horseman drew rein.

'Good day to you, Mistress Nutter,' said a deep voice. Alice turned.

'Good day to you also, Master Baldwin. I am sharing my good fortune with this family who nearly starve.'

Richard Baldwin was dressed in austere home spun. He had long black leggings up to his thighs. His expression was hostile as he looked at Alice.

'The Lord will provide,' he said.

'I am the instrument of the Lord, and without such as I, in these sad days, he is unable to provide,' replied Alice.

'John Hargreaves should be at work on the land,' said Richard Baldwin.

'He has had an accident,' Alice looked sternly at the man. 'I have just dressed a deep wound in his foot, sustained while chopping a tree for fuel. He is unable to walk. Where is your pity Sir?'

Baldwin ignored the remark, and turning his horse he galloped away, without a farewell.

'He is a mean and wicked man,' said Anne, 'I am afraid of him.'

14

'No need to be afraid of him,' said Alice. 'Just avoid him.'

Returning home, Alice and Anne were overtaken by a young man of about twenty years on horseback.

'Good day, Mistress Nutter, and Anne. Why I had hoped to have a word with you today,' he said.

'Good day, Tom. Please escort us home and you may take refreshment with Anne.' Alice smiled at him warmly.

Tom Redfern was a pleasant young man. He worked for another branch of the Nutter family at Greenhead, Fence. This was Miles's brother, another Christopher, for whom Miles felt no closeness. This family made a great show of their apparent conversion to the Church of England, and avoided contact with any who may bring doubt on this conversion. Tom Redfern had showed a quickness and aptitude to learn, and when Christopher's son, also named Robert, had gone to serve the Shuttleworths at Gawthorpe Hall, he had taken Tom with him.

Seated cosily in the farmhouse kitchen, Tom waited for Alice to leave the room, then turning to Anne, he said urgently, 'Anne, I have missed you my dear, let us marry now and you can live with my parents in their cottage at Greenhead whilst I am at Gawthorpe.'

'Oh, Tom,' Anne replied, 'I am so comfortable here with Mistress Alice. Do not ask me to live with your parents in their cottage. I would not even have my own room. Let us wait until we have a home of our own. Maybe a cottage will be available at Roughlee, where I can still be of service to Mistress Alice when you are away.'

Tom caught Anne by the hand, and gazed earnestly into her face. 'I want you for my wife. Please meet me before I return to Gawthorpe at New Year, I must see you again,' He allowed himself to embrace her.

Anne, content in the circle of his arms, replied, 'I go to visit my mother at Greenhead tomorrow.'

'I will come over and escort you back there,' Tom assured her.

'I am worried about my mother,' said Anne. 'She becomes more strange each time I see her and I fear she needs a physician who understands these things.'

Anne's mother, widow Whittle, known as Chattox because of the way her teeth chattered continuously, lived in a cottage on the Nutters of Greenhead land. Her husband had been in service to them all his life. When he died, they had allowed her to stay. She carded wool for Mistress Nutter at Greenhead Farm and eked her miserable living by begging, and by what Anne and her other daughter, Beth, could take to her. Beth was in service at Gisburn, and did not visit often, thereby leaving much of the burden of her mother on Anne.

Tom left after enjoying his refreshments, assuring Anne he would return in the morning.

V

The following day dawned bright and sunny. Tom arrived on horseback, and Anne climbed up behind him, holding her basket of provisions. In just over an hour they were approaching the cottage, little more than a hovel where Widow Whittle lived. They had to pass Greenhead Farm to reach it.

As they cantered slowly by, a young man, aged about twenty-five, dark and saturnine of appearance, dressed in the clothes of a gentleman with leather breeches, matching jerkin, and thick woollen shirt, called to them.

'Tom and Anne. Good to see you.'

He looked Anne up and down in appraisal. She was a pretty girl with fair, curly hair and rosy cheeks. She wore a good woollen cloak provided by Alice Nutter.

'Has Mistress Alice recovered from her brother's execution and her mother's death?' he asked.

'She is as recovered as may be possible after such sad events, but she is happily married to Master Dick,' Anne replied and averted her gaze. Robert Nutter had made advances to her in the past and she was a little afraid of him.

'Please ride on,' she whispered to Tom, and he, looking somewhat surprised, called, 'Good-bye Sir, see you tomorrow when we return to Gawthorpe,' and urged his horse forward.

Robert watched them go, a calculating frown on his face. That girl becomes prettier every time I see her, he thought, I must look for an opportunity to speak to her when she is on her own.

Anne and Tom had by this time reached the mean hovel where her mother lived, and Anne went quickly inside. A few sticks were smouldering in an open grate and smoke filled the room. Rushes were strewn on the floor and a rude table, cupboard and several small chairs, were all the furniture in the entrance room.

Anne went through a doorway, and in the next room, on a bed covered in blankets, once clean when supplied by Alice, lay Widow Whittle, dazed of eye, and with chattering teeth. Anne took her mother's hand as the vague eyes tried to focus on her.

'Who are you?'

'Oh, Mother, it is your daughter, Anne.'

A little understanding appeared in the vacant gaze. 'I am hungry Anne, I have twisted my ankle and I cannot get out for food.' She tried to raise herself from the bed and Anne saw the swollen foot.

'Oh, please Tom, go to your mother's house and ask for some bands to tie up this foot, and some hot water to wash her.'

Tom left, and hurrying across the fields, soon came to his parents' cottage. It was a cottage, somewhat larger than Anne's mother's, and in a much better state of repair. A few hens picked outside, and inside, the rushes on the floor were fresh and new.

The Redferns had been in the service of the Greenhead Nutters for as long as Tom could remember.

'Mother, can you not do any more for Anne's mother?' She seems to be poorly.' His mother looked up from the pot she was stirring. 'Oh, it's Anne, is it. I hoped you would meet someone better bred, now you are at Gawthorpe.'

'We have had this out before Mother. I have always loved Anne, and I intend to marry her soon.'

'She is not coming to live here. We would have her mad mother round every day.'

'Anne will not agree to live with you, even if you welcomed her. She is much too comfortable at Roughlee Hall.'

His mother looked unappeased. 'Anne Whittle has big ideas now she is all but lady's maid to Alice Nutter, but she won't get away from the Chattox, who will live a while yet. Her mind is going but her legs can still carry her into Burnley and Padiham to beg.'

'If you gave her more work, she would not need to beg, and her legs cannot carry her today. She has hurt her ankle, please supply me with bands to bind her ankle and water to wash her.'

Grumbling, Mrs Redfern produced the necessary articles and, with a bad grace, ladled an amount of stew into a container and handed it to her son. He quickly thanked her.

Widow Whittle became more alert when she had eaten the stew and sampled the provisions Anne had brought for her.

Anne gently washed her face and carefully bound up her ankle. 'I wish I could take her to Roughlee,' she told Tom.

'I am not leaving this cottage. I was married here and I brought up my children here.' Her mother looked sharply at Anne.

'Well Mother, you have enough food for a few days, so you may rest your ankle. I will try to visit again soon.' Anne stooped and kissed her mother.

'Anne, I think we should leave now. It has started to snow, and we must try to make good progress in the daylight.' Tom looked anxiously outside.

'I am ready to go now,' Anne replied, looking at her mother who was still eating ravenously. She bade her goodbye.

Outside, they mounted the horse. Noticing that the snowflakes were starting to stick on the ground, they hurried the horse uphill, past Goldshaw Booth, beyond Fence, up the hill over Noggarth, and down the steep gradient into the Pendle Water valley.

As they approached Thorneyholme, the horse stumbled badly and they were both thrown onto the ground. By now, they were in a blizzard, with the flakes of snow cutting mercilessly into their faces.

'We are nearly at Thorneyholme,' Tom gasped. 'If we can get there, Christopher Hargreaves will give us shelter until the snow is over.'

The walls of a house loomed up in front of them, and Tom began to hammer on the door. Minutes went by.

'No one at home. They must be Christmas visiting,' he said. 'I'll see if I can open the barn door.' Tom reassured Anne, who was shivering with cold. The door of the barn opened easily.

'I'll at least be able to tie the horse up. It won't carry us again today. We can rest a while, and then we will have to walk. Do you feel able to walk the rest of the way?' Tom asked.

'When I have rested,' Anne replied.

It was warm in the barn, and several cows mooed uneasily. 'Oh, Tom, I am so cold, my hands are numb,' said Anne tearfully.

Tom took her hands in his, rubbing them. He soon had the circulation going and they became pink and warm. Tom looked into Anne's face, which was now rosy and glowing, and leaned forward and kissed her.

'I seldom see you alone, Anne, and I have longed to tell you how much I love you and whisper words of affection in your ear.'

Cupping her face in his hands he kissed her again. She held up her face to him, kissing him in return. She closed her eyes and he kissed the lids, her cheeks, her chin, and then her throat, and as his hands moved downwards she stumbled backwards and they fell together on to the soft straw. His hands moved over her body and, fumbling with the fastenings on her bodice, he kissed her breasts.

'Oh, Tom, please stop,' she gasped. At the same time, unable to resist, she relaxed in the straw and gave herself up to a new feeling of weakness and longing. Putting her arms around him she held him close.

When later they lay together in the straw utterly spent, Anne said, 'I wanted to wait.'

'I could not wait any longer Anne,' he replied, 'but we will marry on my next home leave from Gawthorpe.'

Tom rose and walked to the door, opened it, and looked out. The snow had stopped and a watery sun was trying to break through the clouds. It was about three of the clock.

'We have about an hour of daylight left,' he said. 'We should be in Roughlee before dark if we set off now.'

Leaving the horse they started along the road, the snow was deep in parts where it had drifted and Tom helped Anne as much as he could. They were silent for most of the way, both engulfed in their own thoughts, reliving their moments in the barn, Anne overcome with guilt, but happy.

'I'm not regretful, she thought, I am going to marry Tom. I have always been going to marry Tom. Ever since I was a little girl I have admired him. Holding on to his arm and listening to his encouraging words, they trudged through the snow and came at last to Roughlee Hall.

Henry Mitton, who ably managed most things round the farm for Dick and Miles when they had business elsewhere, and whose home was a small cottage near the Pendle Water, came out of the barn as they arrived. He was a short, stocky man, ruddy faced and inclined to obesity, but had a cheerful smile.

'Mistress Nutter has been very worried about you Anne. Thank God you are safe,' he said. 'Tom you must stay the night at my home, you should not attempt to return to Greenhead tonight.'

'Thank you Henry, I will be pleased to accept your offer. I have to collect my horse from Thorneyholme when it has rested.' Tom turned to Anne, 'I will see you into the house first.'

As they entered the house, Alice came quickly into the kitchen. 'Anne, I am pleased to see you safely home. What a storm! How is your mother?'

'Oh, Mistress Alice, she is ill. She had sprained her ankle and nearly starved.'

'You must take more provisions for her shortly,' Alice smiled at Anne.

'Mistress Nutter,' said Tom, 'Anne has consented to marry me and I wish to marry her as soon as possible. We would like to rent a cottage from you, if there is one available. Anne would like to remain in your service.'

'I am so glad for you, Anne and Tom. Miles and Dick will find a cottage for you. There are several which require repair. Leave it with me. Now, come Anne. You look frozen. I will ask one of the girls to prepare a bath of hot water for you.' She went out of the room.

'I will arrange for the bans to be called at Newchurch, Anne, and we will be married when next I have leave at Easter.'

20

Tom embraced her. Then taking leave, he hurried out to join Henry Mitton and enjoy a tankard of ale in his cosy cottage.

Roughlee Hall was not short of comforts. A room by the kitchen was set out with a large tub which could be carried upstairs, if needed, by the family or guests. Alice insisted her servants had a bath each week, which was not the usual custom in those days. Alice was democratic for her time, which made her popular with her servants, but unpopular with a section of her neighbours, who did not believe in lifting up the lower classes, as they called them, or treating servants well.

The young servant girls quickly filled the tub and Anne sank gratefully into its enfolding warmth. Alice had called for hot bricks to be placed in Anne's bed, and the fatigued girl was soon asleep.

Tom was a man of his word, and the wedding was arranged for Easter Saturday when he would once more be on leave from his duties at Gawthorpe.

VI

On a blustery day in March, Alice decided she would at last make her promised visit to Read Hall. She was accompanied by James Wilsey, a yeoman of Pendle Forest, who looked to the Nutter's horses, and was happy to accompany Alice on her local visits or shopping trips as far away as Preston. James had arranged to see a horse he might buy from a farm at Read whilst she paid her visit. James, like Henry Mitton, found the Nutters to be fair employers, and considered himself to be their friend also, a feeling which the Nutters reciprocated.

Alice had heard that Mistress Nowell had given birth to a daughter and she hugged the knowledge that she herself would have a child later in the year, and would not be able to ride out on horseback much longer. Sadness overcame her as she thought of her brothers, and how they would share her joy. No word had been heard from them since Christmas.

Alice was dressed in the latest riding habit, a doublet, cut like a man's, with tight fitting sleeves and a cloak of russet wool. Instead of the usual long skirt she wore wool breeches and soft high leather boots. She rode astride her horse, as did many country ladies. It was safer than riding side-saddle in the terrain of Pendle Forest. With her glowing skin, soft-brown eyes and dark-wavy hair, she was the picture of health and happiness.

Roger Nowell was just leaving on horseback as she arrived, and he lifted his hat with a flourish. 'Good day to you, Mistress Nutter,' he said, 'My wife will be most pleased to see you. She has few friends in Pendle, and has talked of you since Christmas.'

'I must congratulate you on your daughter's birth,' Alice replied.

'Thank you, and good day,' he said, wheeling his horse, he was off into the distance.

A man-servant opened the door and Ellen Nowell came into the entrance hall with outstretched hands.

'Oh, Mistress Nutter, how glad I am to see you. Come and see our daughter, Elizabeth.'

Alice followed her, and as she stared down at the sleeping infant in the cradle she confided to Ellen that she herself was also soon to be a mother. The two women became immediate friends, and when James Wilsey called for her at three of the clock, Alice was sorry to leave.

'You must visit me at Roughlee, Ellen. Promise me you will,' Alice insisted.

'I shall indeed, dear Alice. I am so glad to have made a friend. I have been so alone, and the local so-called gentry do not befriend me because they consider I am more lowly born.'

'Ellen,' replied Alice, 'The day will come when class will not matter; when a person is judged on their own merits and achievements, and personality will be more important than who your father was.'

'Maybe, Alice, but I doubt we will live to see it, may be our children will.' Alice kissed Ellen lightly on the cheek, and mounting her horse she rode away with James.

Alice mused on the differences between herself and Ellen. I feel ten years older than Ellen, she thought, and yet I am not. Maybe it is because of what my family has suffered that I have aged, but I see further into the future and hope more hopes than anyone else I know. When I have children, I will teach them to right wrongs, to practise no discrimination and to be fair in all things.

Thinking happily of her first child growing inside her, she entered once more into the forest, with James riding silently behind her.

As Alice descended the hill at Downham, she noticed a crowd of people. James overtook her, and motioning her to wait, went down by the stream, where he saw Richard Baldwin with a whip in his hand, and Elizabeth Demdike, now Elizabeth Device, cowering back, her hands held up to protect her face, her two young children clutching at her skirts.

Alice had by now taken in the scene and, galloping towards them, she saw Baldwin's whip lash out, and as it curled around Elizabeth's waist, it caught one of the children who screamed loudly.

'Whatever is the meaning of this Sir?' asked Alice, white faced.

'Baldwin turned to her. 'Since you ask, this woman has not been to church these last two Sundays and I take her to Read Hall to face the magistrate.'

The woman turned to Alice, tears streamed down her muddled face. 'I am with child, Mistress Nutter. I have not been well. My husband has gone selling his wares and I am unable to make the journey to Newchurch.

'Put your whip away, Master Baldwin. You are inhuman to treat a woman so, and her with child. I will be her guardian and I say you are not to harm her further.'

Baldwin looked at Alice, with eyes flashing murderously. 'Papists guard papists, do they?' he said. 'We shall see. I will report this matter to Master Nowell.'

'Do so with pleasure,' replied Alice, and reaching down, she picked up Elizabeth's younger child, and placing her in the saddle in front of her, she said to the mother, 'Make your way quietly back to Roughlee and collect Beth there. I will have refreshment prepared for you.'

Elizabeth stumbled off with the small Thomas holding stoutly to her hand. The other villagers moved away. Richard Baldwin and Alice Nutter faced each other.

'I will see my day with you, Mistress Nutter,' he said. 'You will interfere once too often.'

'Do you threaten me, then?' she asked.

He made no answer, but turned abruptly, mounted his horse, and set off in the direction of Read. Alice turned to James.

'Well, James, and what think you?'

'I think you have an enemy,' he replied.

'What harm can he do me,' said Alice, and spurring her horse, she galloped off, the small Beth clinging tightly round her waist.

Once at Roughlee she lifted the child from the horse, and taking her into the house, she called Anne. 'Please bathe this child and give her some food.'

'Why, Mistress Alice, it is little Beth from Malkin Tower,' Anne looked questioning.

'Yes. I have just saved her mother from a whipping by Baldwin.'

'What did I just hear?' Miles entered the kitchen.

'Oh Father, come and I'll tell you.' Arm in arm they walked into the dining-room.

Over supper that evening Alice told Dick and his father she was sure she expected a baby in August. Glasses were raised, filled with Miles' famous claret, which he imported from France and a toast was made to the yet unborn addition to the family.

VII

A cottage had been made habitable for Tom and Anne, and two weeks before the wedding – arranged for Easter Saturday – Anne went over to see her mother to try to persuade her to come and live with them at Roughlee. Mistress Whittle was in a more lucid state than Anne had seen her for some time, and she recognised her daughter immediately. The cottage was cleaner, and a pot was boiling on the hearth.

'No, Anne. This was my home when I was married and had my family. I will stay awhile longer. Mistress Nutter, at Greenhead, has given me more carding to do and the Redferns have been kinder to me since your betrothal to Tom. Robert Nutter brought me fire-wood yesterday. He was asking after you.'

'I do not like him. He is too bold,' Anne replied. 'I have something to tell you Mother, I am to have a baby. It will be born in September.'

'But how, when?' her mother asked.

'Something happened between Tom and I at Christmas. I do not regret it. No one else knows, only you and Tom, not even Mistress Alice.'

Anne left some food and clothing for her mother, and bidding her farewell, she set off for Roughlee, feeling happier about her mother than she had done for a while. Taking a short cut, she bypassed Goldshaw Booth, and striking upwards she saw a horseman galloping towards her. With sinking heart she recognised Robert Nutter of Greenhead.

'Good to see you, Anne,' he said, dismounting. Anne looked downwards, 'Anne you do not seem friendly?'

'I am in a hurry to be back in Roughlee. Mistress Alice expects me.' She started to turn away.

'Wait a minute Anne, I hear you are soon to be married. Spare me a while of your company,' he walked towards her. Anne looked wildly around. No one was in sight. Clouds hung low and grey, and fields and trees hid her from sight. He smiled, but his eyes held no humour.

'You are very pretty, Anne. Spare me a kiss. Tom will not miss one,' he laughed cruelly. She shrank away from him in fear.

'You bewitch me, Anne, Why do you choose Tom? I have more to offer than him. He took hold of her by the arm.

'No, no, leave me. You do not know your place,' she said, trembling.

He grew angry. 'Know my place, with the daughter of mad Chattox, from the hovel! What place is that?'

He grabbed her by the hair, 'I will have a kiss,' he said and bent his head towards her. She struggled, and slipping on the damp turf, she fell. He fell on top of her.

She continued to struggle and rolled away, she scrambled to her feet. He rose, and hitting her hard across the head, knocked her to the ground again. He was a powerful man, now angry and lustful, and resentful of her refusal to accept his attentions. He hit her again and she curled up, half-stunned and terrified.

Robert dragged her to the shelter of a clump of trees and, hitting her again until she was almost unconscious, he tore open her clothes and raped her. She lay sobbing until he raised himself from her numbed and pain-filled body.

'So,' he said, 'Tom was there before me? I thought to be the first. Or was it Tom?'

Anne lay sobbing, not looking at him. He kicked her over on to her back, and, with his foot pressed against her throat, he said, 'Not a word about this, or your mother will be swum as a witch and her hovel will be raised to the ground. Understand? Tell Tom and he will not return from our next foray into Wales,' He kicked her again.

'Understand?' His foot pressed into her and she nodded mutely. He strode away towards his horse. Anne, raising herself feebly, called after him.

'A curse on you, Robert Nutter, and on your family, and may you be the one who meets with an accident in Wales.'

All she heard was an ugly laugh as he mounted his horse and rode away. Anne lay for what seemed hours, and then crawling first, then staggering, she came to Roughlee Hall.

'Anne, Anne, whatever has happened?' cried Alice, seeing the battered face and torn clothing, 'Who has done this to you?'

'I don't know, I don't know. It was a stranger', and Anne collapsed on the floor.

Easter Saturday dawned. Anne, now recovered, was being prepared for her wedding.

She had pleaded with Alice not to pursue the matter of the attack, saying she did not want anyone else to know what had happened to her and the attacker would have fled the area anyway.

Alice knew that desperate men often lurked in country places. Indeed, since the dissolution of the monasteries, gangs of vagrants roamed, displaced from their homes and lands, and she thought Anne lucky to have escaped with her life. If she suspected Anne knew more about her attacker than she had said; Alice did not question further.

Anne had confessed she was already having a child, as she was afraid she would lose the baby, and she wanted Alice to know it was Tom's, but she pleaded with Alice not to tell Tom of the attack. He had been away and had not seen her bruising, and she feared if he knew he may question her, and she would tell him, and then what would happen between him and Robert Nutter?

Anne went happily to Newchurch with Alice and Dick, and was married to Tom in a quiet ceremony. Returning to Roughlee, the happy pair entertained the villagers, who cared to call, to ale and meat in their cottage. Miles, Dick and Alice joined in a toast to their continued health and happiness.

On Easter Sunday, at Newchurch, Roger Nowell made his way over to Alice after the service.

'Greetings, Mistress Nutter. I have had a report from Richard Baldwin, who informs me that you interfered with the course of justice recently,' he said, with a hint of a twinkle in his eye.

'If justice be whipping pregnant women, then I interfered,' she replied.

'I am afraid Richard Baldwin has little pity in him,' Roger said. 'I told him he should temper justice with mercy, but he was not appeased. I am afraid he will hound the family whilst the pedlar is away.'

'Elizabeth gave birth to a boy last week. He is to be called James, so she will be excused from church for a while,' said Alice. 'The old woman, Demdike, is nearly blind, and they rely on the pedlar to return soon. I hope he does.'

'Why, Alice, how are you my dear?' Ellen had walked up behind her husband. 'When will you visit us again?'

'I am not riding now,' replied Alice, 'but you have not returned my visit.' Turning to Roger Nowell, she said, 'Please accompany your wife to Roughlee soon.'

'I will indeed,' and bowing, he turned to Nicholas Assheton. 'Good to see you, Nick.' The two men walked slowly to the gates. Ellen smiled at Alice and assured her she would see her soon. Then she hurried after her husband.

Richard Baldwin, his wife and small daughter, walked past Alice. His wife smiled shyly, but Richard merely nodded, with a hostile gaze.

27

VIII

On a warm July day, Alice was cutting roses in her walled garden. She was happiest here, and had copied the layout of the garden from one in Douai, where she had been taught in a convent. There were beds of roses divided by small paths, with a sundial to record the passing time in the centre. In another part of the garden Alice supervised the growing of herbs and vegetables, she spent many hours there, particularly since she was well advanced in her pregnancy.

Anne came into the garden to tell Alice that Will Device, the pedlar, would like to show her his wares.

Alice quietly asked Anne to send Will into the garden. He may have a message from one of my brothers, she thought. Will had his usual supply of braids and ribbons, and Alice chose a selection, then she spoke to him about his family. 'Will, you must give Elizabeth more support. Richard Bladwin means her harm.'

'I know, Mistress. I do my best and I leave what money I can, but as you know, I am needed in many places, by many people. I thank you Mistress, for your defence of my wife at Downham.' Saying this, he moved a comb aside in his tray, and Alice saw a rolled piece of paper. She quietly retrieved it, placing it in the pocket of her kirtle. She invited Will to step into her kitchen for refreshment.

When she had instructed Anne to serve Will with food and ale, she hurried upstairs, and with trembling fingers opened the roll of paper. It was, as she had hoped, from her brothers Robert and Christopher. She learned that they were both well and Robert promised to visit her soon. Oh, how I long to see him, she thought, but he is placing himself in danger if he comes here.

Later, discussing the letter with Miles and Dick over supper, she and Dick were surprised when Miles, after first checking the parlour door was bolted, walked to the fire-place, and pressed a rose designed in the panelling. A panel swung back revealing a flight of steps.

'Go down, Dick. Alice, you stay here. The stone steps are damp and you may fall.'

Dick disappeared, returning a couple of minutes later.

'I built this hiding place myself,' Miles said, 'No one else knows of it. If Robert comes he will be safe here. It has ventilation, and a cess drain. I have disguised the water outlet into a drain from the barn. A person could remain there several days without fear.'

However, no word was heard from Robert, and in early August

1585 Alice gave birth to a son. As she and Dick gazed on their sleeping infant, Dick said, 'What are we going to call him?'

'Miles, after your father, and John, after my father and brother, I thought. What do you think?' Alice gazed apprehensively at her husband.

'That is a wonderful idea,' said Dick, 'I will tell my father now,' and leaving the room, he searched for his father. They returned together and Dick said to him, 'Let me present your grandson, Miles John Nutter.'

Miles felt tears of joy cloud his vision, and bending he kissed the small puckered face. 'God grant you a happy life,' he said.

Invitations were sent out for the christening, the following month, and on a mellow September day, with the trees alongside the river golden in their autumn colours, Alice and her baby son were conveyed by carriage to Newchurch for the baby's baptism.

Thomas Firber and his wife, Martha, from Firber House, near Barley, were the godparents, and everyone of eminence in the area were present. Roger and Ellen Nowell, Ann and Henry Towneley from Carr Hall, Sybil and William Bannister from Bawle House, old friends of Alice and Dick, with Henry Mitton and James Wilsey rubbing shoulders with richer men in this democratic gathering.

Alice allowed herself a moment's sadness when the baby was christened Miles John, as she remembered what a fine young man her brother had been, and how he had been prepared to die for his faith.

Back at Roughlee Hall, Alice happily introduced Sybil to Ellen Nowell. Looking round the guests Alice felt glad that, in this area at least, there were no social barriers as existed in other parts of the country. Feeling the need for fresh air she wandered into the garden, where she was joined by Roger Nowell. He complimented her on her cooking and asked if she had grown the herbs which flavoured her meat dishes.

'Yes, I brought my recipes from Douai. The French cook their food in more interesting sauces than the English generally. I like to emulate them.'

'I wish that I had met you before I met Ellen,' said Roger momentarily forgetting himself.

'You speak out of turn, Sir,' said Alice. 'I was always promised to Dick. I love him dearly.'

'Forgive me. I was admiring of your education and culinary expertise, and your skilful way with entertaining. Ellen does not have your graces.'

'Remember, Ellen brought you a large dowry, so I hear,' retorted Alice, and turning from him, she hurried into the house.

'Well said! Madam,' Roger replied, following her into the house, a sardonic smile on his face. Inside again, Roger looked around him. The Nutters had a lovely home. He had been in great houses where the hospitality was poorer than he had received today.

Miles walked over to Roger. 'You have been admiring Alice's garden?'

'Yes, and Alice too. She is a most remarkable girl. She appears older than her years.'

'Sadness and realism have caused that Sir, and the times in which we live. However, let us talk of other things. Have you heard of my latest venture?'

'And what is that?' asked Roger.

'Coal,' replied Miles. 'I bought several hundred acres a few years ago. They extend from Blacko hillside towards Gisburn. Dick and I have had several men excavating for some time now and we have found stocks enough to supply this area.'

'I am impressed,' said Roger. 'As you know, my wife's parents own a large pit in Newcastle on the river Tyne.'

'I believe we are standing on deposits of coal throughout Lancashire,' said Miles. 'I have orders already for most of the large houses in the neighbourhood, and I can employ many who have been unable to work to support their families.'

'I heard you bought the Greystone land,' said Roger. 'I was interested in it myself, but I had not thought of coal.' The two men moved towards the servants who were refilling glasses.

Roger Nowell, deep in thought, watched the proceedings and enviously observed Alice's demeanour as she attended to her guests. Miles, always generous with his wine, mingled with his friends. The atmosphere was happy and congenial. May it always be so for Alice and Dick, Miles said the prayer within himself.

When the last of the guests had said their farewells, Miles, Dick and Alice stood together in their dining-room and congratulated themselves on the success of the day. The baby, Miles junior, crowed happily in Alice's arms. He thrived, Alice would not allow him to be put to a wet nurse, but fed him herself.

IX

Word came that the pedlar Will was gone again, leaving his wife once again with child. Richard Baldwin watched the family closely, ready to pounce at the first sign of poverty, but for now the family were comfortable.

Anne Redfern's baby was born the week after the christening, and Alice employed another villager, Jane Bulcock, to help her during Anne's confinement. Jane soon learned to make the sauces Alice excelled in.

Tom Redfern came home as often as possible, and although Anne could not now visit her mother regularly, Tom arranged for his mother to see that the Widow Whittle always had enough to eat and fuel for her fire.

As soon as Anne was fully recovered she brought her baby daughter with her to Roughlee Hall every day. She and Tom had named their baby Maria and she slept in a basket every day whilst Anne did her work.

Anne's sister, Beth, in service to the Listers at Gisburn, visited Anne to see her baby and was also able to go to Greenhead and check on their mother, who seemed abler and stronger than she had been.

Autumn passed. There was a new baby at Wheathead, but no celebrations were held at his christening. Richard Baldwin's wife was a shy, reserved woman who did not mix with the villagers.

One frosty evening when the family at Roughlee Hall were sitting down to supper there was a knock on the door. Shortly after, Jane entered the room to say a pedlar visited. Miles, expecting it to be Will Device, asked her to bring him in to the room. They looked towards the doorway. The pedlar entered, and closing the door behind him, turned to face them.

'Robert,' cried Alice, and rushing to him, she threw her arms around her brother. Joyful tears rolled down her cheeks as she was enclosed in his warm embrace. Miles and Dick gathered round him, shaking his hand and pressing refreshments on him. Alice called to Jane for extra savouries, chicken and ham. Miles opened a bottle of the best Bordeaux wine he had been saving for Christmas.

However, Robert's news wasn't good. He described to them his landing at Warley's Creek and the dour-faced constables waiting to question all of the ship's crew in their search for returning priests. He had been able to avoid detection, had bought a horse from a friendly farmer and ridden first to Samlesbury Hall, where he had

31

received a warm welcome from Sir John Southworth, and a change of horse. His next refuge was Towneley Hall, from where he had come that day. He was aware of dangers faced by those who harboured him.

'I have left the horse in the stable, Dick. You will be able to return it for me?' Dick nodded.

'Now, let me see my nephew.' Alice took him upstairs to the room where young Miles was sleeping, pink fingers in a little rosebud mouth.

'May our Dear Lord preserve him from all harm,' he said, kneeling and crossing himself. Alice knelt beside him. 'Whilst I am here, Alice, let us celebrate a mass with our close friends.'

'Robert stayed in the house, not using the hiding place, but keeping to his bedroom most of the day. Anne and Jane were totally trustworthy and saw to his meals. The younger servants, keeping to the kitchen and dairy, were unaware of the extra resident in the house. When they had gone home to the village in the evenings, Robert shared the family meal. Only Anne and Jane were trusted, the other servants might talk to their families, given the opportunity of seeing Robert. But no one came to the house, the weather was wet and cold and the days were short, and it was not difficult to keep Robert's presence a secret.

Miles had extended his invitation and on Christmas Eve, after darkness fell, the Nutters were joined by their friends to celebrate a mass. Sybil and William Bannister, Ann and Hugh Towneley and John and Mary Towneley, with their cousin John of Grays Inn, only recently released from prison as a recusant and recovering from his ordeal at Towneley Hall. The Firbers completed the gathering. Prayers were said for Robert's safety whilst in England.

He left Roughlee on Christmas Day, being a day when most people were too busy feasting to be interested in escaping priests. Alice kissed him goodbye, with tears in her eyes, but she had enjoyed his company for longer than she had expected and did not urge him to stay longer and endanger himself. He rode towards York and friends.

He left behind him an atmosphere of happiness and well being at Roughlee Hall.

X

In the small cottage by the river, Anne Redfern nursed Maria. She was melancholy, missing Tom, who was once again serving with Sir Richard Shuttleworth, somewhere in Cheshire. Anne had begun to visit her mother again but she was always terrified of meeting Robert Nutter. She knew a visit was due. Her sister Beth could not travel from her position at Gisburn very often, and she was worried about her mother. She determined to visit the next day.

Leaving Maria with Jane at Roughlee Hall and carrying items of food provided by Alice, Anne set off. It was a brisk April day, with blue sky and white clouds scudding before the sun. Pussy willows waved in the breeze and ivy peeped out of cracks in the stone walls. An hour and a half or so later she was passing along the top of Greenhead Lane and she saw smoke curling from her mother's chimney. She quickly crossed the field and went into her mother's house. It was empty and she looked round, the fire was burning brightly and the room was clean and tidy. She held out her hands to the blaze when a shadow darkened the room. She turned, and saw, filling the doorway, Robert Nutter.

'Go away,' she cried, feeling trapped.

'So, you have left our child behind,' he said.

'She is not your child, Maria is Tom's,' Anne cried.

'Oh, I was right, you laid with him before me. You are a slut, but a pretty one, methinks. I will let Tom follow me again.' He strode forward, and lifting her in his arms, carried her into the bedroom and threw her on the bed. Ignoring her struggles, which were useless against his brute strength, he ripped open her clothes and raped her. She sobbed, her whole body shaking. She pushed at him, cursing him over and over. He rolled off her on to the floor as she scratched at his face, she rose from the bed and lunged at him, grabbing his legs and screaming.

'I'll get even with you, if it takes me all my life, I'll get even with you.' He tried to kick her hands from his legs, and she heard her mother's voice.

'What is happening, Anne, is that you?'

Robert pushed the terrified woman to one side and, without another glance in Anne's direction, left the house.

Anne cried helplessly and hopelessly. 'He will not leave me alone. What can I do? He threatens Tom if I tell. He did it before. Oh Mother, tell me what I can do?'

'When did it happen before?' her mother asked.

Anne sobbed out the story of the rape and beatings in the wood. Widow Chattox sat quietly for a moment, digesting this information, then she said, 'I was told by an old-wise women how to bring pain.' She disappeared into the kitchen returning with a mug of ale for Anne. 'Drink this and lie down until I return.'

Half an hour later Anne was recovering and warming herself by the fire when her mother returned. In her hands she held wet clay, and as Anne watched intrigued, she began to mould it into human shape.

'This clay is Robert Nutter,' she said. Then in a frenzy, or so it seemed to Anne, who wondered if her mother had taken leave of her senses, she threw the image to the floor, stamping on it and screaming obscenities at the name of Robert Nutter.

As the Chattox sliced the head from the image, Christopher Nutter, Robert's father, appeared in the doorway.

'What is this screaming and ranting woman? I heard you from the road?'

'Your son Robert has raped my daughter!'

Christopher Nutter went outside. They heard him call, 'Robert, answer these charges!' Robert Nutter lounged in the doorway.

'I had a dalliance with the girl. She did not object, she is a slut.'

Anne shrank back. 'I did object! Oh, Sir, I did! He raped me,' she sobbed.

Chattox flung herself on Robert, clawing him and scratching his face. Now out of control, she cursed him over and over.

Christopher pushed his son before him out of the house and turned to him.

'You have brought our name to this. Are there not enough women in the towns without you forcing your attentions on Tom Redfern's wife?'

'You heard her cursing me. She means me harm,' Robert replied angrily.

'The woman was out of her mind in defence of her daughter, you fool. Return to Gawthorpe and I'll try and smooth things over.'

'Turn the old woman off our land if you want to see me again,' Robert shouted to his father.

'Be grateful I will keep this from your mother and sister,' his father replied as Robert swung himself on to his horse. 'Get you gone!'

Christopher Nutter returned to the house. 'I apologise for my son's conduct. You have my word it will not happen again. I can only say to you, Anne, that should this matter be reported further, more distress will be brought to you. Your husband will want revenge on Robert. They may injure one another. Indeed, one of them may be killed. Do you want that?'

'No, no. I fear for Tom. Robert has raped me before Sir. Honest to God. I am afraid to visit my mother.'

'You need be in fear no longer. You have my protection whilst I live, and your mother is safe in her house. I will undertake to provide her with food and fuel.'

'Thank you Sir. I will trust you,' Anne replied.

'You have my promise. I will see to your mother.'

Christopher Nutter smiled briefly at the two women and left the house. Further along the road, Robert Nutter was approaching Burnley when he met his brother John.

'I had a little dalliance with the Redfern woman and her mother has cursed me. I am bewitched by her daughter, but the hag means me harm.'

'You imagine it. What can she do?' replied his brother, but Robert was in no mood to continue the conversation and spurring his horse he rode to Gawthorpe.

XI

In 1586 Alice gave birth to her second child, a girl, Margaret, and as they welcomed their friends to Roughlee Hall after the christening at Newchurch, it seemed their happiness was complete.

Miles raised his glass and made a toast to the health and happiness of the baby. The deep red claret, rich in the fire-light, reflected on the glasses of pure crystal as their friends echoed the toast.

Few letters came from France with news of Robert and Christopher, no bad news either, but the persecution of Catholics in England continued. Queen Elizabeth was kept in a constant state of anxiety and suspicion regarding a claim to the throne by her Catholic cousin Mary, Queen of Scots, who was supported in her claim by many English Catholics. The Nutters' neighbour, Thomas Southworth, of Samlesbury Hall was foremost in the attempt to bring the Church of Rome back to its former glory. Edmund Campion had been arrested for sending Catholic literature from a secret press at Stonor Park, and following torture on the rack, he was executed at Tyburn.

Margaret Clitherow of York was arrested for harbouring a priest and was sentenced to the punishment known as *peine forte et dure*. She was stripped and a sharp stone was placed under her back and heavy weights crushed her. She took 15 minutes to die.

All these pieces of news filtering through to Roughlee, warned the Nutter family, and their friends, of the importance of maintaining an outward appearance of acceptance to the Church of England.

In 1587 came the news of the execution of Mary, Queen of Scots, following an alleged plot to overthrow Elizabeth, and the persecution and hounding of Catholics continued.

In the spring of 1588, Sir Richard Shuttleworth, and a contingent of men, rode through the Roughlee Valley. He drew rein outside Roughlee Hall, and Miles and Dick walked forward to greet him.

'We have received orders to prepare beacons on the highest points across England. They are to be ready to alert the country in the event of an invasion,' he told them. 'The constables of the village will need help and assistance and I would be grateful if you could organise the beacon on Pendle Hill.'

'Is it feared the Scots may retaliate for the execution of Queen Mary?' asked Dick.

'No, young man,' replied Sir Richard Shuttleworth, 'worse. We have received information that Philip of Spain is preparing an Armada of ships in order to attack us. He no doubt wishes to see the Inquisition set up in England. I say thank God we have said goodbye to the evils of the Roman faith,' and wheeling his horse and signalling his men, he rode away.

'What is happening?' asked Alice, coming towards the two men, holding Margaret in her arms, young Miles trotting beside her.

'Do not fear, dear,' said Dick, 'there is a possibility that Spain will invade us and we are ordered to prepare a beacon on Pendle Hill.'

The whole village, it seemed, assembled the following day. No work was done in the fields or in the mine. Men, women and children from all the surrounding areas gathered at Barley with carts and trucks. Relays of men toiled up the side of Pendle and erected a bonfire such as had never been seen before.

In the village the alehouse keeper was busy distributing hot stews and pies, bread and ale, and it became more of a festival than a preparation for disaster.

Guards were organised to watch the beacon through the day and night. They were to watch for the flare from Beacon Fell, at Preston, which would signal the time for lighting of theirs. Roger Nowell, Nicholas Assheton, or Miles Nutter were to be contacted immediately this flame was seen. The beacon was not to be lit without one of them to give the word.

There was excitement and apprehension. Young Miles screamed with terror when the largest animal he had ever seen was led past him on a chain by a man playing a flute. Another walked beside him crying, 'bear baiting tonight. Come and see the bear baiting tonight,' ringing a bell as he walked.

'Oh Dick,' said Alice, 'I must take the children home, it is becoming more like a fair day than a day of national emergency. Someone has even produced a maypole.' Sure enough, in the centre of the village, a maypole fluttered gaily. Richard Baldwin rode grimly towards the merry-makers and demanded that the maypole be taken down.

'This is a time for praying, not for tomfoolery and pagan pastimes. Get down on your knees and pray for deliverance,' he shouted, laying about the crowd around the maypole with his whip.

Miles Nutter rode over to him. He, too, could lose his temper if he must. 'Stay, stay your actions Baldwin,' he cried, 'these people are not breaking the law, merely making light of a situation which may prove deadly, but in the meantime they do no harm. I demand that you stop your unlawful punishment.'

James Wilsey rode up behind Miles, then Dick, and Thomas Firber appeared, with John Bulcock bringing up the rear. A silence descended on the throng of villagers. Baldwin realised he was outnumbered by the Nutters and their friends. Wheeling his horse he cried, 'I will see my day with you, Sir. Your championing of these common, ignorant people will bring you pain in the future. They should be taught humility not pagan licentiousness. There will be drunken brawling this night through your leniency.'

He galloped away and the yokels sent up a cheer, but Miles Nutter held up his hand. 'Carry on and enjoy yourselves, but do not betray my trust in you. Be to your beds by midnight and at work again tomorrow.'

37

Miles rode off in the direction of Roughlee, accompanied by his friends, and sitting over supper in the dining-room, Alice said she feared the repercussions from Wheathead.

'Baldwin's children are never allowed to enjoy themselves,' she said. 'He is a bigot, a puritan at heart. There is no gaiety in their home.'

'What can he do to us, dear?' Dick asked her gently, 'his mill is dependent on the water that runs through our land, and he mills our flour. We are his good customers.'

'Nevertheless,' she said, 'I always fall foul of him, and now you, all in defence of the poor people.'

'Baldwin is a feared and hated man,' said Thomas Firber. 'He is welcome nowhere and he rules his family with a rod of iron. He has a son and two little girls who are always dressed in sober clothing. They never smile, are never allowed to play with the village children, and their mother is a drudge. You should hear how Baldwin speaks to his wife. We treat our servants better.'

'No more of Baldwin,' put in Miles. 'Do not spoil our supper. Eat and enjoy. I have received a consignment of the best Bordeaux wine. Go to the cellar, Dick, and bring up a bottle. We will drink to the defeat of any Spanish Armada which sails against us.'

The villagers remembered for years the great beacon which was lit on Pendle Hill when word came that the Armada had been sighted. The sky had been alight from Ingleborough and Pen-y-ghent, right up to the Scottish borders when they climbed the hill. There was excitement and apprehension in the farmsteads until a horseman brought the news that Sir Francis Drake had sailed his ships out of Plymouth Hoe and destroyed the Spanish Armada, with the help of a great storm which many believed had been sent by God to help in the destruction of their enemy.

Services were held in the Newchurch, at St Mary's at Gisburn, and in the church at Whalley, to where the Nutter family rode on the following Sunday. Miles now had an even bigger carriage for his family, and Alice was wearing a riding habit ordered from London, and a high-crowned velvet hat. Margaret was a miniature of her mother in her small habit and hat, and young Miles was proud in his leather jerkin and high-leather boots like his father and grandfather. They were a prosperous family and it was obvious to all who saw them pass by.

Roger and Ellen Nowell were alighting from the Nowell carriage. Ellen hurried towards Alice. 'Do come for refreshment after the service,' she said.

'Yes, please do,' echoed her husband, 'it is a while since we have talked with you.' Miles and Dick were happy to accept, and the arrangement was made.

The service over, the two families rode back in the brilliant sunshine to Read Hall. The men talked in the panelled lounge, whilst Ellen and the children walked in the lovely garden.

'I expect another child at Christmas,' Ellen told Alice. 'I would like more children,' Alice replied. 'Maybe next year.'

Returning to the house, luncheon was served in the large dining-room. Roger Nowell was a pleasant host, although Alice still felt reservations about him and could never relax in his company. The conversation was lively. It had been an eventful year and there was much to comment on. The new vegetable sweet potato, was served, buttered and glazed with orange juice, recently brought from America. Roger invited Miles and Dick to try the new habit of pipe smoking introduced by Sir Walter Raleigh.

'Come, Alice. We will excuse ourselves,' Ellen rose. 'The pipe habit is unpleasant, smoke everywhere. I cannot understand Roger's infatuation with it.'

Alice wanted to see the long pipes with small round bowls lighted, but she felt she must accompany Ellen. Taking the children, she followed her hostess upstairs. The children played happily together, whilst Ellen and Alice chatted.

Later, riding through the valley homeward, Dick remarked that Roger seemed to be mellowing. 'I don't trust him,' Alice replied. 'He was very arrogant when he came to Reedley and I don't forgive him.'

'I think he is sorry for the shock be brought your mother,' answered Dick.

'He should be,' Alice retorted.

'He was enquiring about buying some land adjacent to mine at Greystones,' Miles told them. 'He wants to start mining near us.'

'Why near us?' asked Dick, 'your survey showed coal deposits under a large part of Burnley.'

'He is covetous. He wants what we have,' remarked Alice.

'Well,' said Miles, 'he surprised me actually. I didn't encourage him. I intend to expand myself next month when I start more workers digging. I need women to collect the coal. Elizabeth Device has asked me for work. The pedlar has been long gone.'

'The old Demdike is hardly fit to care for those children when she is working. They run wild. The youngest is only a few months old,' remarked Alice. 'I am not keen on giving her indoor work. She is not as comely as Anne, nor so willing.'

'Nevertheless,' said Miles, 'she will be suitable for the work I have in mind, and her eldest boy will be of some use. In that way the family will not starve when the pedlar is absent for so long. His life is in constant danger anyway, because of the messages he delivers. One of these days he will be discovered and there will be no hope of a reprieve. He will hang. He is a brave man and is true to his beliefs, or he would settle down in one place.'

'I know he carries messages, but his family must suffer because of it,' Alice sounded sad. 'I have been glad to hear of Christopher and Robert via him. Why does it have to be at someone else's expense all the time?' She lapsed into silence, her mind ranging over the sea to her brothers in France.

They rode on towards home, Miles deep in thought, planning his extension to the mine, and Dick alone amusing Margaret and Miles with stories of the animals in the hedgerows they passed. So they came to Roughlee as the evening shadows were beginning to shade the trees.

Anne was waiting to welcome them, and together she and Alice prepared the children for bed, little Maria dancing round the room where she shared a bed with Margaret.

Miles and Dick walked amicably round the farmyard, checking their horses and talking over the events of the day.

XII

In 1589 Alice had another son, Charles, and at the christening Richard Towneley, who was shortly to marry Jane Assheton of Downham became his godfather. Roughlee Hall saw another gathering of friends, Anne and Hugh Towneley, and the Nicholas Asshetons, while the Nowells were again included in the party. Ellen was to be Charles' godmother, and their daughters and baby son were with them.

They rubbed shoulders with the wealthy Towneleys and the poorer Wilseys. The Nutters, always a democratic family, had friends in all classes. They were rich themselves, but never lorded it over their servants, and for this they were respected. Henry Mitton was helping to serve the food and Anne, busy as always, bustled happily to and fro among the guests.

Sybil and William Bannister and their children, the Foulds, Thomas Firber and his wife – all were there to give their blessing to this latest addition to the Nutter family.

Early the following spring, Miles Nutter started to excavate deeper into the hillside beyond Greystone. The track was now known as Coalpit Lane, and the poorer people of the area were often to be seen collecting the coal which had dropped from the carts near the mine workings. Dick rarely went to the mine. He preferred to oversee the farm and busy himself with the sheep, cows, dairy milk and cheeses, and the marketing. They also had pigs, geese, hens and ducks. Kitchen maids milked the cows and made butter and cheese. Their produce was taken to Gisburn market every week.

During April, Miles and one of his workers, James Hargreaves, and Elizabeth Device's brother, Christopher Howgate, entered the tunnel which had been hollowed out by a small gang of men employed from the local villages. The sides of the tunnel were shored up with small trees, and now it was possible to pass about a quarter of a mile into the hillside. The coal seam started immediately. Elizabeth Device and several other women worked hard piling up the coal into carts. These carts were pulled by donkeys out on to the hillside, where they were emptied into large carts ready for delivery to the local houses.

They worked from seven in the morning until noon, when ale and pies were passed round. They then carried on working until Miles packed the children off home at four of the clock. He was a man of compassion and did not believe in keeping young children working

41

until they dropped, as many of his contemporaries did. For this work the women were paid fourpence a day and the children received twopence. Alice Nutter's house servants received eighteen shillings a year and their keep, and considered themselves comfortable.

The weeks went by and Miles' coal stocks grew. James Wilsey and Henry Mitton were now taking the coal out twice a week. They supplied all their friends, from the Bannisters at Bawle House to the Firbers at Firber House. They supplied the houses in Barrowford, where a new bridge had been built over the river on the site of an old Roman one, and the pack-horses went that way to take the road to Burnley.

In July, Roger Nowell escorted Ellen and the children to spend the day with Alice at Roughlee Hall. Leaving the women chatting, he spurred his horse in the direction of Greystones. There was an inn on the hillside, and he stopped. Handing his bridle to a youth standing near, he went in and called for ale. Exchanging pleasantries with the innkeeper, he enquired as to how the mine was progressing.

'Miles Nutter has found a good seam of coal, Sir, quite near the surface,' he said, 'he buys ale and mutton pies from me and keeps my fires going, so I am not complaining.' He smiled his satisfaction.

Roger drained his tankard, and throwing some coins down he thanked the innkeeper and continued on his way. He reined in his horse on the top of the next incline and cast his eyes covetously on to the hillside opposite where Miles' sheep nibbled the sparse grass. Lowering his gaze to the mine workings, he spurred his horse to a gallop and was soon hailing Miles, who was hard at work loading the larger cart.

'Miles,' he called, 'the older you get the harder you work. Do you not leave the heavy work to a labourer?'

'No, Roger, work is life to me. I enjoy my leisure in the evenings by my fireside. I trust you will dine with us today? I have a good bottle of claret you must taste.'

'Excellent, Sir, although I have Ellen and the children with me, so we must not stay too late.'

'Late enough to enjoy some hospitality anyway,' Miles laughed. 'I think you smell my consignment of wine as soon as it arrives!'

Laughing, the two men walked towards the tunnel and Miles explained to Roger how the workings were progressing, and how much coal they produced. Roger stayed to partake of the pies and ale, and threw himself into some of the activity.

They returned home together in the late afternoon and Ellen exclaimed in dismay at Roger's unusual dirty appearance.

'I'll make a labourer of him yet,' teased Miles. 'He has been fed too much on cream and needs more exercise.' Calling to Anne to prepare hot water, he assured Ellen he would soon have Roger restored to his former appearance.

'I have enjoyed myself today, Miles,' Roger said.

'I live by the rule that I never ask a workman to do a job I cannot undertake myself. That way you gain their respect.'

'I'll remember that, Sir,' Roger smiled warmly at the old man.

Ellen and Alice were discussing the price of English soap, and Alice said she got hers direct from Bristol at fourpence a pound. Alice's washroom was hung with posies of herbs, and small bowls of potpourri were placed around the house.

Dick came home and soon the dining-room was noisy with the sound of children and the murmur of adult voices. The servants brought in pastries, roast chickens, quince jelly and preserved raspberries. Jugs of sauces, prepared by Alice to her own recipes accompanied the repast, and Miles replenished glasses with his favourite wine.

When the good-byes had at last been said, Alice and Dick wandered down towards the river, arm in arm.

'I wish for our lives to be as tranquil as this for many years,' said Alice.

'I am sure it will be,' replied Dick.

'If only I had word of Robert and Christopher, all would be perfect,' Alice spoke sadly.

'You haven't received any bad news dear, so they must be well.'

They returned to the house, and whilst Alice helped Anne to settle young Charles, Dick bounced Margaret and young Miles on their beds, each shrieking delightedly.

Downstairs, in the parlour, Miles puffed contentedly on the pipe of tobacco Roger Nowell had brought for him.

XIII

Anne was still worried about her mother. On her frequent visits she found her to be stranger than ever, not always knowing Anne when she called, and calling to a cat in her imagination.

Anne told Alice she intended to visit her mother and asked her advice about samples and infusions for her mother's sleeplessness.

'An old remedy which I have in my cabinet is the juice of poppies and hemlock. My mother took it for years at bedtime, and I keep a supply. Come, Anne, I will fill a bottle, but your mother must only take one glass at bedtime.'

'She would not understand that, I fear,' said Anne. 'I will take two or three smaller bottles, only half full. She may drink one at a time, anything to calm her down. She is growing stranger every time I visit. She sometimes behaves like a child.'

Alice searched for suitable bottles, but could only find several empty Bordeaux wine bottles, so carefully they poured in Alice's mixture. When they were half full they put in the stoppers and Anne stowed them away into saddlebags with the food she was also taking to her mother.

'Are you taking Maria with you?' asked Alice.

'No, I will leave her with Margaret. She is happiest to stay. My mother doesn't know her anyway. I hope I do not inherit my mother's failing as I get older, so that Maria has to worry about me so.'

'Perhaps your mother will recover?' said Alice.

'I fear her mind is too far gone, now, although she varies. On some of my visits she is quite lucid and remembers incidents in my childhood. I feel guilty leaving her alone so much. Perhaps if she lived near to me I could visit her more often and she would be more stimulated, but she always says she wishes to remain where she is.'

'You have your own life to live and your first duty is to Tom and Maria, and yourself. I am sure your mother is quite happy in her own way. Now let me help you up.'

Anne mounted the pony, and coming out of the farmyard she turned right towards the river, reflecting as she rode how fortunate she had been to serve Alice Nutter. I would give my life for Mistress Alice, she thought. She is more to me than a sister.

As Anne had dreaded, she found her mother in one of her vague moods, peering vacantly and chattering as always. 'Mind the dog, mind the cat,' she said.

'There is no cat or dog here, Mother,' Anne replied. Her mother became agitated. 'Calm down, Mother. I have brought you medicine and provisions.'

'I need no medicine. Take it away!' she shrieked.

Anne had a brilliant idea. 'Mistress Nutter also sends you French wine Mother. Drink it. I will take the medicine back.'

Anne's mother fastened her vacant gaze more steadily on her daughter and said, 'Yes I will have wine.'

Anne passed a bottle to her. 'Do not drink it all,' she said. 'I won't, I won't. Give it here.'

'Mother, it is not good for you to drink it all at once. Save it.'

Anne left the other bottles in her saddlebag, reluctant to let her mother see them. She will make herself ill if I give it all to her. I had better take it back, or hide it somewhere, she thought.

Anne walked slowly into the house. Looking round she shuddered. In her father's day it had always been bright and clean, new rushes on the floor and a pot of food simmering on the hearth. She seldom found her mother cooking these days. Anne threw some wood on the fire and flames shot up, giving a warm glow to the room, showing briefly dirty pots, and in the corner, on its side, a small clay doll.

'Mother, get rid of that doll. What have you been making it for?'

Her mother's eyes brightened as she remembered. 'The Nutters of Greenhead do not help me. He said he would, remember? Your father worked himself into the ground for them, curse them.' She kicked the clay doll.

'Robert Nutter still means you harm. He comes and looks for you. He brings wood for my fire and tries to ingratiate himself. He told me he was sorry for what he did. I don't believe him. Go quickly, daughter.' Her eyes brightened, and she looked at Anne with some urgency. 'He is still at home. Go.'

'Mother, have a rest now, then I will go.' Anne tenderly helped her mother into her shabby bed. 'You look tired, the wine will help you rest.'

Anne tidied the room and stacked the fire with logs. I will bring some more logs in and then I will go, she thought. Outside she began to collect the logs from the woodpile at the side of the cottage, and turning to go back in the house she heard the hated voice.

'Anne, my lovely. So you gather the wood I brought for your mother. See how I look after her.' Robert Nutter swung down from his horse.

'Your father promised me you would not trouble me again. He gave his word.' Anne shrank from him.

'My father is not here, my dear, and I come to make amends. I am sorry you do not give me chance to show my true feelings. Come, what have you in your saddlebags? Do you bring wine for your mother? She is strange enough without wine. I will sample it for her,' and taking the stopper from the bottle with his teeth he drank deeply.

'Please leave it. It is a potion to make my mother sleep. Do not drink any more.'

'Pass me another bottle,' he demanded, 'and less of your lies.'

'No, no. Please do not drink it,' Anne pleaded.

Anne sent up a fervent prayer that someone would deliver her from this man. She was terrified and ran into the house. He followed her, drinking deeply of the wine bottle.

'Do not run from me, Anne. We are old friends, are we not? You really enjoy my attentions. Give me a kiss. Your protestations only make you more desirable.' He took her arm, drawing her towards him.

'No, no. I shall tell Master Nutter if you touch me again, I will. I will complain to Roger Nowell,' she cried.

'No you won't, or harm will come to Tom, I promise you, and I will have your mother floated as a witch. She is mad,' he moved towards her.

'Please let me go. I have to go to my daughter.'

'Maybe she is my daughter,' he said, looking carefully into her face.

'No, she is Tom's daughter,' Anne replied.

He took another draught from the bottle, then threw it to the floor. He leaped towards her, grabbed her round the waist, bent her backwards, and kissed her hard on the lips.

'My mother is asleep in the bedroom. Please let me go,' she pleaded, but he was again consumed by lust and hit her hard across the face. She fell, half-fainting to the floor. In her terror she was unable to struggle, and she wept silently as he ripped open her clothes. Thinking her life was always to be in fear of this man, she lay like stone until he had finished.

'So, you no longer struggle,' he said. 'Methinks you enjoyed it. We must meet here again. Admit it, you like me better than that milksop Tom.'

She lay unspeaking, shocked and helpless. He bent to pick up his hat and saw the clay image on the floor.

'What have we here?' he inspected the doll closer. 'Come on, tell me what this is?' Anne gazed dumbly up at him. 'Tell me,' he kicked her roughly.

'I'll tell you what it is, you evil beast,' Anne's mother appeared in her bedroom doorway. Shocked into sanity she took in the scene. 'It is you. I will kill you before I am finished. You defile my daughter and walk away. Your time will come. I will pray for you still and loud.'

He lashed out at the older woman with his fist. She fell backwards. Robert strode through the doorway. Ripping open the saddlebags on the pony, he grabbed two more bottles. Pulling the stopper with his teeth again, he drained one bottle and flung it to the ground. He mounted his horse with the other bottle in his hand. Stopping further down the field, he drained that also, hurled it to the ground and rode away.

Anne was numb, shattered by the experience, terrified because she knew he may be poisoned by the mixture he drank, hating him and fearing him, wishing he were suffering some effects from the potion.

'Anne, Anne, speak to me, Anne.' Her mother stroked her poor bruised face and tears ran down her cheeks, as Anne sobbed harsh choking sobs of despair.

Anne was still in a state of shock when, hours later, as her mother added extra wood to the fire to warm her as she lay on the floor covered with a ragged blanket, there came a banging on the door and Christopher Nutter and his son John entered.

'My son, Robert, writhes in pain. He says you gave him poison. What is your explanation?' Christopher asked sternly.

'Your son raped my daughter and stole wine meant for me,' Anne's mother's voice was clear and lucid, and Christopher Nutter's gaze fell on Anne's shivering body and her pitiful gaze spoke the truth.

'Is it true?' he asked. She nodded mutely.

'He is ill,' cried John, 'he says you gave him a foul potion.'

Anne whimpered, 'I brought a sleeping potion for my mother in wine bottles. She does not sleep well. He drank it all. I begged him not to.' She collapsed back on to the floor sobbing.

A clatter of hooves announced the arrival of horsemen and the door was again thrown open to admit Dick Nutter, Henry Mitton, James Wilsey and Tom Redfern. They crowded into the room.

'What have we here, Uncle?' Dick addressed Christopher Nutter.

'These women have worked a mischief on my brother Robert,' shouted John.

'No, no,' screamed Anne loudly, 'He raped me. I cannot bear to live. He has raped me before. Your uncle knows.'

'Is this true?' demanded Dick. His uncle had the grace to stare downwards, nodding. His sons were a sore trial to him.

'Yes, Robert has always persecuted Anne. It is to my shame I never brought it into the open before. I wished to save further trouble.'

'Do we settle it here among the family, or do we call a magistrate?' asked Dick. 'Remember, Anne's state is evidence enough, and your son is known for his excessive drinking habits. I will ride to Read now and make charges of rape and violence against him.'

'I will deal with him now!' said Tom, striding to the door.

Dick nodded at James Wilsey, who immediately hit Tom hard, knocking him to the floor.

'Oh, Tom, Tom.' cried Anne, suddenly jerked into action, she ran to him.

'Why did you do that, James Wilsey?'

'To protect him,' said Dick. 'He would have killed Robert, and what good would that be to you, or to him, or to any of us?' Turning to Christopher, he said, 'Well, do we call the magistrate?'

'I would be grateful if you would keep this in the family, Dick. I will see my son is punished, if he is not punished enough by his own excesses?'

He walked out of the house, followed by his son John who, glancing balefully at Dick, said, 'You take your papist army back to Roughlee. My father is too soft, but I will remember.'

Dick bent towards Anne. 'Are you happy with this decision Anne? If you are not, we will send for Roger Nowell?'

'I don't want my degradation to be made public, Sir,' she whispered, not knowing that she would live to regret that decision.

The small procession reached Roughlee, and Alice hurried out in pity when she saw Anne, and quickly called for hot water to bathe her. When she was eventually warm in bed, with Maria hugging her close, Alice said, 'And that time, long ago, when you were attacked, it was he also?'

Anne nodded dumbly. 'What could I do, Tom was in his employment?'

Tom came into the room. 'Be kind to her, Tom,' Alice said gently.

'I will always be kind to her, Madam,' he replied. Kneeling by her bed, Tom said, 'I will not return to Gawthorpe. Miles will give me work in Roughlee. You must never visit your mother alone again.'

Robert Nutter recovered enough to rejoin Sir Richard Shuttleworth in Cheshire, but several weeks later he collapsed with severe stomach and bowel disorders, and died in agony the following day.

At Newchurch the Sunday following his burial, his mother and father, brother John and sister Anne, passed the Roughlee Nutters without a word, and no communication was to occur between the two families for many, many years.

XIV

There was a disturbance in the village just before Christmas when Will the pedlar arrived home to find his wife heavily pregnant. Answering the door one night, Henry Mitton brought one of Elizabeth Device's young children into the room. Alice, Miles and Dick were having their supper. He was almost hysterical and rushed to Miles, grabbing at his arm and urgently pleading with him to go to Malkin Tower, where, he said, his father was killing his mother.

Miles and Dick saddled their horses. Taking the young boy up on his horse, Dick called to Henry Mitton to follow them to Malkin Tower. In about twenty minutes they drew rein before the cottage and Miles was off his horse and up to the door before Dick had time to dismount. Miles opened the door, and through the smoke which belched everywhere, he saw old Demdike kneeling on the floor by her daughter, who was sobbing. Standing over them was the pedlar, with a whip in his hand.

'What goes on here?' asked Miles.

'That slut is carrying Sellars's child,' was the reply.

'How can you judge her?' asked Miles, 'you go missing for nearly a year, and your family would starve if they didn't work. I have your two eldest in the mine, and Elizabeth, too, when she is fit. If Sellars had not given her employment at White Moor when my work was too hard, they would have near starved. You are feckless, man; feckless and unreliable. I've a mind to drive you from the district. Life is hard for a family without a man to provide on a regular basis. Touch your wife again and I'll have you in the pillory! Now get out!'

Miles stood aside and Will Device walked past him. Casting a venomous look at the other man he hissed, 'Mayhap you will regret this interference in my family affairs. You forget yourself, and my importance to you.'

'Threats, threats!' Do your worst, Sir. I fear you not!'

Miles turned towards Elizabeth who was sobbing, half-sitting, half-lying on the floor. 'Now, if he touches you again, inform me immediately and I will have Hargreaves the constable on to him.'

Throwing some coins down towards the children, he walked out.

The three men rode back towards Roughlee, passing the pedlar on the way. I wonder where he will spend the night thought Miles. Maybe he will return to Malkin Tower when he has calmed down.

Back at Roughlee Hall, Miles and Dick discussed the situation with Alice. 'I wonder what this child will be like' The last one of Device's, young James, is certainly moonkissed,' Miles mused.

'Well, the woman hadn't much choice but to give in to Sellars. He is a noted womaniser and it won't be his first bastard, nor his last,' replied Alice. 'He has provided well for Elizabeth whilst the pedlar has been away. The whole family are kept well fed.'

'I wonder whether the pedlar will make his way back to Malkin Tower this night. It was starting to snow when we were riding home and it is a bare moor, without shelter for him.' Dick looked worried, despite his objection to Will whipping his wife. He had always liked the pedlar and knew he carried dangerous messages.

The pedlar did not return to Malkin Tower that night. His frozen body was found in the Pendle Water, his pouch had been opened, and there was no sign of its contents. James Wilsey brought the news from one of the villagers at daybreak. Miles, Dick and Henry Mitton helped to lift the battered body out of the water.

'He threatened me with cryptic words,' said Miles. 'I wonder if he was carrying a letter for us.' As he spoke a shadow darkened the light before him. Miles looked up and met the sardonic smile on the face of Richard Baldwin, who had just ridden up.

'So,' he said, 'the pedlar was a papist messenger. He carried letters I have taken to Read Hall.'

'Well, Sir,' said Miles, 'if you removed letters from the body of a dead man and left him lying in the river, you are a felon. Robbing the dead. Or maybe you know something about his death?'

'Have a care, Nutter. The penalty for harbouring priests is death,' and turning, he rode away before Miles could reply.

'What did he mean, Father?' asked Dick.

'I can only assume he carried a letter from Robert or Christopher and would not give it to us last night because of the circumstances. Now, was his death an accident or not? We shall probably never know?'

Later the same day, Roger Nowell rode into Roughlee with Nicholas Assheton. Approaching the hall he met Miles, who immediately offered them hospitality. As he and Nicholas warmed themselves before the great fire burning in the pleasant room, Dick joined them.

'I expect you are here to investigate the pedlar's death?' he said.

'Baldwin thought it was an accident but who saw him last, do you know?' asked Roger.

'Father and I, and Henry Mitton. We rode to Malkin Tower last night after one of the children came and begged us to go because the pedlar was whipping his mother. We warned him off and last saw him heading into the village. Richard Baldwin told father and I he was carrying letters. The callous fellow left the body in the water. I suppose he was dead when Baldwin found him?'

'We will never know that,' replied Roger. 'He brought the letters to me, of course, but there were no names on them. I think if Baldwin had got him alive he would have had a confession from him, you can be sure.'

Dick saw the relief on Alice's face, and so did Roger as he turned to take his food, but nothing was said. Roger's eyes met Alice's and she quickly turned away.

Will Device, the pedlar was buried at the Newchurch on Christmas Eve, Elizabeth and her children walking behind the coffin all the way. As the bedraggled party made their miserable way back through Roughlee, Alice sent Anne to bring them round to the kitchen.

'Elizabeth, you are in no state for all that walking,' she said. 'What else could I do, Mistress? I have no horse or carriage. I had to see my husband laid to rest. I loved him, yet he was absent so often, and now I am truly alone.' She began to cry. Alice pushed a tankard of spiced, mulled ale towards her.

'You must rest here. I will make a meal for you and the children before you return to Malkin Tower. The night grows cold. Rest awhile.'

Alice rushed round finding footwear for the family whose shoes and hose were pitiful. She wrapped the children in woollen shawls and gave enough provisions to Elizabeth for Christmas Day, then watched them go wearily in the direction of Malkin Tower.

'Richard Baldwin will hound them now that the pedlar is dead,' Dick said, as he watched them go, 'although Sellars will be a match for him. He is a strong man. He may take the child she is expecting to White Moor, if it is his?'

'Oh, I am sure it's his,' Alice replied. 'Elizabeth has never ventured far. She will become bitter now she is a widow with five mouths to feed, as well as her old mother.'

XV

The New Year's Eve festivities were tainted for the Nutter family by the fear that Baldwin had, in fact, spoken with Will Device before he died. In any case, Baldwin must have seen the letters before he took them to Read. Had the letters given any indication that Robert or Christopher were in England? Were they likely to visit Roughlee Hall? Did Baldwin and Nowell know if this was the case?

Miles and Dick discussed the possibility of Robert or Christopher arriving. 'I have no way of warning them now,' Miles said. 'I dare not worry Alice with my fears, but we are in danger if they come. I swear Baldwin and his henchmen come round here more often, and chat to the servants.'

'I feel it in my bones also,' replied Dick, 'but I dare not say this to Alice.'

'I think we will give a feast for our friends at Candlemas. I dare not seek them out secretly, but if we get them all together our fears can be extended to them. I am sure word has spread regarding the pedlar's letters. Nothing is a secret long, and there was great interest in his death.' Miles looked cynical.

'William Bannister tells me that Sellars and Baldwin are at odds over Elizabeth Device, so that is a diversion. The old woman has been hanging around Wheathead recently and Baldwin set his dogs on her,' Dick told his father.' She told him she would pray for him still and loud, and Baldwin is now saying she is a witch.'

'Let them think of witchcraft if it takes their minds off priests,' remarked Miles.

The Candlemas feast duly took place. Alice was always delighted to entertain, and again Roughlee Hall saw yeoman and squire mixing together. Dick and Miles were able to warn their friends of the possibility of Robert or Christopher arriving in the area without arousing suspicion in anyone else.

Talk around the table was of the discovery of further seams of coal on Nutter land. Miles was planning a trip to Newcastle, where German miners were being employed to advise on mining expertise and Ellen Nowell insisted she would contact her parents who would afford him hospitality.

Thomas Firber arranged with Miles and Dick to keep in close touch should any word be received of a priest's visit. At Firber they had a large hiding place underground where Robert Nutter had sheltered in the past and which was always stocked with provisions.

Firber was further off the beaten track, so warning came early of anyone approaching on the hillside beyond Barley.

Roger Nowell always found time to engage Alice in private conversation, usually to compliment on her culinary expertise.

'Your servants do you proud, Mistress Alice,' he said. 'How do you train them so well?'

'By constant supervision,' she laughed easily, and continued, 'I intend to journey to France later this year and I will no doubt bring back more recipes and herbs, certainly fresh garlic. I fear the winter will have killed off most of my herb garden.

'When do you go?' he asked.

'In June, when the weather is likely to be most calm. I have friends in Douai, where I studied, and now that Charles is older, I am taking the opportunity to renew old acquaintances.'

'And see your brothers?' he asked, 'if you do not see them before.'

'Why do you say that, Sir?' Do you know more than I?' Alice felt a sinking sensation in her stomach.

'I know nothing, my dear, other than that I am constantly bombarded with documents and warnings of my fate should I consort with, or give assistance to Roman Catholics,' he replied grimly.

'Queen Elizabeth keeps up the pressure,' Alice remarked sadly.

'She is afraid, my dear. There are always plots to usurp her from her throne,' he said, 'Does Dick sail with you?'

'No, James Wilsey will accompany Anne and I. Also, I am taking young Miles to see his uncles. Jane Bulcock will care for Margaret and Maria and we will only be away four weeks.'

'You will be missed,' he replied.

Blushing, Alice moved away, picking up Charles who was toddling towards her with Margaret, always the little mother. Charles was a great favourite with everyone, continually smiling.

Young Miles, dressed as a miniature version of his father, leaned against Dick's knee. He was never far away from his father's side and already helped on the farm when he was allowed. He fed the hens and watered the horses. He was to go to Towneley Hall daily when he was eight, as his father and uncles had done. He could already read and write, as Alice had taught him. He would take his lessons with the young Towneleys, Asshetons and Nowells.

XVI

A week after the Candlemas feast, Sybil Bannister rode into the yard at Roughlee Hall with her man-servant. As she dismounted, he took her horse immediately to the water trough. Alice came out of the house.

'Why, Sybil.' She moved forward with outstretched hands. 'How nice.'

'I felt the need for fresh air. I had such a bad headache,' she said loudly. 'I thought a gallop would be beneficial to me.'

They walked into the house arm in arm. Alice helped her off with her cloak and the two walked into the cosy parlour. As soon as the door had closed behind them, Sybil whispered, 'Christopher is at Bawle House. He arrived late last night. I have explained about the letters found on the pedlar.'

'Oh, Sybil, how is he?'

'He is very well, but he dare not ride for Roughlee with Baldwin's spies around.'

'How can I visit him? It will arouse suspicion if I come tomorrow, so soon after you have been here.'

'Why not return with me now?' asked Sybil. 'I will seem to be dizzy and nauseous in the yard and you must insist on coming back with me. I have already said I have a headache.'

'You are clever, Sybil.' Alice opened the door, and calling to Anne, asked for refreshments.

When they felt a reasonable time had passed, Sybil made preparations to leave, and Alice escorted her to the door. As Ruth, the little servant girl, ran to open it, Sybil leaned against the door post, and putting her hand to her head, she said, 'My head aches so badly I feel faint.'

'Do come in and sit down again, dear.' Alice held the door open and Sybil walked back into the comfortable parlour. The two young women allowed a half-hour to pass, then Alice rang the bell. She told Anne she would require her outdoor things as she would be escorting Sybil home.

'Please send out for Henry Mitton, Anne dear. He will go with me, I'm sure.'

As Alice donned her riding clothes, little Charles and Margaret clamoured for attention, little Maria always with them.

'Anne,' Alice called, 'please see to the children, I may not be back tonight.'

'They will be quite all right with me. I am sleeping here tonight, anyway, as Tom has gone to Preston with Master Dick.'

Alice gave her a quick kiss. 'I don't know what I would do without you, Anne,' she smiled.

Walking down the stairs she met little Ruth hovering in the doorway waiting to tell her that Henry Mitton was ready and waiting.

Leaving a note with Anne, Alice and Sybil were soon cantering down the road, alongside the river, with Henry Mitton and Sybil's man-servant close behind. The road climbed slowly upwards. They passed several rude cottages on the way, and just before the hamlet of Blacko they turned left and proceeded along a rutted track which took them below Malkin Tower. The wind blew icily around them and flurries of snow began to drift downwards.

'You will have to stay the night, Alice,' Sybil remarked loudly as the wind began to set up a howl.

'I told Anne I may do that,' she answered, just as loudly, then lapsed into thought.

It must be eights years since I have seen Christopher. Certainly not since mother died. He has been teaching students, here and in France. He must not stay, he risks his life. Head bent against the weather, Alice rode on.

As they approached nearer to Malkin Tower, the two older Device children, Beth and Tom, suddenly broke from some bushes and headed for home, the wind howling around them and plucking at their shabby clothes.

Sybil rode closer to Alice. 'I believe the Demdike has been feuding with old Chattox again,' she called over the roaring wind.

'Yes,' Alice replied, 'Elizabeth believes Beth stole some clothing from Malkin Tower. They were robbed recently and Beth was seen wearing some article of clothing, which she says she found. I cannot see her breaking into Malkin Tower. It is a long way from Gisburn. I also can't see that there was anything really worth stealing at Malkin Tower. The place gets more and more dilapidated.'

'Richard Baldwin is forever hounding them,' Sybil replied sadly.

'I try to help as much as I can, but it seems to be a losing battle,' Alice remarked.

'Baldwin is dedicated to hounding them. He quotes passages from the bible and applies it to the family, accusing them of witchcraft.'

'I know.' Alice still had to shout above the wind. 'He has stopped the village children coming to me for lessons. Says they can learn enough at church services. He doesn't believe in the lower classes being educated. His own children are not being tutored.'

'The time will come when all are treated equal,' Sybil replied, as the wind whistled and tossed the words between them.

The snowflakes were swirling thicker now and Henry urged them to ride faster. Crossing a deep gully, they cantered down White Moor Lane, then turning right again they espied ahead of them the welcoming glow of the lantern outside Bawle House. William was anxiously waiting for them, and they were happy to enter into the enfolding warmth. Bawle House had been built at the same time as Roughlee Hall. The rooms were large, great fires burned in the ingle-nook fireplaces and sheepskins were spread over the large stone flags of the floors.

Henry Mitton went off with Sybil's man-servant. Bolting the huge parlour door, William walked towards the fireplace and raised one of the stone flags to reveal a flight of steps. A figure came quickly up, and Alice cried, 'Christopher.' Brother and sister embraced. Tears streamed down Alice's cheeks, which were bright and ruddy from the snow and wind.

'You look very well, my dear sister,' Christopher spoke at last.

The four friends knelt together, and with bread and wine blessed by Christopher, they celebrated a mass. Alice had so many questions to ask him.

'Later,' said William, 'we must eat. Back into your hiding place my friend, whilst I call the servants to prepare food. I will send them to bed once we have eaten.'

A repast was soon placed before them and William again bolted the door. Christopher joined them.

'Oh, remember when we were young and carefree?' Alice said, 'having our parties at Reedley. When you and William were married, Sybil. What fun we had, John and Robert here as well. Now our lives are turned upside down. I wish mother and father were here to chide us for our noise.' They all looked into the flickering flames of the fire, remembering together.

Noticing that Christopher was falling asleep, William took a candle. 'He must sleep in the guest room tonight. The servants are in bed and I will rise early in the morning to rouse him. We will devise a plan to smuggle him to Roughlee.'

'I wonder how long he can stay in the area,' Alice remarked to Sybil. 'He told me he landed at Hull this time, but he expects to leave from Warley's Creek and sail round the coast. He has to go to Samlesbury first, where he has business, and where he is sure of a welcome.'

56

William went to the door. 'I told Katherine Hewitt to wait on us. She holds fast to the faith. We are lucky to have her here. Her husband died last year, following imprisonment for recusancy, and I offered her a position and a home with us. She was glad to accept.

'I remember Katherine,' said Alice. 'I have seen her at church long ago, and on fair days at Whalley.'

XVII

Back at Roughlee Hall, Dick and Miles were pondering over the note Alice had left, and on the information received from Anne.

'It isn't like Sybil to be taken ill. She is a strong girl,' said Miles, 'she must have messages from Christopher or Robert. We must wait and see.'

Alice and Henry returned to Roughlee the following day. She and Dick were closetted in the privacy of their parlour for a long time, whilst Alice told him of William's suggested plan.

The following day a large cart of coal lumbered towards Bawle House, driven by Miles himself, with James Wilsey seated beside him. A thaw had set in and the snow had turned to slush. An evil wind cut their faces and their leather jerkins were poor protection. They were glad of the mulled ale awaiting them.

James and William carried a large old wardrobe out to the cart, tying it down with rope and covering it with layers of rough cloth. 'I must return quickly. I think it may snow again,' Miles remarked to William. James leaped up beside him as they turned the cart homewards. When they reached the track by Malkin Tower they saw a horseman reined in by a coppice of trees, and recognised Richard Baldwin.

'So, you drive a cart yourself, my fine squire of Roughlee?' he said sarcastically.

'Watch your words, Baldwin. You know as well as I do that I never ask my men to do something I would not do myself. And I ask you what brings you to spy on Malkin Tower and its unfortunate inhabitants on this winter's day?'

'I am a churchwarden, and it is my duty to bring malingerers to trial if they do not attend church.'

'It seems to me you are somewhat preoccupied with the Demdike's brood. Have you no work at your mill?'

'This family are noted for their failure to attend church. It is not your business, I am the churchwarden.'

'It is winter, Sir, and the Devices have no horse. Would you have little children tramp through the snow? Let them alone. See to your own family, the loveless ones. I pity them.'

Baldwin's face was red with anger and he half raised his whip to Miles.

'Be careful of your whip, Baldwin. One day it may be raised against you. You take a wicked delight in using it methinks. I shall speak to Hargreaves, the constable, if I hear you have used it on the Device children again. You have a warped mind.' Miles jumped down from the cart, but Baldwin wheeled his horse, and as he spurred forwards he called, 'I have said it before and I will say it again, I will see my day with you and yours.'

'You do not frighten me you bigot,' Miles called after the retreating figure.

The door of Malkin Tower opened as they passed, and Elizabeth Device, her children clinging to her skirts, tumbled out.

'Oh, Master Nutter, you have saved us. Baldwin whipped my Tom last week until he bled. We fear him.'

'Have no more fear, woman. I will make a report to the constable, Hargreaves, as I fear that Baldwin is over-zealous in his duties. He will not trouble you again if I have my way.'

The cart creaked and rolled over the rutted track towards Roughlee, and as they drove into the yard, Alice came rushing out, her eyes alight with welcome. Dick followed her.

'Why do you need more furniture, Alice?' asked Dick, for the benefit of anyone spying on them.

'Help me to lift the wardrobe,' Miles asked James, and the three men carried the heavy furniture up the stairs.

Locking the bedroom door, Miles took a large key from his pocket and opened the wardrobe door. Christopher literally fell out of it.

'Uncle Miles, I am all but dead. I must be bruised from head to foot. I vow I shall never be able to walk again, I'm sure.' He rolled about on the floor. Alice knelt beside him.

'The stiffness will be gone tomorrow. Be glad you are home with me,' she said.

'It was lucky we did not risk him riding, Alice. We were observed by Baldwin, and passed some rude remarks to each other. I was ruder than usual to allay his suspicions.'

Rising, Alice said, 'I think I will have the bath tub brought up here, and Christopher can soak his bruised limbs.'

Going to the door, she gave orders for the bath to be placed in her room with plenty of hot water. 'Master Miles has taken a chill today. Hurry, and use my best Bristol soap,' she said.

Christopher was persuaded to go into the wardrobe once more, whilst the serving girls ran up and down with hot water. An hour later he was in Alice's guest room with hot warming pans at his feet. Miles grumbled at having to go to bed early because of his 'chill'. Alice and Dick promised to bring him a bottle of wine from the cellar.

Christopher stayed until the following Sunday. Alice enjoyed the days spent with her brother, maintaining long conversations with him, but being unable to bring him downstairs for fear the children may talk.

Christopher was seated in the carriage before the servants were awake, hot warming pans at his feet, as the day was chilly. Dick and Alice, with Miles, left early for the service and Henry Mitton rode his horse beside the coach. Henry would, like James Wilsey, have given his life for one of the Nutter family.

In a plantation of trees by the River Ribble, Christopher alighted from the coach. Henry dismounted, and Christopher swung himself into the saddle.

'I will see you in June in Douai, Sister, God willing.' He waved his hat as he rode away.

'He has been lucky so far,' said Miles. 'Pray he transacts his business successfully and reaches his ship safely.'

'It saddens me that he could not talk with the children,' Alice remarked, 'but they are too young to keep secrets. Miles will learn to know him in Douai. I am pleased he will see both his uncles whilst we are there.'

The Nowells were also at church in Whalley, and once again invited the Nutters to lunch with them, but pleading a desire to return to the children in case of further snow, they made their farewells and drove home.

XVIII

The spring was a busy time for Alice as she made her preparations to visit France. Miles junior was excited to be going too. Small Margaret stood sadly watching the preparations one day.

'Can I go next time, Mama?' she said.

'Of course you can, my lovely, and Charles too. But you know how I rely on you to comfort Charles when I am not here, and you will have Maria to help you.'

'Oh, yes, Mama, I would not leave Charles, but I will miss you. She looked troubled. 'Why must you go?'

'Margaret,' Alice drew her daughter gently towards her, 'I have two brothers, like you have. Once I had three, but John died because he wanted to worship God in the way he had been trained, and that isn't allowed any more in England. So, if Robert and Christopher come to see me here, they are in danger of losing their lives, and would certainly be put in prison, and maybe your father and grandfather also if they visited us here. So I must visit them in France, where they are safe.'

The little girl turned and put her arms around her mother and kissed her gently.

'I understand why you have to go, Mama,' she said.

'I will bring you a new gown and cap from France, and one for Maria also, and a toy for Charles, of course. Four weeks will soon pass, my dear.'

'Oh, Mama, I have heard there are storms at sea and ships sink,' Margaret looked anxiously at her mother.

'Not in June, my dear. The weather is usually most calm. We will be quite safe,' Alice reassured her.

The beautiful spring weather continued into summer, and on a day of sunshine and clear blue skies, Alice, Anne and young Miles, James Wilsey, Henry Mitton and Dick, who were escorting them, left Roughlee intending to stay the night with friends at Ripon on their way. No one seemed to take any notice of their departure from Roughlee and the countryside was quiet as they took the coach routes on roads that were little better than tracks, stopping at lonely inns to refresh themselves.

When at last they reached Hull and had obtained lodgings, Dick and James went off to arrange a passage. Alice could not calm Miles, so excited was he at the prospect of his first sea voyage. He ran up to Alice in their room, then excitedly out to the stables where Henry was settling the horses, chattering and laughing until Alice eventually managed to calm him down.

Sea captains were always ready to accommodate wealthy travellers, and Dick and James were soon back with the news that, weather winds permitting, they could leave the following day. Alice had made the trip many times in her teens and knew how arduous it

61

could be, but Anne was apprehensive as it was her first trip away from Pendle.

They boarded the ship the following day, and Dick and Henry Mitton stood waving on the quayside. Miles and Anne were speechless with delight watching the seabirds screeching overhead. The sails were unfurled and the ship slipped quietly out to sea, seamen swarming up the masts to the amazement of Miles.

When Dick and Henry returned to Pendle several days later it was to find Miles in bed with his leg propped up in front of him.

'One of the tunnels in the mine was not shored up enough. I was lucky I was first in, or others may have been hurt,' he told them.

'Father, you are too old for the heavy part of mining. I wish you would leave the work to the other men. They are having to do it anyway now you are injured,' said Dick.

'I cannot let others do what I cannot do. It is not my nature,' returned Miles. 'Roger Nowell sent a physician to attend my leg. He said it was not broken, but I must rest. He has bound it with comfrey and hemlock. Excellent cures, he said, and Tom Redfern has taken over the management whilst I am resting.'

The two men discussed the departure of Alice and Anne, and Miles reported the many incidents of farm life which had occurred during Dick's absence. Then Margaret and Maria started excitedly calling to Dick, he joined the children, tossing Charles in the air to his delight and giving them sweetmeats he had purchased in Hull.

XIX

The four weeks of Alice's absence flew by, and Dick and Henry prepared the carriage to collect the party from Hull. Little Margaret was to go to meet her mother as she had been a great help in looking after Charles, Dick thought she deserved a treat.

Leaving Maria and Charles playing on the floor in Miles' bedroom, where they had spent a great deal of time since his accident, Dick and Margaret said good-bye and left for the long journey to Hull, Henry Mitton as usual riding alongside the carriage. They rode into Hull on a bright July morning. The lovely summer weather had continued and the wayside grass was brown and scorched for want of rain.

Alice, young Miles, James and Anne were already waiting in the inn.

'Mama, Mama,' Margaret ran to Alice, who enfolded her in her arms. Then Dick was clasping them both to him.

'How I have missed you, heart of my heart. Pray never leave me again,' he murmured, his lips brushing her silky black hair.

Chatting happily, the reunited family exchanged news, and Miles was anxious to hear about his grandfather and the news from the farm.

That night, in the warmth and depth of a feather mattress in the low-beamed bedroom of the cosy inn, Alice lay content in Dick's arms.

'I am so pleased to have spent time with my brothers in unbridled circumstances, but I have missed you and the children, and father. Poor father. I am anxious to see him. I hope he recovers fully,' Alice said sadly.

'I have missed you,' Dick replied. 'I hope you do not want to venture away again for a long time.'

'The sea journey is tiresome, but we were lucky with the weather. I don't know how Robert and Christopher suffer the wild winter journeys,' replied Alice.

'I have never loved you more, Alice,' said Dick sleepily.

'I love you. You are my life, Dick,' and safe in his arms she slept.

Leaving Hull the following day, they made their way quietly back towards home, staying on the way in the best inns they could find, making a holiday of the few days. Alice and Dick wandered down country lanes when the children were in bed, breathing the sweet honeysuckle-scented air, and later dining well in the quaint dining-rooms, served by innkeepers anxious to offer hospitality to this obviously well-to-do family.

When at last the familiar shape of Pendle Hill loomed ahead, Alice's heart lurched within her. Dear old Pendle, she thought. It is good to be home in your shadow.

They rode into the yard of Roughlee Hall to a welcome from all the servants. Alice was eager to gather Charles into her arms, and likewise, Anne and Maria embraced each other tearfully and joyfully.

When later Alice explored her garden to see what plants were flowering, she buried her face in thick tufts of mint which threatened to take over. She gathered a clump of rosemary to flavour the evening meal.

'Let us have our home roast lamb,' she said, 'I have missed our family meals.' Charles clung to her skirts, afraid she would go away again.

Anne went happily to her cottage with Tom, excused any duties at the hall for the next couple of days. When she returned, she confided in Alice that she and Tom had visited her mother and found her to be very strange, although physically quite able.

'Might I speak to the physician about her next time he visits Master Miles?' she asked Alice.

'Most definitely yes,' Alice replied.

The physician arrived soon after their talk, clad in a cloak of grey with red slashes cut into the sides, and wearing a black-velvet cap. He introduced himself as Doctor Gabriel and told Alice he had been trained by doctors who themselves had trained under the famous Johannes Mirfield, of St Bartholomew's Hospital, in London, many years before. He was a man of tall stature, with a way of sweeping his hands around when describing illnesses or cures.

Alice introduced him to Anne and he questioned her closely about her mother.

'From what you tell me, my dear, your mother's illness is not physical but is influenced by phases of the moon. The lunar cycle has some effect on certain people. When the moon is full be kind enough to observe her behaviour and make a report to me, but today, I will see her myself if you will escort me.'

When Doctor Gabriel had refreshed himself, Alice and Anne, both mounted, the former on her fine chestnut mare and the latter on the pony, accompanied him to Greenhead. Anne's mother was sitting outside her cottage in the warm sun, handling lumps of clay which she was fashioning into shapes.

'What is she doing, Anne?' asked Alice, curious.

'Oh, mother is always making dolls. It keeps her occupied,' Anne replied with a sinking feeling. What was mother up to now?

'Mother,' she called, 'how are you today?'

Her mother raised her eyes. 'Who is this you have brought here?' she asked, shading her eyes to the sun.

'This is Doctor Gabriel, who can help you to get well, Mother.'

'I am quite well. What do you mean?' her mother asked indignantly.

'You are not always well, you know that, Mother,' Anne replied.

Doctor Gabriel talked quietly to Mistress Whittle, then turning to Anne he said, 'I am ready to leave when you are.'

Anne felt rather disappointed, but mounting her pony, she followed Alice and the doctor.

Doctor Gabriel looked at Anne. 'It is sometimes possible to make a diagnosis without great examination. The twitching eyes, the chattering teeth, the jerky movements all suggest that your mother has a sickness of the mind, rather than a physical disorder, which I had suspected from your previous descriptions.'

He continued, 'We are only in the early days of diagnosing such illnesses, and the cure is not known. All we can do is to calm down such sufferers and sedate them. I will prepare a potion for you. I have noticed similar symptoms in other villagers we have seen today. Is your mother related to anyone living near?'

'I do not know of any relations. My mother knew very little about her parents. They lived in Gisburn and died when she was young. My mother was in service at Gisburn when she met my father, and my sister and I were born when my mother was approaching middle age.'

'For your mother's malady I would recommend a potion made from henbane, and the juice of poppies. Mistress Nutter will prepare some for you, and on my next visit, I will bring a potion of my own.'

XX

The mine was in full production again and Miles returned to it at the beginning of September. Dick pleaded with him to stay at home and Tom Redfern had assured him that everything was running smoothly, but Miles liked to be amongst the industry and action.

Alice packed the usual ale and cheeses, while pies were collected from the Greystone Inn each day. The atmosphere around the mine was good. The workers were pleased to be earning steady wages and to receive free coal, which in the inclement northern weather assured them of good cooking and heating fires.

On a mild September day work was progressing well on the preparation of the new tunnel. James Hargreaves, Elizabeth Device and her half-brother Christopher Howgate were inside the first tunnel filling the small trucks with coal. Elizabeth's eldest son, Tom, was running about outside waiting to load the carts. The children were paid pennies to do small jobs, and hung around when the pies were being handed out!

Quite suddenly, without any warning, a rumbling noise started and grew with intensity. Miles shouted to them to come out of the tunnel. Realising they couldn't hear him, he rushed inside, shouting again.

'Come out quickly! Get out!'

Christopher Howgate came over to him, but Elizabeth was further in. Pushing him to one side, Miles started forward. Earth and stones were dropping around him. Elizabeth and her son hurried passed. Miles waited for them, before he turned and ran towards the opening of the tunnel. Suddenly a beam fell in front of him and with it tons of soft earth. Miles plunged forward into blackness.

Outside, Tom Redfern realised what had happened and despatched several boys to the Greystones and Roughlee for help. Then he began tearing at the mounds of earth, helped by Christopher Howgate. They made little progress until a half-hour later when Dick and a contingent of men began shovelling the mounds of earth aside, shoring the tunnel up as they went.

Alice was informed of the accident. Sending word to as many houses as she could, she mounted her horse and set off towards the mine. She arrived just as they were lifting Elizabeth and James free. Elizabeth's head was covered in blood and James was unconscious but alive.

'Where is father?' Alice asked.

'Inside,' Dick tersely replied, shovelling the mounds of earth. Christopher Howgate was beside him.

'If he hadn't come in to warn us, he would be safe now,' he said with a sob in his voice. A great man, Miles. Never was another like him. Always in there with the workers, but always at home with the gentry.'

It was another hour before they reached Miles. His body was caught under a large beam and he must have died instantly. Silently, they carried him to one of the carts. Dick, white faced and grim, jumped up behind the horse and drove off in the direction of Roughlee, Alice riding behind. Once again she was tasting the gnawing, familiar smell of tragedy. When I am happiest, something always happens to fill me with despair again, she thought.

Sadly, the little cavalcade reached Roughlee Hall, the house Miles' father had built when Miles himself was young and where Miles had spent his married life. Henry Mitton and James Wilsey helped to carry the battered body into the house. Alice called for hot water. She and Anne washed him and laid him on his own bed. Not until then did Dick give way to his anguish, and with harsh rasping sobs he sank to the floor by his father's bed. Alice held his head in her hands and together they let their grief overflow. Margaret and Miles came slowly into the room. This was their first experience of grief and the children tried to comfort their parents.

Five days later the funeral procession set out from Roughlee to Newchurch. Everyone of any note was there; their close friends, the villagers, and those from the mine who were not injured.

Richard Baldwin rode slowly in the background. He and Miles had not seen eye to eye, but he had to show his respect for the dead man who had always been good and honest in his dealings with everyone.

Roger Nowell and his wife joined the congregation at the church, and after the burial, the party returned to Roughlee Hall. How different was the atmosphere to the merry party spirit prevailing at Candlemas. It seemed impossible that Miles would not come into the room and ask everyone to try his new wine from France.

Later, when everyone had gone, Alice and Dick sat together by the roaring fire. 'This is how it will be now, dear,' said Dick, 'just you and me, until the children are older. It will not be long before Miles joins us.'

'As long as I have you, Dick, I know I will be safe. We will always miss your father. He was a good man and we have so many happy memories. He never seemed to recover fully from his accident. I wish he had stopped working at the mine.'

67

'Father could not stay at home by the fire like an old man. He did not suffer, and for that, we must be grateful,' Dick replied.

Elizabeth Device was badly injured. Alice went to Malkin Tower with James Wilsey, to take provisions and to see how she fared. It seemed her sight was impaired, a beam had fallen right across her face and moved the bone structure. Now one eye was slightly higher than the other. Her face was bruised and cut, her legs unable to hold her.

'Mistress Nutter, I fear my legs are broken,' she said.

'I am sorry I did not come before. I will send for Doctor Gabriel immediately.' Alice looked sadly down at the broken figure on the rude bed.

'We have no money for doctors,' a shrill voice spoke from the shadows. Old Demdike shuffled forwards.

'The responsibility for the physician is ours. Dick and I are most concerned for your daughter. Your son was not injured. Why hasn't he helped you?' Alice asked.

'Howgate help me?' Demdike laughed a bitter laugh. 'He and his wife will not help me. He has forgotten us already. We are too poor, but he will pay. I will see that he pays,' she added on a threatening note.

'Mistress Demdike, your threats will not help your daughter. She needs to regain her strength.'

'To work in your mine? Not likely!' Demdike replied angrily.

'I do not expect her to work in the tunnel again. We will find her lighter work when she is well.'

Alice left the house. Outside, the four children were playing with a wooden cart and the baby was in a makeshift cradle.

'Has Sellars been of any help?' she asked Demdike, who had hobbled after her.

'He don't want her when he can't bed her, he, he, he,' she cackled.

Alice felt she was getting nowhere with the old beldame, and mounting her horse, she rode off with James Wilsey.

'Send Henry with whatever they need,' she told him.

'No sign of Sellars round here,' James said, 'I would have thought he'd try to help them.'

'He is a dark horse,' Alice replied. 'I would have expected him to take some interest in the baby. It looks healthier than the others.'

'Maybe he will when it gets older. His wife seems to be barren,' James said thoughtfully.

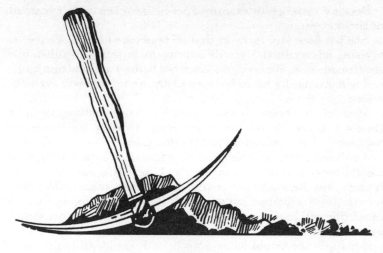

XXI

Doctor Gabriel called at Roughlee Hall the next week.

'Roger Nowell thinks you may have need of me. I have potions to help you sleep and calm your grief,' he said.

'Dear Sir, grief is no stranger to me,' replied Alice, 'but I have a women in great pain who was injured in the mine accident. It would please me greatly if you would visit her with me.'

'Tell me more about her state,' Doctor Gabriel enquired.

'Her face appears crushed and she cannot see properly,' Alice told him.

Again, James Wilsey and Alice rode to Malkin Tower, this time with Doctor Gabriel in attendance. Alice opened the door of the rude cottage. Through the smoke she saw Elizabeth still lying on the bed, and the old Demdike crouched by the fire. Several children crawled listlessly around the floor, looking half-starved.

'I sent food and fuel for the children. Why do they look so neglected?' Alice asked her.

'I am too old to deal with children. We have already eaten the food,' she whimpered.

Doctor Gabriel had followed Alice into the room. Peering down at Elizabeth he slowly turned her face from side to side.

'This is the good Doctor Gabriel,' Alice informed the sick woman gently, 'he will help you.'

Doctor Gabriel gently examined her poor broken body. Eventually he spoke.

'She has been very lucky in that no bones are broken. Very severe bruising has occurred. She will walk again, but she will stiffen up if she remains here. She needs massage, hot baths daily, and nutrition.'

'I will arrange for her to be taken to my home and I will attend her myself.'

Alice left the house. Doctor Gabriel remained talking gently to Elizabeth for a few minutes. He joined Alice by the horses and together they and James rode back to Roughlee.

'I will have to reset the bones in her face. It is a difficult task and should have been done immediately. I suggested she came to my hospital but she would not hear of leaving her children. The bones have set into a strange pattern, with the one eye higher than the other. She will be disfigured for life. The old crone does not seem to be much help,' he told Alice.

'I thought she would refuse your help. I would willingly pay for any surgery required. I will try to persuade her. I intend to bring her to Roughlee. Anne will care for the younger children. The older ones can fend for themselves with her mother for a few weeks, if we see that they are fed.'

'Surgery is quite new to this country,' he told her. 'Although the Romans were adept with the knife, their skills were lost for centuries, but we are learning again. The facial bones could be reset.'

Doctor Gabriel stayed with the Nutters for their evening meal. They were glad of the different company, still missing Miles' lively conversation. Alice was interested to hear of new remedies for healing, and his forward thinking in relation to the cure of illnesses. He described how he had cured a patient who was suffering badly from dropsy, by a juice obtained from the leaves of foxgloves.

'We call it digitalis,' he said. 'It is not easy to find the correct dosage, but the lady's legs are now back to normal after years of swelling and pain.' He continued, 'You will find cures for many things growing in the hedgerows.'

'I know quite a lot about herbs,' Alice told him, 'I was educated in France and herbs are used more often in cooking than they are in England, especially garlic. I always bring back the fresh garlic when I visit. It is just the thing for the common cold, as well as for food flavouring.' Alice passed a small jug to the doctor.

'Do try my rosemary sauce,' she said.

'I must compliment you on your cooking, Madam,' he said.

Dick poured the doctor a glass of red wine.

'This was my father's favourite wine. Let us drink to his memory. We will never forget him.' They raised their glasses.

The conversation was animated as the three continued their meal. They were immediately compatible, and the servant girls scurried in and out with the many and varied dishes.

Doctor Gabriel was an interesting man, learned and far-seeing. He said to Alice, 'many of my fellow physicians have a great belief in the supernatural, and prior to Henry VIII's founding the College of Physicians they often had no means of studying disease objectively. Apothecaries served the needs of most neighbourhoods.'

To which comment Alice remarked ruefully, 'We have to go to Preston to find a decent apothecary. The local farmers consult the old women, such as Whittle or Demdike for potions for their cattle and children alike! It is common to see a child in Pendle with a rabbit's foot tied around its neck to ward off evil spirits that bring sickness!'

'Of course, Queen Elizabeth's Poor Laws, with their basic hygiene legislation are at least a step in the right direction,' he said, 'now medicine is a recognised and esteemed profession. If people will only listen to us we can stop the more barbaric treatments. My basis is the book written by Andrew Boorde in 1542, *Dietary of health*, I find it most enlightening,' he said.

Doctor Gabriel described his time in Padua, where the great Doctor Linacre studied, and where he himself had met John Caius, who had made a long report on the sweating sickness, in English, too.

'He was a devoted Catholic,' said Alice.

'And was persecuted for it,' the doctor replied.

When at last the meal was over, darkness had begun to fall. Doctor Gabriel rose to take his leave.

'You have been most hospitable. I will come this way again.'

'You will always be most welcome,' Dick replied.

The following day, Alice arranged for a cart to be made comfortable with mattresses and blankets. With James Wilsey and Henry Mitton, she rode to Malkin Tower. Elizabeth Device was tearful, and objected to being moved, but when Alice assured her the children were to go to Anne's cottage she became calm. Only the older ones insisted on staying with their grandmother.

The old beldame shrieked and cursed, complaining she was being abandoned.

'There is food and fuel,' Alice told her curtly,' and Tom and Beth are to remain with you. You will survive, but your daughter may not unless she receives care and attention.'

71

Back at Roughlee Hall, Alice gently bathed Elizabeth, who was in great pain, and massaged her body with balms and herbal plasters. Elizabeth's face was wet with tears as she tried to thank Alice.

'I will never be able to thank you enough for what you have done for me. I have never been in a hot bath before. You are so kind.'

'We have known each other a long time, Elizabeth. The years have been kinder to me than they have to you. Now drink this hot posset and try to sleep.' Alice gently held a cup to the other woman's lips.

Anne was in the kitchen talking to the other servants when Alice went downstairs.

'Mistress Alice, whatever have you let me in for?' Anne asked. 'Those children are like little wild animals.'

'It will not be for long, Anne,' Alice replied. 'Elizabeth was in danger of being unable to rise from her bed. I intend to help her to move her legs a little more each day. When she can walk again she will be going back to Malkin Tower.'

Alice tended Elizabeth devotedly, saying to Dick that she felt it was helping her to recover from the grief of Miles' death. Anne brought the children to see their mother two or three times a week and the whole house was disrupted by their presence. There were sighs of relief all round when Elizabeth was able to walk around the room and asked to return to Malkin Tower.

'You have been good to me, Mistress Alice, but my place is with my mother and my children.' She was quite definite, she wanted to go home.

Alice had spent many hours trying to persuade her to have surgery to her face, but she would not hear of it.

'I do not care about my looks. I can see all right and I am able to care for my children.'

So Alice was convinced at last, and a cart was prepared to take her back, with her children, to Malkin Tower.

XXII

Christmas had been a quiet affair because they missed Miles, but the children had been to the Manger at Newchurch to see the baby Jesus in his stable on Christmas Day. On their return, a feast had been prepared. Tom, Anne, and Maria Redfern, as always, were guests at the table. Other servants waited on the family. One or two of them were jealous of the closeness between Anne and Mistress Nutter, but Anne had been in the service of Alice for many years before she married Dick, and they were more like sisters than servant and mistress. So both happily discussed their forthcoming babies, expected in the summer.

'I am hoping for a son this time,' said Anne.

'I do not mind,' Alice replied. 'I have a daughter and two sons already. Let us pray they are well and strong.'

After the meal the children received their presents from the Three Wise Men; Dick, James Wilsey and Henry Mitton dressed in Eastern garments. With shrieks of pleasure they pounced on the toys, books and sweetmeats.

On New Year's Day 1592, the family went once again to Newchurch for the service. Roger and Ellen Nowell were outside, and the two families conversed.

'We all miss Miles,' Roger said to Dick.

'None so much as us, Roger, but life goes on. If you have no other arrangements, why not bring your family along to Roughlee for meat?'

'We will be delighted,' he replied.

Ellen Nowell was pregnant with her fourth child, and back at Roughlee Hall, the two women happily compared notes.

'Anne is expecting a baby also this year,' Alice told her. 'Next Christmas there will be three more children to buy presents for,' and she laughed.

Little William Nowell rushed into the room. 'Charles has a rocking horse, may I have a rocking horse?'

Dick took him on his knee, 'I will make you a rocking horse. In fact, if you come with me you may find one already made.' Dick was clever with wood and he took William to his workroom upstairs, and there in the middle of the floor was a rocking horse, surrounded by piles of wood shavings.

'Now we will find a bridle and perhaps your mama can make a saddle for you?' Dick carried the wooden horse downstairs and the grown-ups admired it.

'I have some velvet, and I will make you a fine saddle,' Ellen told her son.

'Now, William,' said Dick, 'I made our horse for Miles, then Margaret rode on it, and now Charles. Soon we will have a new baby who will play on it too. You will share your horse with your brothers and sisters, won't you?'

'Oh yes, Uncle Dick, I will,' he assured him solemnly.

After the meal there was more conversation, then farewells were said, and the Nutter family promised to visit the Nowells in the near future. On the way home, riding in the carriage with Ellen and the children, Roger leaned towards his wife.

'We never receive better entertainment than we do at the Nutters. They are a rich family.'

'They are a generous family, Roger,' Ellen rebuked him quietly, 'I love Alice. She is my dear friend.'

'Well, they hide their papist leanings these days. Alice does not mention her brothers. They stay in France, much better for everyone.'

'I do not mind if she is a papist. She is nicer than anyone I know,' replied Ellen firmly, 'your other friends have not been so kind to me, nor so welcoming in their homes. In fact, I would feel friendless in Pendle without her.'

'I am sure you will never be without her, dear,' replied Roger, 'I am grateful to her for her kindness to you.' He covered her hand with his in a rare show of affection.

The horses were making good time along the deeply rutted road, and the thought of the warmth awaiting them in their comfortable home made Ellen snuggle deeper into her cloak.

'I wonder if Dick will sell the coal mine now his father is gone. He never showed any interest in it. I think I will ask him in a month or two,' said Roger.

'Oh, Roger, you always look to your own advancement,' Ellen replied.

'Well, are you not glad I looked to advancement and married you, my dear,' he asked with a twinkle in his eye.

'You are cruel, Sir. Surely you did not marry me for my money alone?'

'Well, Ellen, my father thought I had been single long enough and he sought to make me settle down. It is my good fortune he found you for me. You are very patient with me, and you bear me beautiful children. What more could I ask?'

'I could ask that you spend more time with me and talk to me more, as you are doing now,' she replied.

'Oh, it is the excellent Bordeaux wine talking, Ellen,' and he laughed. Taking William on his knee, he said, 'Now, when we arrive home, we shall find the horse a saddle.'

XXIII

In June, Anne gave birth to a baby boy several weeks earlier than expected. She was very ill and the child was small and fragile. Anne was unable to return to serve Alice and rested in her cottage, where Tom hovered anxiously. Her baby was christened Jacob. Alice and Dick became godparents at the ceremony at Newchurch.

Two months later, Alice also gave birth to a son, lusty and strong. They called him Christopher. A large party was held to celebrate the christening, the house was full of well-wishers. Roger Nowell walked in the rose garden with Alice, who had strolled out for some fresh air. She showed him the bed of Damask roses. The original cutting had been brought to England from Padua by Doctor Thomas Linacre, a learned fellow of All Souls' College, Oxford, who had died several years ago. John had brought her the cutting, and she treasured it, remembering her brother each time she filled a vase with the perfumed flowers.

Alice always felt at a disadvantage with Roger Nowell. He was always presumptuous, and as usual he spoke bluntly.

'I admire you, Mistress Nutter. Whatever disaster strikes you, it never bows you for long.'

'Master Nowell,' she replied, 'I have my children to consider. In my quiet moments I have plenty to disturb me. I lost my mother and my brother in one month when I was very young, and last year, we lost Dick's father. But I have my prayers to sustain me.'

'How are your brothers?' he asked.

'I have had no news recently, but I trust they are safe in France,' she replied. 'I enjoyed seeing them last year.'

'You may not be allowed to visit them again,' he replied. 'I hear a law is to be passed forbidding travel to France, and also forbidding children to be sent there to be educated.'

'Do you threaten me?' she asked.

'You give nothing away, Mistress Nutter.'

'There is nothing to give away, and I am ever mindful that you are a Justice of the Peace.'

'May that never come between us, Madam,' he replied, and together they walked back to the house between the beds of roses which were in full bloom.

When the last of the guests had departed, Alice suddenly looked at Dick in surprise.

'I half expected Anne to call in, even for a short time, just to toast the baby. I missed her. Maria and Margaret are tired or I would send them to enquire whether she is well.'

Dick was standing by the window. 'Tom is here now, probably to give Anne's apologies.'

Alice joined him at the window and watched Tom walk down the garden path. They walked to the door to meet him.

'Whatever is the matter, Tom? You look grievously sad?' said Alice, looking enquiringly at him.

'Jacob died this morning, Madam. Anne would not let me tell you sooner. She did not want to spoil your day.'

'Oh, Tom, I am so sorry. I will go to Anne now.'

Alice sped from the house, down the garden path towards the riverside to Anne's cottage, where she and Tom had been so happy.

It is always thus, thought Alice. My happiness has always to be impaired by misfortune and tragedy. Reaching Anne's cottage, she went quietly inside. Anne was sitting holding her head in her hands. Alice knelt down beside her and put her arms around her friend.

The baby was buried at Newchurch several days later.

Book Two

I

The Demdike family continued on their downward spiral. Although Alice tried to help them her offers were often spurned, but Elizabeth would always accept food and clothing for her children. In 1595 Elizabeth gave birth to another daughter, Alison, whose father was not known. Alice and Dick discussed this event over their evening meal.

'Do you think Sellars is the father?' asked Alice.

'I suppose it is possible,' Dick replied, 'although it was said he had cooled off after her accident, and her appearance hasn't improved. He isn't admitting it, although he acknowledged the other child as his. The children are all growing up, but James is ever backward and not much use on the farm. Young Roger Mitton is my best apprentice.'

'Will you ever start the mine again, Dick?' asked Alice.

'No, I have no heart for it. People can get their coal elsewhere now, and while the farm prospers there is no need. I collect enough coal for ourselves, dear,' he replied.

'Mama, Mama, Papa, come and see the puppies.' Children's excited voices preceded the entry of Miles, Margaret and Charles, with their ever present shadow, Maria. Alice rose to her feet smiling. Margaret took her hand and led her through to the kitchen, Dick following. In the basket was their wolfhound, licking four small puppies.

'Don't touch them, children. She will be on her guard now,' Dick warned them.

'Can we keep them?' asked Miles.

'Not all of them, just one. Roger Mitton has asked for one. Sybil and William would also like one, so we shall see,' their father replied.

'Can Christopher come down and see them, Mama?' asked Margaret.

'If he is not asleep, but you must not wake him,' Alice said firmly. Margaret disappeared upstairs, and shortly, the servant girl, Ruth, came downstairs carrying the small Christopher, who struggled to reach the ground. Alice came forward to stop him touching the puppies.

'Black one, black one,' he pointed.

'Yes, we will keep the black one. Now back to bed with you.' Alice passed him to Ruth who carried him, complaining, up the stairs.

Back in their comfortable parlour, Alice told Dick that the Demdikes had fallen foul of Baldwin again.

'Old Grandmother has been up to Wheathead again, begging, so it is said. I am surprised that any of the family go near Wheathead. Baldwin has always been against them,' Alice said.

'She's asking for trouble,' Dick replied.

'Well, apparently she was more or less in the kitchen one day begging for milk. Young Anne Baldwin gave her a drink, then Richard turned up with his whip and drove her away. Demdike had told Anne she could cure her cough with herbs. When Richard heard this he grew very angry.'

'Where has this story come from?' Dick asked.

'Christopher Baldwin told Ralph Bannister. They are quite good friends when Christopher can escape from his father for a few hours,' Alice replied.

'Ralph says Anne Baldwin is very delicate,' she continued. 'It's damp around Wheathead, and it is said Baldwin keeps poor fires. Sybil says Baldwin was raging. He said he didn't want Demdike's spells and potions.'

'I've heard the boy receives many beatings from his father. The man seems to take a pleasure in it. He is warped,' replied Dick.

'To happier subjects,' Alice continued. 'Let us give a feast at Hallowe'en. The children can dook for apples and we will have turnip lanterns.'

'An excellent idea, my dear. It will do us good to relax?' Dick replied.

Alice turned her mind to the preparations, happily discussing who they would invite.

'We'll invite almost everyone,' Alice said, and a list was hastily made.

October 31st was a bright, frosty day. The sky was blue and the sun shone on to the changing colours of the giant oaks, sycamores and limes which lined the river bank. Alice was busy all day with her final preparations. Guests started to arrive about five of the clock, welcoming lanterns hanging outside the Hall to light the dusk.

'Daylight Gate,' said Dick to Alice as they stood for a while looking out on to the road for their visitors, 'the time of day I like the best, just before dark.'

Servants ran to stable the horses and lights shone out of Roughlee Hall in welcome.

'Christopher Baldwin can't come, Mother,' young Miles told her. 'Ralph and I both asked him. His father says it is a pagan festival. What is a pagan festival, Mother?'

'Oh, Miles, it's just fun. Baldwin sees wrong in everything. Pagans were people who had not heard of Christianity, and they had their own festivals. They had never heard of God, so they worshipped other things, like the sun and the moon. They were not wicked people, just ignorant. Who knows, their ways may have been better than ours? Maybe they didn't hang, draw and quarter their priests, as our people do?'

Alice looked sad. Then brightening she said, 'Go and enjoy yourselves. Baldwin shall not cast a blight upon this feast. He has never heard of warm-hearted happiness. His children are deprived of everything. You can give Christopher some sweetmeats tomorrow.'

James Firber, his wife and children swept into the room. James twirled Alice round. 'You grow prettier each year,' and Alice blushed.

'I tell her that also.' The tall dark figure of Roger Nowell appeared in the doorway. 'If it wasn't for the Nutters, we should lead a boring life, I say. Thank goodness for yeoman farmers who allow us to let our hair down once in a while, no disrespect, Dick.

'No offence taken, Roger. I agree we all need to relax occasionally and my lovely wife has been preparing these last weeks. Come and try the Bordeaux, Sir.

Maria and Margaret, pink-faced and pretty in their gowns and caps, their flowered kirtles becomingly ruched into frills, danced excitedly round the many buckets where they were to dook for apples. Turnip lanterns hung from the ceiling. Alice and Dick had never presided over a merrier feast. Henry Mitton was skilled with the flute, and feet tapped to the music.

Around ten o'clock the guests began to leave, and only a few close friends remained. Sybil and William Bannister, and James Firber and his wife, whose children had begged to stay the night, and who were even now being prepared for bed by the patient Anne. Maria still had her own bed in Margaret's room and spent more time at Roughlee Hall than in their own small cottage down by the river.

When the children were asleep, the adults talked contentedly by the fire. Affairs of state passed them by in Pendle, and their Roman Catholic faith was well hidden. Talk moved round to Alice's brothers, Robert and Christopher.

'Christopher Southworth brought me a letter from Christopher. He stayed two days,' Alice said.

'He stayed two days with us also,' replied James Firber.

'He was safer with you, James. You are more isolated at Firber,' Alice told him.

'When he left us, he was off to York. I trust he is safe. We never hear news, and it is dangerous to enquire.'

'As the children get older, it is not easy. They do not understand it is a matter of life or death to harbour a Catholic priest in these times.' Alice looked into the fire. The flames flickered, casting shadows on the walls, and she sighed.

James Firber rose to his feet. 'I think we should go, dear.'

His wife arose, and Sybil and William Bannister also. 'We, too, need to be going. Your mother will be anxious, Sybil. She expects us back tonight.'

Good-byes were said, then Dick and Alice returned to their fireside, lingering in the warmth and talking companionably together. Quite suddenly there was a clatter outside and a tapping on the lighted window. Dick hurried out of the room. As he opened the outer door, a man almost fell into the house.

'It's Christopher Southworth,' said Alice, rushing forward, 'are you hurt?'

'Please move my horse. I am being followed,' he gasped.

Dick ran outside, quickly led the horse around the back of the farm to a barn in the field, and then returned to the house.

Alice came to the door of the parlour as Anne came down the stairs.

'Boil a kettle, Anne. One of our guests has returned. His horse cast a shoe.' This was for the benefit of Ruth and her fellow servant girl now peering through the stair rails.

'To your beds, girls. You have an early start in the morning,' Alice called peremptorily. They scuttled off.

'Anne took in the scene at a glance and hurriedly prepared a hot posset. Dick opened the secret door in readiness.

'What has happened, Christopher?' Dick asked.

'Baldwin is on my trail. I found a poor, unwanted new-born baby dying in a pool of water. I was baptising it when Baldwin came upon me and suggested I had drowned it. Some poor servant girl's downfall, more likely,' he said.

'Well no one from here,' said Alice, 'what happened to the poor little thing?'

'I had to leave it and escape as quickly as I could. I was near the mill, but cut off up hill and he lost me. I don't intend to stay, just change my horse.'

'You must stay in the hiding place. You're in no fit state to venture out again tonight. Take off your wet clothes when you are inside. There are clean clothes already prepared.' Dick opened the secret door and ushered him inside.

'He may have gone for Nowell,' Christopher suggested.

'Roger will not be interested in Baldwin's allegations. He has been feasted here tonight and has supped well. He will be asleep. Now down into the cellar and rest. We will speak in the morning.'

They had no sooner closed the secret door when they heard the sound of horses, loud shouts, and a pounding on the door. Dick opened it to find Baldwin, his face like thunder, standing by his horse.

'We search for a popish priest. Is he here?' he asked.

'How dare you disturb our peace so late! We've had guests all evening, but all have left now. You have no authority to question me. Now leave!' Dick spoke angrily.

'Yes, you had guests. Turning a peaceful October evening into a pagan celebration. No wonder evil is abroad! We have found a dead child left as a sacrifice to Satan.'

'What rubbish you speak, Master Baldwin. Why should the dead child have been a sacrifice?' Alice appeared in the doorway with Dick, 'How old was this child?'

'New-born, Madam. New-born, and left for the Devil,' he replied loudly.

'Left because its mother wished to hide her evidence. Some poor servant girl brought low, out of marriage. Why turn everything into Satan's work, Sir? It is simply human failing.' Alice was angry now.

Baldwin looked disconcerted and ill at ease for a second, and Dick seized his chance.

'Do not trouble us further with stories of the Devil, dead babies and lost priests! Why are you not at home with your wife and children? It is late to be out riding, is it not?' he asked.

'It is All-Hallows Eve, and I do not trust these heathen villagers. I am a churchwarden and must be vigilant against the powers of darkness.'

'You are a dangerous man, Sir. You see evil where there is only ignorance and fear,' Alice told him sharply.

'What of the priest?' Baldwin suddenly remembered his mission.

'What priest is this?' asked Dick.

'There was a priest with the child,' stated Baldwin.

'With a new-born baby?' Alice sounded incredulous.

Ignoring her, Baldwin said, 'He would make for the nearest papist stronghold, which I consider to be here.'

'Watch your tongue, Baldwin!' said Dick with a steely glint in his eye, 'We attend the Newchurch and we worship there every Sunday.'

'Your wife's brothers are priests. You do not fool me with your apparent about turn.

'Are you suggesting that one of my brothers is here?' asked Alice.

'It was not one of your brothers. I know them both and would have no hesitation in summoning the constable had it been one of them.'

'Good neighbour that you are,' said Alice sarcastically,' and what have they ever done to you or yours?'

'They follow the papist doctrines of Rome, which are heresy to me. I will search them out where I can,' Baldwin replied with a fanatical gleam in his eyes.

'I feel sorry for you, Sir. You miss so much happiness by your bigotry.' Alice turned and went into the house.

'Leave my land immediately!' Dick told him. 'The matter of a dead baby is for the constable. The matter of a man you say to be a priest is none of my business!' So saying, he stepped into the house, closing the door.

Baldwin turned to his companions. 'We will inform the constable.' They left the yard and all was quiet again.

On the stairs young Miles crouched. 'What is it Father? What did Baldwin want?'

'He thinks we have a priest here, because your mother's brothers are priests.'

'Uncle Robert and Uncle Christopher are good men. They were kind to me in France. Why should they be in danger if they were here?' Miles asked.

'We have tried to shield you from persecution, Miles, but as you grow older you will become more aware of it. Their way and our old way of worshipping God is forbidden. It started with the Queen's father. She continues it because she is afraid. The Pope has excommunicated her. So priests, and those who harbour them, are punished.'

Alice took her son's hands. 'Uncle John was put to death because of his beliefs, before you were born. He was my dear brother, but he died brave and true to his beliefs. You must always be true to what you believe, Miles.'

Alice took her son in her arms. 'I hope you never have to choose, dear,' she told him lovingly.

Alice and Dick lay in bed unable to sleep. 'I didn't go to Christopher again. He would probably be asleep,' Dick said.

'Baldwin will not get authority to search here tonight. Roger would not believe his story. He was here himself only hours ago.'

'They may come tomorrow, dear, but Christopher is safe where he is. We must make a plan for his escape.'

Dick fell asleep planning the escape.

II

The following day, Roger Nowell J.P. and Nicholas Assheton J.P. rode into the yard of Roughlee Hall. Dick had been expecting them and raised his hand in greeting. He signalled for Henry Mitton to take their horses. Dismounting, Roger and Nicholas followed Dick into the house.

'Sorry to be returning so soon, Dick,' Roger said and on seeing Alice, smiled, 'an excuse to see you again, Madam,' he bowed.

'We half expected you, Sir. Master Baldwin was quite hysterical last night, speaking of priests and dead babies,' Alice told him.

'He had me from my slumbers early today,' Roger replied, 'and, of course, I am bound to ride out and investigate the complaint. Having spent the evening here myself, I assured him I saw no priest, but he would have me harass you.'

'I can believe it, Sir. Baldwin has no love for us,' she replied.

Anne carried tankards of mulled ale into the pleasant dining-room which only the night before had resounded with happy laughter. The two men drank deeply, then bowing to Alice, they took their leave.

'I am sure Baldwin's spies will have seen us make this visit,' Roger said to Dick as he walked up to his horse. Dick nodded in understanding.

Sybil Bannister arrived to collect her children and looked at Roger and Nicholas in surprise.

'Back so soon, Sir?' she asked. 'What is the attraction?'

She grinned at Alice, who replied, 'Oh Sybil, Baldwin has been on a witch hunt again. This time he has been talking of sacrifices to Satan and hidden priests.'

'Good gracious, and all in the short time since we left?'

'I am afraid so,' said Alice, 'Come inside and I'll tell you about it.' Arm in arm they walked into the house.

As Dick watched Roger and Nicholas disappearing in the direction of Wheathead, Thomas Firber galloped into the yard leading two ponies.

'You have had visitors early today, Dick. What has brought Nowell back so soon?'

Dick led Thomas into the house, and calling for ale, they joined the ladies. With children and puppies tumbling all over the floor, there was no opportunity for private conversation. They all stayed to dine, and in the early afternoon, the Nutters waved them goodbye.

Dick and Alice dared not open the hiding place until the children were asleep and the servants had retired to their own quarters for the night. Christopher looked well and rested despite his cramped conditions. He ate ravenously the fresh food they gave him.

'You cannot leave tonight, Christopher. There is still a hunt for you. I managed to account for your horse because of all the visitors. Thomas Firber has ridden off on it and left his own for you.'

Dick continued, 'My plan is for you to ride in the coach on Sunday. James will ride your horse and change places in the coach with you at a suitable spot.'

'Oh Dick,' said Alice, 'will this plan work again?'

'Have you a better suggestion? It worked last time and there were no enquiries. If we send him off alone, he will not get far. No, he must dress as James and go out to the coach house early. James will already be there. Christopher will get in the coach. We will join him. Miles and the children can miss church this Sunday.' He was quite adamant.

Sunday dawned bright and sunny. The Nutters departed for Whalley early, Henry Mitton driving.

'I think Baldwin has been persuaded that the priest he saw did not make for Roughlee,' Dick said, 'probably because we had a feast and there had been too many people about.'

'Anne said a servant girl from Barley has admitted abandoning her baby. Poor thing, she is to be tried for murder. She cannot have been in sound mind so soon after childbirth. If Baldwin has one victim he may be satisfied for now.' Alice spoke sadly.

'I think I will leave the coach before we had planned,' said Christopher, 'I will ride to Towneley, where they will arrange the next safe house.'

Dick felt relieved. The sooner he was out of the coach the safer they would be. He did not relish the thought of serving a prison sentence, or perhaps even the death penalty, for hiding a priest. Christopher, dressed in James Wilsey's clothes, would not attract undue attention.

Reaching the clump of trees above Goldshaw Booth, James dismounted. Christopher took his place on the horse, and he climbed into the coach.

Christopher waited until the coach was on its way to Whalley, then, breaking cover, he galloped past the home of the Nutters of Greenhead, down the hill past Wood End Farm.

I must not visit my father at Samlesbury this time. He has already suffered enough because of me. I will ride for Towneley, then make my way back to the coast, he thought as he urged his horse on.

Arriving at Whalley, Alice and Dick relaxed in the church, giving thanks for the safe disposal of Christopher, and praying he reached Towneley safely. Gathered outside, following the service, were the Asshetons, Bannisters and Nowells. Roger Nowell approached them.

'I trust things have quietened down in Roughlee. You will no doubt have heard that Hargreaves, the constable, brought a young girl to be questioned regarding the dead baby?' he said.

'I believe so,' Alice replied, 'surely she is in no state to be held responsible so soon after the birth?'

'I am afraid Baldwin is pressing for her to be sent to the next Assizes,' said Nowell.

'Surely the poor girl has been punished enough?' cried Alice.

'Madam, we cannot have servant girls disposing of their unwanted children in this way. Others will follow suit. However, the girl is ill with fever and Ellen has taken pity on her. It may be a blessing if she does not live to be taken to the gallows. Her mother has walked from Barley to be with her.'

'Let's return home quickly, Dick,' said Alice, 'I have such a feeling of depression. I have a mind for a quiet afternoon with our children. There are too many sad stories these days.'

Ellen came up to Alice as she walked towards her coach. 'Do you go so soon?' she asked.

'Yes, Ellen. This matter of the servant girl you have in custody at Read has upset me,' Alice replied.

'I am caring for her, Alice, she is very ill. I will do what I can,' Ellen replied.

Saying goodbye, Alice and Dick climbed into their coach and Henry urged the horses forward. Just over an hour later they were removing their cloaks in the warmth of their own home. The children were happy to see them, and they enjoyed their Sunday meal always a happy affair and as very often happened, Anne and Tom Redfern shared it with them.

Later that week came news that the poor servant girl had died at Read. Crossing herself, Alice gave a silent prayer of thanks that the girl had been spared certain execution.

III

The whole family attended church at Whalley a few weeks later. No word had been heard regarding Christopher Southworth, and it was assumed no news was good news.

'We should go to Whalley more often in the summer,' Dick said to Alice, 'the Newchurch is nearer but it is nice to go further and encourage the children to extend their acquaintances.'

As they left the church, Ellen Nowell came forward.

'Please come and take meat with us before you go home. It is so long since I talked with you.'

'Can we, dear?' Alice asked Dick.

'Yes, of course. Anne will not prepare the meal until she sees us. It will be a change for you and the children.'

Roger Nowell was ever the genial host. Alice and Dick stood by the window sipping a glass of red wine, whilst Roger pointed out new plants he had introduced to his garden.

'The damask roses are from Padua,' he said.

'Did Doctor Gabriel obtain them for you?' she asked, 'he saw the ones I had brought back from France, given by Doctor Linacre. He said he would look out for some on his next visit.'

'I should have known that you would beat me to it in the matter of plants and herbs,' he said, smiling. 'I shall gather you a posy and see how yours compare with mine!'

After the meal, Roger offered Dick some tobacco and Alice wrinkled her nose.

'You set a bad example, Roger. Since Miles died, Dick has not indulged in tobacco.'

'Come, Alice, let us go to my parlour and talk,' Ellen took Alice by the arm. They could hear children tumbling excitedly in the large airy nursery overhead, so they were glad to retire to Ellen's parlour for some peace.

Once inside Ellen turned excitedly to Alice. 'Have you heard about the Starkies?'

'Roger's cousins at Padiham?' Alice asked.

'Yes. Well, the children have been ill, falling on the floor, foaming at the mouth and biting their tongues.'

'I have heard of such an affliction when I was in France. It is very distressing, and can be passed down through families if the blood is too close,' Alice replied.

'Oh, Alice. It is said they are bewitched.'

'Oh Ellen, you do not believe such stories?' Alice laughed. 'Who is supposed to have bewitched them?'

'I do not know that, but I do know there is a priest who says he can cure them and he is to live in the house until they are better.'

'You mean someone who once was a priest? Surely he is not openly practising?' Alice asked.

'Oh no. He has studied medicine, though, in France. His name is Edmund Hartley and he comes from Leigh. The children have not foamed at the mouth since he came and Nicholas Starkie is so grateful he is giving the man a living at home.'

'I am sure Doctor Gabriel would have been able to treat the children,' remarked Alice.

When the good-byes had at last been said and the children safely in the coach with their parents, Alice told Dick the Starkie story.

'What rubbish! I am surprised Ellen believes in witchcraft,' he said.

'She is a simple girl and believes anything told to her. I fear Roger is not too kind to her, and she cannot stand up to him,' Alice replied.

More than a year later came news that Edmund Hartley had become arrogant, making many demands on Nicholas Starkie. He was asked to leave. The children began again to have fits such as they had suffered before. Nicholas accused the man of witchcraft. Roger Nowell sent him to Lancaster for trial, where he was found guilty and hanged.

So began the rumours of witchcraft, the belief in which had lain dormant in the hearts of the people of Pendle Forest for many years. Someone had been found guilty, so they must have been a witch, folk said, and neighbour looked at neighbour with new eyes.

IV

On Christmas Eve 1599, Alice and Dick gave a feast for their friends who lived nearby. The weather was already bitterly cold, and a hard frost had frozen most of the river. Flakes of snow struggled down from a grey sky as the Firber, Bannister and Wilsey families arrived.

Henry Mitton and his son Roger, were helping Dick serve the mulled ale. Anne and the other servants moved quietly around the dining-room where the long table was piled high with food; there were platters of cooked meat, whole roast fowl, and in the centre of the table was a decorated pig's head, with dishes of pastries and pickles.

Dick had arranged for a travelling musician, and his friend, a juggler, to entertain the company. After partaking of the lavish feast, they all gathered in the large parlour to enjoy the fun. Later, the Three Wise Men appeared with gifts for all the children, then the ladies, to their great delight, were presented with trinkets. Never was a merrier party celebrated at Roughlee Hall. It rang with children's laughter and the musician's songs.

As the evening ended, Alice asked the musician if he would accompany them as they sang the *Agnus Dei*. Though prohibited by law, all were in accord and they joined in. Without fear, Alice's voice rose high above the others in the beautiful hymn as, with tears in her eyes, she remembered her father and mother and Christmases at Reedley with her brothers long ago.

Sybil approached her as she was leaving. 'I admire you for the music, Alice. It is well we are all friends.'

All the good-byes said, and the children settled at last, Alice and Dick stood by the fire in their bedroom.

'I hope our guests arrive home before the snow really settles. I wanted them to stay but they wished to be at home for Christmas morning.'

'Don't worry, dear. They're all only an hour's ride from their homes. Now, I have something for you. Suffice it to say there are wandering players in the village at the moment,' and he handed Alice a letter.

With trembling fingers, she opened it. 'Oh, Dick, read it with me,' she said.

Together their eager eyes took in the messages from Robert and Christopher, the blessings for Christmas, and the information that they would try to visit England soon, but in the meantime, their love and prayers were with the Nutter family at Roughlee Hall.

As Alice lay in Dick's arms that night she felt a peace and happiness which had eluded her for a long time.

Christmas Day was bright and sunny, the snow crisp under their feet as they prepared together to go to the service at Newchurch. Christopher was to stay at home with Anne, but the other children would go with Alice and Dick.

Margaret, Miles and Charles rode on their own ponies behind their parents, who were astride handsome horses. Alice's plumed hat and russet cloak were of the latest fashion, and she wore leather breeches and boots to ride through the forest. Margaret, bright eyed and pink cheeked, was a miniature of her mother. Richard Baldwin, waiting outside the church when they arrived, looked disapprovingly upon the glowing hats and cloaks. His wife and daughter, were dressed in sombre black. His other daughter, Anne, was ill and never left their home at Wheathead. After the service the family rode home to collect Christopher. Their Christmas feast was to be at Bawle House.

Sybil, William and their children were waiting to welcome them.

They had been to Colne for the Christmas service and so returned much sooner. Alice told Sybil about her letter from her brothers, whilst she was changing out of her cloak in Sybil's bedroom.

Leaving for home in the late afternoon, they saw smoke rising from Malkin Tower, and a lantern at the window.

'It looks as though the Devices have warmth. I sent them chicken and pork, so their bellies will be full,' said Dick.

'Yes, things seem to have settled down again, thank goodness,' Alice replied, 'perhaps Baldwin is leaving them alone at present.'

V

In May came a letter signed 'R. Askew' suggesting that Alice and Dick journey to York to visit him. In the quietness of their bedroom, Alice said, 'Please let us go to Robert. No one suspects who the letter is from, and I may not chance having him here. It will also be a change for us, Dick.'

So, several days later, Dick and Alice, accompanied as always by James Wilsey and Henry Mitton for safety, rode off towards York. Staying two nights in inns, they reached York at noon, and were soon housed in an inn Robert had suggested on Micklegate. Dick and Alice spent two days with Robert, walking around the city wall, and mingling with the worshippers in the Minster. They celebrated Mass with Robert, and his friend, in a country house before saying their farewells.

Alice's heart was full as the quartet rode in the direction of home. 'Why is the Queen so frightened of us? Does she not know we are her loyal subjects?' They stayed for a while in Ripon and then struck off across country to spend the last night at Heber, where they had cousins, renewing friendships, before returning home.

Alice was to remember those few days as her last period of lightheartedness. Cruel fate was once again waiting to destroy her happiness.

Later that month a rider splashed with mud cantered urgently to the back door of Roughlee Hall. Dick, coming across the yard, hurried forward to help the man dismount.

'I carry a message for Mistress Alice Nutter,' he said.

'I am her husband, Richard Nutter. Come into the house and my wife will give you refreshment whilst we talk.'

'Henry,' Dick called, and the man moved forward.

Dick took him to one side. 'Wash the horse down and put him with ours. We want no questions asked.'

Inside the house Anne was organising food and drink for the stranger who was now with Alice. As Dick walked into the room he introduced himself.

'I am Roger Ashton. I have bad news for you. I am afraid Robert, and several other priests, were taken at Wisbech and are imprisoned.'

Alice put her hands to her face. She knew what that meant.

'Oh, why didn't he stay in France?' she said.

'It is no good to be in France, Madam, when the word must be kept alive here. We hope for the day when the real church is once more recognised here as the one true church,' said Ashton.

'I know,' Alice replied, 'and I am a good Catholic in my heart. But why can it not be recognised that all men do not worship in the same way? Why do we have to wage war against the different ways of worshipping God?'

'The Queen fears for her life, Madam. Some Roman Catholics would overthrow her,' remarked Ashton.

Alice turned and said, 'My grandfather visited the Holy Land and he told me of how the Saracens worshipped and how we tried to convert them to Christianity. Will we never be at peace and content with our own ways? Oh, Robert, Robert, my brother! Will he be tortured?'

'If they want the names of others, he will certainly be, Madam. Your brother also knows this. He is strong in his faith, and in his loyalty to his friends.'

Dick went to Alice and held her hands.

Roger went on, 'Parliament is afraid of infiltration by Roman Catholic priests. It is so strong in Lancashire, they intend to make some examples.'

'You must rest here,' Alice said.

'Thank you. I would be grateful for a meal and a wash, but I must be at Samlesbury Hall by midnight. Sir John Southworth's son is also held prisoner.'

'Your horse is tired. Take mine,' said Dick, 'and a change of clothes.'

Alice hurried out and called to Anne to prepare the bath tub in the room set aside for that purpose.

'You are soaked through,' Alice said. 'At least leave here comfortable.'

'What can we do for Robert?' Alice clung to Dick, 'I feel so helpless.'

'We can only wait, my dear. We cannot endanger ourselves, we have our family to consider. Our lives must go on. Remember, you promised your mother to pay lip service to the Church of England and have a secure life. She did not want you to take up the faith as your brothers did.'

'I know mother wanted me to have a happy family life and I have, dear Dick. You are the most wonderful husband.' He held her close.

Later, Roger Ashton rode out and made his way in the direction of Samlesbury Hall.

Three days later a contingent of soldiers rode into Roughlee, Sir Richard Shuttleworth of Gawthorpe, leading them. He approached Roughlee Hall, dismounted, and banged on the door. The whole village was agog with excitement, and gathered to watch. Those who were jealous of the Nutters hopeful of seeing them brought low.

Alice opened the door. 'Madam, we search for your brother, Robert Nutter,' said Sir Richard. 'I have orders to search for him. He is a notorious priest and has escaped from captivity at Wisbech. I believe he may be here.'

'I did not know my brother had escaped,' she said.

'Oh, so you knew he was arrested? Word travels fast for an area with no means of communication.'

'Do not intimidate my wife, Sir,' Dick stated sternly. 'We do not harbour her brother here. He would not place us in danger. Search elsewhere.'

'I understand, Dick, but I have orders to search this house. I will not trouble you too much. We are old friends, but I must ask you to allow me to search your home. You and your family will not be molested, nor will your property be damaged.' He beckoned to one of his men.

Dick stood aside. 'You have written orders, Sir?'

'From the Earl of Derby, no less. He orders me to seek out more than Robert Nutter.'

He produced a document. Dick glanced quickly at the parchment with its red seal, and his eyes took in the list of names. Most were well known to him from his childhood.

The soldiers searched the house whilst Sir Richard accepted refreshment from Alice in the parlour. Anne and the two scullery maids were huddled in the large kitchen when Alice entered.

'Do not be afraid, and certainly do not show them any fear.' she said.

Taking a ladle and filling a tankard with ale from the barrel in the buttery, she carried it back to the parlour.

'Your men are welcome to quench their thirst when the search is over' she said.

'Thank you, Madam,' he said as he drained the tankard. 'I must apologise for this intrusion into your home, but I have my orders.'

'I quite understand, Sir, but I promise you my brother is not here. He will not return. He would not put us at risk.'

'I believe you, Madam. I remember your brother, of course, from our youth, but as I say, I have my orders.'

Alice hurried back to the kitchen and soon the maids were serving ale to the twelve or so men. Afterwards, Sir Richard saluted Alice. Calling the men together, they mounted their horses and rode out of the village. Disappointed, the villagers dispersed, and calm returned. The whole episode had taken less than an hour but to Alice it had seemed an eternity.

'What list did he have?' Alice asked Dick.

'I saw Thomas Hesketh's name, and the name of Lawrence Yate who taught me years ago at Towneley. He will be accused of giving shelter, I am sure. I would like to know who has given such a list to the Earl of Derby.'

'Some traitor who has been bribed,' said Alice grimly. 'Sir John Southworth will be in danger of being banished from the county again, as he was in 1584, if Christopher is there.'

'He was excluded after John's execution,' said Dick. 'I think he will be careful to have a hiding place for Christopher further away from home this time.'

'Pray that Robert does not risk coming home,' Dick said. 'He may not realise there is already a hue and cry out.'

Two miles away, Robert was in fact approaching from Gisburn. Dick was right when he suggested Robert may not know the search was on, but the Earl of Derby had decided to teach all priests and recusants in Lancashire a lesson. As Sir Richard Shuttleworth and his men rode out of Roughlee, it was their intention to drop down into Colne. Where the road from Roughlee meets the Gisburn road and the Downham road, he stopped his horse, waiting for his men to catch up.

The track was stony, wet with rain, rivulets of water trickled down the road from which they had come. Mist hung damply over the trees as Shuttleworth and his men started to descend the road to Colne.

All would have been well had the last rider's horse not stumbled. The soldier was thrown clear. The horse in panic galloped up the road. The soldier scrambled to his feet and chased after it, just as Robert rode into view. Realising he calmly turned his horse down Roughlee track but the soldier shouted, 'Stop my horse, Sir!'

Hearing the shout, Sir Richard turned and saw the solitary horseman. He spurred his horse uphill towards Robert. The latter sensed danger. He, too, turned his horse, cleared a ditch and was soon on Wheathead Lane. But Sir Richard and his men were now on his trail. Robert knew Pendle well, and his first thought was to lose them and reach Firber. There he would be safe, he was sure. He cleared another ditch and headed for Admergill.

Looking back he saw the troop were catching up fast. He turned his horse up Burn Moor, then on to Brogden, passed the site of the mine and out towards Weets Hill. He passed the farmhouse at Far Newfield Edge. Looking behind again he saw that the troop were now losing ground. With a feeling of relief, he spurred on towards the old Roman Road, passing Brogden Hall. He was soon on hard ground on the road and made good progress. But Shuttleworth and his men had made a detour and outwitted him. As Robert came on to the road at Greenber Field, he was surrounded.

His thoughts, as they led him away, were of Alice, and how near he had been. Thank God, he thought, I was not taken there.

VI

Later in the week Roger Nowell and Nicholas Assheton rode into the yard at Roughlee Hall. Roger, grim faced, asked to speak privately to Alice, then he asked Henry Mitton to bring Dick quickly in to the Hall. He then followed Alice into the parlour. With a sinking heart, she looked at Roger.

He said gently, 'Won't you sit down?'

She sank on to the oak settle as Dick came through the doorway. 'It's Robert, isn't it?' she asked sadly.

'You know he is in England then?' Roger looked at her. Alice bowed her head.

'What has happened, Roger?' asked Dick.

'Robert is to be executed at dawn tomorrow in Lancaster,' said Nowell. Nicholas Assheton nodded in affirmation.

'Can I go to him?' asked Alice.

'You would put yourself into danger if you tried, and you would not be in time, my dear. Robert has lived this last dozen years with the knowledge that this could happen.'

'Why, oh why did he not stay in Douai?' she asked.

'Why not indeed, Mistress Nutter,' Roger looked at Nicholas. 'We will leave. I do not wish to trespass on your grief.'

'Please accept some refreshment,' said Dick, 'You are merely the messenger. I am sure that despite everything Alice would rather hear the news from you than from anyone else. Isn't that so, dear?' Alice nodded mutely, then raising her eyes, she asked to be excused. Dick summoned for Anne, who helped Alice from the room.

'It is a bad thing to lose two brothers so,' said Nicholas. 'It is a sad end for another of our childhood friends, dying drawn and quartered. Let us hope Christopher stays in France and does not join the priests here.'

'I hope he stays in France,' Dick replied. 'I do not think Alice could sustain a third such loss.' Ringing the bell he called for ale and pasties for the two men.

'I shall ask Ellen to ride over and see Alice. They are fond of each other.' Roger looked at Dick.

'Please do,' Dick replied.

The door swung open to admit young Miles. Grown tall and strong, he was now sixteen and working with his father.

'Is something wrong, Sir?' he asked Dick.

'I am afraid your Uncle Robert is to be executed at Lancaster tomorrow,' Dick explained.

'Oh no! He was so good to me at Douai. It's not true, say it's not true. He's a good man. Oh poor mother' and turning, he ran down the passage and up the stairs to his mother's room. She was sitting on the bed with Anne kneeling beside her when Miles rushed in. She held out her arms to him, Miles clasped her in his arms. Tears poured down their faces.

Alice stayed in her bedchamber for a week. Dick was worried at her lack of energy and will to do her household tasks. Sybil Bannister and Ruth Firber had been to console with her, and on a grey, miserable day, Ellen Nowell rode into the yard with her eldest daughter. Alice took refreshment with her and Ellen pleaded with her to walk in the walled garden.

'Yes, Ellen, I do need some fresh air,' she spoke sadly, but allowed herself to be led outside.

Dick, leading his horse into the yard, was relieved to see Alice out once again, and smiled gratefully at Ellen.

Walking round the rose garden, Alice stooped to remove some dead heads from the roses and when she returned to the house she felt calmer than she had done at any time since the news of the execution.

'Doctor Gabriel has sent you a potion to help you sleep, dear,' said Ellen.

'I will accept it now. I have slept very badly since Robert's death and Dick has suffered with me,' she smiled. 'Dear Dick, through all my tragedies he has remained solid. With him at my side I feel I will surmount anything,' and going through to the kitchen, she told Anne she would dine with the family that evening.

When Ellen left, Alice continued to sit quietly in her pleasant parlour. Margaret and Maria came in, and without speaking, sat on either side of her, smiling happily to see her downstairs again. Christopher rushed in.

'Mama, Mama, are you well again?' he cried.

'Yes, dear. Mama feels much better,' she replied as he climbed on to her knee. She buried her face in his soft hair and tears ran down her cheeks.

'Mama, why are you crying?' Charles asked.

'Because I am happy to have such lovely children. God has given me so much, and taken so much. You are my dear consolation.'

Dick was happy to see Alice in the dining-room, and holding her close he whispered, 'You have me, and you have the children. We will give thanks for them.'

'Pray God Christopher stays in France, Dick,' Alice whispered.

VII

At Christmas the whole family were invited to a feast at Read Hall. Maria was included in Ellen's invitation.

'Isn't Ellen kind to remember how close Maria is to us,' said Alice, passing Dick the letter to read.

'We must go, Alice,' Dick said.

'Oh, I know. I will look forward to it, although Roger Nowell always brings me bad news.'

'He is the Justice of the Peace for this valley, he has no choice,' Dick replied, 'if he delegated it to someone else you would feel slighted.'

'I hope he never has to bring more bad news,' Alice looked sad. 'I may not see Christopher again. I do not relish the thought of a trip to Douai, and he must not come here.'

'You have always enjoyed your visits and you could take Margaret next time.'

'Oh Dick, I love Douai. The gardens, the weather, and meeting old friends. It's the long journey to the port, and the sea voyage I find exhausting.'

'We will see how you feel next year,' he said and squeezed her hand.

Alice told the family about the Christmas feast as they sat down to supper that night. Maria blushed with pleasure when she realised she was included in the plans.

'I wish Christopher Baldwin was going,' she said.

'The Baldwins never socialise with anyone. Indeed, Richard Baldwin would put a cloud on my revelry,' said Alice.

'Oh, Maria doesn't want Richard to go, just Christopher,' Miles winked at his mother.

'So that is the way of it. I wondered why Christopher rode to church and back with us now. I thought it was to accompany Miles!' Alice said.

Maria blushed at the banter. 'Maybe Christopher will be able to lead his own life some day,' she said.

'He will not find it easy with a father such as he has,' said Dick, 'and he will have to work in the mill.'

'Christopher would like to be a farmer. He tires of the corn mill,' said Maria. 'He is planning to rent a cottage and start with a few animals. Have you a cottage he could tenant, Uncle Dick?' Maria asked.

'It would start a holy war if I gave him a cottage, or attempted to lure him away from his father,' Dick replied.

'Only you can stand up to his father,' Maria said sadly.

'Well, I never. This is a surprise to me. Have you spoken with Christopher often?' asked Alice.

'Mama, she speaks to him at every oppurtunity,' Miles grinned.

'Yes, as often as I can, like you do to Ruth Bannister,' retorted Maria.

'Oh, what is this? Secrets are out today,' Alice smiled. 'And what of you Margaret? Do you seek to share confidences with anyone we know?'

'No, Mama, there is no one I am drawn to. I would like to do what you did and go to study at Douai. Charles would like to go also. May we?'

'Why, Margaret, this is indeed a day for confidences coming my way. I had no idea you had this inclination. Your father has already suggested I visit there next year. I was hesitant. But if you would like to go, and Charles too, we will arrange it, won't we, dear?' she smiled at Dick.

'So you want to leave me for a while, my dear? Dick asked. 'You had better not decide you want to stay until you visit. It may not be what you expect, so we will keep an open mind and just arrange a visit.'

'I will stay and learn to speak French, like Mama, and return a lady,' said Margaret.

'I hope Charles does not return a priest,' said Miles suddenly.

'If I feel called to follow my uncles, I will,' Charles said.

Alice's heart sank. This was something she had kept to the back of her mind, hoping for their own sakes, her sons would embrace the new religion at least on the surface.

Charles saw her stricken face. 'Do not worry, Mama. If I stay to be a priest, I will not risk my life in England,' he said.

'Let us eat, the food grows cold,' said Dick. 'We will discuss all these new affairs again.'

The gathering at Read Hall was attended by all their friends and acquaintances, and the Nutters talked of it for weeks afterwards. The jugglers and magicians, Roger on his lute, the men smoking their pipes, and the interesting people they had met.

'There was a man there who had been to the New World,' Christopher said, 'Ralph Assheton's uncle. He said there are dangerous coloured men, and the weather is always warm and sunny. I will go there when I grow up.'

'You must do as you wish, dear, when you grow up. Your father

99

and I will not stand in your way, but when we are old, you must return and visit us,' Alice said smiling.

'Oh, I will always come back to see you, Mama,' he replied.

Alice smiled to herself, thinking how her children were growing up. *When Dick and I are old I hope we will have some grandchildren near to us.* She remembered Miles and Ruth Bannister dancing together at the Nowell's party. *If they marry, I will be so pleased. Sybil's daughter and my son, and Miles working on the farm with his father,* she mused happily.

VIII

The winter of 1601 was hard. The fields were frozen. Dick, young Miles and their labourers transported fodder to the sheep spread over many acres as far as Pendle Hill. They had grazed in the lower fields at the bottom of the hill in November, in tupping time, but this year was more difficult than normal. There was a hard frost, night after night, and regular snow falls. When Dick and his party had to dig the sheep out of drifts, they came home each afternoon glowing and hungry.

Alice and Anne cooked pastries and pies and made hot soup for the villagers who were poor and unable to travel far for food. They roasted chickens and sheep, and decided to set out for Malkin Tower one day. Elizabeth Device received the food thankfully and the children clamoured round the horses. The old Demdike hobbled to the door.

'My Beth's face will never be the same, thanks to your mine,' she shrieked.

'Remember, we lost our dear father in that accident,' Alice retorted. 'I offered to arrange for Doctor Gabriel to operate on her face but she refused.'

'Leave be, Mother, leave be. Take no heed of her, Mistress Nutter,' Elizabeth said. 'I am well enough, I can still look after my children.'

Alice noticed a large stack of wood at the side of the building and was reassured that Sellars had obviously provided the family with the means to keep warm. Anne and Alice rode on.

'Tom and I must visit mother shortly. She grows worse, and the Nutters shun her since Robert died,' Anne said. 'I dare not pass their house alone, and tremble when I remember the past. But at least they allow mother to remain in her cottage.

'Robert Nutter of Greenhead was a bad man, Anne. You were not responsible for his death, although I know his mother accuses you. He took the potion meant for your mother, but that didn't kill him. I have heard, just recently, in fact, at Christmas at the Nowells, that Robert drank ale and wine heavily and often had a stomach disorder,' Alice told Anne.

'His mother still blames me though. She did not know what he did to me. His father wished to spare her the knowledge, but I can't help thinking she would judge me differently if she knew. His brother knew,' Anne replied.

'Never mind, dear, those of us who love you know the truth,' said Alice gently, and taking the road to Roughlee, they broke into a gallop.

IX

The winter passed, and as often happens, spring came unannounced. On a cloudless day in late March, suddenly the birds were singing, small flowers raised their faces to the sun, and Alice wandered in her walled garden inspecting the ravages of the long cold winter.

The dogs, unused to the warmth of the sun, rolled on their backs on the path. As Alice paused to look around, she saw Sybil Bannister entering the garden.

'Why, Sybil, so pleased to see you. Are you alone?'

'No, Ruth has stopped to talk to Miles along the road. I think those two feel something for each other.'

'Yes, I know,' Alice replied. 'I do hope they marry.'

'I do, too, dear, and we will have grandchildren to share.' The two friends linked arms and strolled around the garden together.

'Richard Baldwin has been riding round Malkin Tower again, warning old Demdike to keep from his land. Anne Baldwin is very ill. The cold winter has taken its toll and he is accusing the old woman of cursing her.'

'I am sorry for Baldwin's daughter, but she has always been delicate and this is a harsh climate for such as she. He is obsessed with the Demdike, I don't know why?' Alice turned to her friend, 'Did I tell you Maria has a fondness for Christopher Baldwin?'

'Oh, no, the poor girl. Baldwin will never let his son marry someone so close to you. It will have to be a girl from a pious and puritan family, who dresses in black.' Sybil smiled ruefully at Alice.

'I don't know about that, dear. It will depend on how much of Baldwin's hard will has been inherited by his son. Christopher is not so soft and holds his own with his father. He may oppose him. We will have to see. Maria has already asked Dick to find Christopher a cottage, but up to now, Dick has refused, not being willing to cause trouble in Baldwin's family. Christopher stays to supper a couple of times every week and always rides with us to church on a Sunday. He and Miles have been buying and selling stock at Gisburn market. They are very sensible, and hold on to their money. I feel Christopher may indeed break away.'

'Baldwin is building a bigger house at Wheathead. He expects to finish it in a couple of years. It's higher up than the mill, quite near the road to Firber. He is doing most of the work himself and expects Christopher to work on it too.'

'Yes,' Alice replied, 'Miles has mentioned it. They're digging a water supply from the hillside. Thomas Firber has seen him up there.'

'The Firbers have sunk another well. We are invited up there on Good Friday. Are you going?' Sybil asked.

'Yes, I am looking forward to it. Their house is so warm and friendly, though quite small,' replied Alice.

On Good Friday, the Nutter family rode on horseback to Firber after the church service, the Baldwin family travelling behind them. When they reached Wheathead, Richard Baldwin turned right into the track leading to his mill. Christopher followed the Nutters.

'Halt, Sir,' Baldwin shouted to his son. 'Where are you going?'

'Father, I told you I was invited to Firber House for meat this day.'

'Your mother needs you here,' said Baldwin. 'I do not approve of you joining a papist gathering.'

'I can manage today.' His mother seemed to take a deep breath as she opposed her husband for the first time. Baldwin looked ready to boil over as he stared at Christopher, and at Miles, who had just ridden up. He turned, followed by his wife and daughter, and disappeared down the track.

'Your mother may suffer for this, Christopher,' Miles said.

'I have talked to her,' Christopher replied. 'She has urged me to stand up to him. She says it is too late for her now, but not too late for me. She knows I love Maria, and intend to marry her. My father may disown me if he will, but he will have no help at the mill. He finds it difficult to get people to work for him. Anyway, I have money of my own now, enough to buy some stock. It will be a start. Maria and I will marry as soon as I find a cottage.

The two friends urged their horses to catch up with the rest of the family. They passed Higher Wheathead, and pressing on by Jackson's Farm, they soon reached Firber. The Bulcocks and Bannisters were already there, with the Wilseys and other friends. A merry feast followed.

Christopher had time to walk outside with Maria, who realised he had made his first stand against his father.

The whole matter of Christopher's opposition to his father had to be forgotten when his sister Anne died. The Nutters attended the service at Newchurch, together with all their neighbours. Sympathy was extended, particularly to Mistress Baldwin, a sad, thin figure, holding on to her son and remaining daughter at the graveside.

On the following Sunday afternoon, Maria and Christopher walked through the fields below Wheathead where the yellow primroses were just budding. The stood together on a small stone bridge in a hollow, and Christopher picked a primrose. Giving it to Maria he said, 'Press this in your bible. It is a token of my love and a promise that you and I will be married soon.'

They climbed the hill and stood looking down into Roughlee.

'One day you will be mistress of a house such as Roughlee Hall,' he said.

'Oh, Christopher,' she replied, 'a small cottage is all I need, as long as I am with you.'

'You have grown up in Roughlee Hall and I will make you mistress of one as grand.' Then laughing, he swung her round and, hand in hand, they ran down the hill to the house below.

The plans to take Margaret and Charles to Douai were not making much progress. Communications were difficult and replies to letters were not received.

'You will have to wait till next year, I fear,' Alice told Margaret, 'unless your father will go to Hull himself to arrange a sailing.'

'Margaret, must you go?' asked Dick.

'I would love to go, if only to visit for a short time,' Margaret replied. 'I have never been, and neither has Charles. Miles has. Why can't we go?'

'Travel is not as easy now,' replied Dick.

'I will go with them,' replied Alice resignedly, 'provided I can return no later than October, which, if I stay four weeks, means we must not set off any later than August. It will be warmer then, there is a difference in the climate.'

'I will despatch James forthwith,' Dick said, 'and a sailing shall be organised for July or August.'

X

On May Day the Nutter family were no exception in their enthusiasm to attend the fair at Whalley. They set off early, leaving Henry Mitton behind at Roughlee.

'I am too old for fairs,' he said. 'Enjoy yourselves.'

'Henry is not as well as he used to be,' Alice said to Dick. 'I am afraid he is too heavy, and his weight makes him breathless.'

'Too much of your excellent cooking my dear and, I suspect, too many glasses of ale from the cellar!' Dick grinned. 'He is a good and faithful servant and I grudge him nothing.'

It seemed the whole county had turned out for the fair at Whalley. The maypole was erected on the village green, and the girls selected their ribbons. A man passed them, leading two bears, and Christopher clung tightly to Alice's hand in excitement.

Miles had gone off to join his friends and Charles and Margaret walked ahead with Maria. Hawkers were selling their wares, beggars held out their hands for alms and, in the stocks, two scolds were suffering an onslaught of eggs and rotten vegetables.

'It is time we had a better form of punishment than the stocks,' commented Alice.

'What do you suggest?' Dick asked.

'Well, for one thing, women shouldn't be put in the stocks for being a scold. They may simply have bad husbands,' she replied. 'Do you ever see a man in the stocks for beating his wife?'

'You answer my question with a question Alice,' Dick said laughing. 'Come, I will buy you a trinket to remind you of this day,' and they wandered round the fair, nodding to acquaintances and chatting to their friends.

Alice, Dick and Christopher dined at the inn. The older children had gone off to wander where they wished. Leaving the inn, they once again started to push their way through the crowds, stopping to watch some jugglers whose antics delighted Christopher. Moving on, they realised there was quite a commotion ahead.

'Oh dear, what is going on? Someone is having an argument,' said Alice. Simultaneously, Alice and Dick became aware of a young boy facing a bloated red-faced man, and realised it was Charles. Dick hurried forward.

'Father, father, see the poor cat.'

Dick looked up. Hanging from a tall pole was a cage containing a cat, hissing and spitting. A notice proclaimed a prize for whoever killed it. A pile of stones, obviously for aiming at the cat, was set out on a tray in front of the bloated man.

'Please buy the cat. He won't sell it to me,' pleaded Charles to Dick.

'Take the boy away, he is ruining my trade,' demanded the man.

Alice pushed her way through the crowd, pulling Christopher with her. The crowd jostled, annoyed at temporarily being deprived of their fun.

'How much for the cat?' Dick asked. The man's cunning eyes took in Dick's prosperous appearance, and named a price.

'I could buy a sheep for that!' Dick expostulated.

'Well buy a sheep,' the man replied.

Charles and Christopher were also pleading with Alice to buy the cat. Dick said, 'The cage must come with the cat. It is too terrified to let out. It may attack my sons in its present state.'

With the handing over of the large sum, the cat was delivered to its new owners and the cat-man headed off for the first ale stall!

The cat continued to hiss and spit and Dick grimaced at Alice as they pushed their way through the jeering crowd. When they returned to their horses at the inn, Dick was annoyed with Charles.

'He will just get another cat, you know,' he told him.

'But Father, we couldn't let it be killed so cruelly.'

'No, but I cannot buy them all. On your ponies now, we are going home before you cost me more.'

'I want to call the cat Tibs,' said Christopher.

'Tibs it is,' said Charles, 'we will soon tame it when we get home.'

The cat did indeed recover from its fright and in no time at all was an accepted member of the family, holding its own with the dogs who tried to chase it, by facing them and hissing and spitting. When Alice pottered in her rose garden, Tibs could be seen rolling in the sun and following her progress through the garden.

XI

Plans were arranged for the trip to France. In August, Dick set off with James Wilsey to escort Alice, Margaret and Charles to Hull. Miles insisted on accompanying the party at the last minute.

'You will be glad of company on the way home, Father,' he said.

'Of course I will, Son. Do you wish you were going to Douai with your mother?'

'Not this time. I enjoyed my visit before, but it won't be the same now.'

'You mean since Uncle Robert's death?'

'You mean Uncle Robert's execution,' Miles said bitterly.

'We cannot dwell on these things Miles. Life has to go on.'

'When I went to Douai, grandfather was still alive and Christopher wasn't even born,' Miles ruminated.

Staying at their usual inns on the way, the party finally rode into Hull a week or so later. Dick and James arranged the sailing whilst Miles, Margaret and Charles enjoyed the hurly burly of the seaport and watched the tall ships swaying in the wind.

'We must ask father to bring Christopher to meet us when we return. He will love to see the ships,' said Alice.

The sailing arranged, good-byes were said, and the following day, Miles and Dick started for home.

'Has Charles talked to you of Douai?' asked Dick.

'Oh, yes. He is obsessed with it,' replied Miles.

'Your mother and I have discussed the possibility that he might wish to become a priest. We will not deter him.'

'Become a priest? Isn't he too young?'

'Not really, if he is to begin his studies.'

'Will Margaret study too?' asked Miles.

'It will be better for Charles to have Margaret there with him, and if she wants to stay, she may do so.'

'But we didn't talk about that. I didn't know they were to stay now. Oh, Father, I thought they were only going to see what it was like. I thought they would return with mother and go to study in a year or two. I didn't say good-bye for years! I thought I would see them in a month.' Miles looked distressed.

'Do not distress yourself, Son. I think your mother hopes they will return with her, but I am sure they will decide to stay. That is why I did not dwell on it. I know your mother will miss them dreadfully,' his father assured him.

'I will miss them, too, all the time,' Miles looked miserable.

'You have chosen to be a farmer and follow after me. You will keep the estates for the family. When mother and I are gone we will know it is in safe hands,' Dick assured him again.

'Father, I pray it will be many years before I am left alone to run the farm.'

'Life is capricious, dear Son. Fate deals cruel blows. We live in a cosy corner of a vicious society and we are not immune from disaster, as you know. Your mother has seen two of her brothers executed for their faith, and some of their friends also. We lost grandfather tragically. You must always be prepared for misfortune so that you can face it when it comes.'

The two horsemen cantered slowly along the track, each busy with his own thoughts.

Aboard ship Alice, James and the two children dined with the captain in his cabin. Margaret and Charles had been overawed by the sailors' expertise in swarming up and down to hoist the sails, and chattered continuously about the events of the day. When Alice and Margaret were preparing for bed, they said their prayers together.

'I pray you have a happy future, Margaret dear, and that you are always strong in your faith.'

'I hope to learn much at Douai, Mother. I do so wish to remain there.'

108

'Wait and see what it is like, dear. You may decide to return,' her mother replied.

'Charles and I have talked about it and we know we will stay.'

'It may not be what you imagine, my dear,' and smiling, she kissed her daughter goodnight.

Towards the end of August a messenger brought the news Dick was expecting. Margaret and Charles were to remain at Douai and Alice was sailing back with James on 1st September. Round the table that evening talk flowed excitedly between Miles, Christopher and Maria.

'Can I go to visit them when I am older?' asked Christopher.

'We will all go, but you must promise me you will not stay. I don't want to lose all my children to France,' Dick smiled.

'I do not want to be a priest. I am going to be a sailor like Sir Francis Drake, and sail to other lands and see coloured people and wild animals.'

'We will see, Christopher,' his father assured him.

'So no one will stay and help me run the farm' said Miles shortly.

'You have good men to help you, and when you marry Ruth Bannister, things may change,' Christopher retorted.

'Hold your tongue! Who says I will marry Ruth Bannister anyway?' asked Miles indignantly, and hurriedly picked up his knife.

Dick smiled and cleverly steered the conversation into more relaxed channels.

A week later, Dick and Miles set off to meet Alice's ship. Christopher, who was delighted to be accompanying them, was also sad because Margaret, his 'little mother', would not be returning with her. When they arrived in Hull, they booked their rooms at the usual inn, Christopher, although very tired as he had never been on a long journey before, was anxious to see ships for the first time. After breakfast on the following day they joined the milling throng on the quayside, and Dick made enquiries about the arrival of ships in the next few days.

Communications were always poor. Permission should have been sought for Margaret and Charles to travel to France, but Dick always felt they could move about more freely if they did not tell anyone they were going. Up to now this had been the case. No one had asked any questions in Roughlee regarding the whereabouts of Margaret and Charles. Only when it was known they had not returned would he have to find a reason for them leaving the country. As always, Dick would meet that situation when it arose. Alice had booked a passage on the *Martha Rose*.

'Sailings, good, Sir. Winds favourable,' said one bearded seaman, 'no storms reported. She should be in late today or tomorrow.'

'Well, Christopher, we can't wait about the quayside all day. We'll explore and then return.'

'Oh Father, do not let us go too far away. I wish to see the ship sail in,' Christopher replied.

'It will take an hour or two from first sighting. We'll keep coming back.'

He led Christopher away, passing the heavy nets of fish, the bartering seamen, the cries of hawkers and the shrill screaming of the sea birds. They wandered up and down the narrow streets, pausing to buy cockles, mussels and hot meat pies.

Dick, Christopher and Miles arrived back on the quayside in the late afternoon to the cry *'Martha Rose* ahoy.' Christopher exclaimed in delight to see the graceful ship in full sail heading slowly into port.

Christopher could hardly contain his excitement watching the preparations for docking the ship. It seemed an age before the ship finally slid into the dockside, and another age before the gangplank was lowered and the tall figure of James Wilsey strode down it with the smaller one of Alice, clad in her green riding suit, behind him. Holding her long skirts, she stepped daintily from the gangplank into Dick's arms.

Alice hugged Christopher, then Miles, and Christopher again. Tears were streaming down her cheeks.

'I have two tall sons left to me, thank God, in this country. Tell me how Maria and Anne are?' and linking up she set off along the quayside. Dick sighed as he looked at James.

'Seemingly we are left with the baggage,' he grimaced ruefully.

As they reached the inn, Alice turned to see Dick and James not too far behind.

As they caught up, Alice said, 'I was so excited I could not eat.'

Dick ordered food from the innkeeper. They had so much news to impart to each other. It was a merry gathering.

Alice's news of Charles and Margaret was eagerly awaited. She told how Charles was immediately content with life in the seminary at Douai, and of Margaret's pleasure in being taught by the nuns.

'Margaret and Charles are happy,' said Dick. 'We will all visit them next year.'

XII

The Christmas feast most remembered in 1602 was given at Downham Hall. The Asshetons threw open their doors to all the local landowners and gentry.

Yeoman farmers, prospering more since the dissolution of the monasteries and church land, were often better off than the gentry, but in Lancashire and Yorkshire there was little class distinction when it came to prosperity at least.

Dick and Alice drank hot punch and discussed various local affairs with Roger Nowell and Nick Bannister.

'Baldwin tried to indict Demdike as a witch last week,' said Roger, 'he blames her for the death of his daughter.'

'What rubbish!' Alice exclaimed defensively, 'Anne Baldwin was delicate from birth and always had a racking cough. It's damp and cold at Wheathead. The girl died of natural causes. Baldwin has an obsession about the Demdikes.'

'I have received a copy of the *Daemonology*, written by King James of Scotland. He obviously believes witches can do great harm. He even lists events in Scotland, and draws attention to certain circumstances which he pleads us not to ignore. He offers rewards for the discovery of witches.'

'Demdike is too ignorant to understand such matters,' said Alice.

'It is said she brews potions for healing sickness in people and animals which sometimes go wrong,' Roger added.

'Reputable physicians have patients who die also. They are not God,' argued Alice.

'There is also the story of the Chattox making clay images. The Nutters of Greenhead blame her for Robert's death.'

'I thought that story was long dead. It is not a pretty one, if the truth were known,' said Alice emphatically. 'It was years ago.'

'So you know something of Robert's death? Of course, Anne Redfern is your servant. Have a care of her, Mistress Alice.'

'Anne is my dear friend. She has been with me since she was eight and I love her dearly. She was ravished by Robert Nutter.'

'I was never informed of this,' said Roger.

'Some matters are dealt with in the family,' Dick broke in. 'Remember, Robert Nutter was also cousin to Alice and I.'

'I believe in God, and not in witchcraft,' Alice turned to Roger.

'Why, yes, but doesn't the Bible tell us to beware of witches?' he asked.

'Enough! The subject is distasteful. Please take my arm and dance with me.'

Alice, who sought assurance from Dick, took Nowell's arm. Dick smiled and nodded to her.

'You look as young as ever, Mistress Nutter. Adversity certainly becomes you.'

'I have come to terms with the loss of my brother. I have a rock in Dick. He is my life support.'

'You indeed have a happy marriage, unlike many others I know, including myself,' said Roger.

'Please do not talk of such things. Ellen is my friend.'

'Maybe, but a dullard in comparison to you. You are well travelled, Mistress Alice. How found you France this year?'

'I enjoyed France, but I missed Dick. Next year, we all go to visit Margaret and Charles.'

'So, Charles leans towards the Roman Church. That must trouble you. If it should reach certain ears that your son trains as a priest, you know the penalty,' he grimly reminded her.

'I would know who was the informer. He promises that he will stay in France,' said Alice.

'I seem to remember your brother Robert promising his mother the same thing.'

'Master Nowell, you distress me. Please may I sit down.'

Roger Nowell, holding her closer than was necessary, whirled her through a door into an oak-panelled study.

'The mistletoe hangs here,' he said, and kissed her soundly on the lips.

'You forget yourself, Sir,' Alice spoke coldly. 'Kindly return me to my husband.'

Roger smiled a sardonic smile, and holding her elbow, he led her into the room and through the crowd.

'You make a handsome couple,' Nicholas Assheton teased, looking Roger up and down.

Roger was resplendant in wine velvet, and Alice's gown of dark blue complemented it. He bowed towards Dick and then drifted away. Dick teased Alice. 'You didn't dance with him very long.'

'I do not like him, Dick. Despite his apparent friendliness there is something inside him which disturbs me. I fear he patronises us. Maybe he considers himself our superior.'

'He was born into wealth and gentility, but if he hadn't married Ellen he would have had to search for another rich wife. He and his father were in great debt, for all they were gentry. Don't let him

112

worry you. I will always be your staff to lean on. Come, let us dance.'
Dick and Alice joined the line of couples in a lively jig.

In the library, Roger Nowell was in conversation with Nick Bannister, 'I will make Dick Nutter an offer for the Greystone land and the coal mine.'

'I doubt he'll sell,' Nick replied, 'though he's never been up there since his father's accident. Wilsey and a few others take what coal is needed for Roughlee Hall and the village.'

'Nevertheless, I believe the area worth further investigation.' Roger seeing Ellen peering from the doorway, muttered to Nick. 'My watch and ward is here. We'll speak of this again.'

'My dear, you are looking for me?' Taking Ellen's arm he left the room. Nick watched with sardonic amusement.

Supper was served in the large hall. Servants replenished plates as quickly as they were emptied, with a selection of hot and cold meats, roast, baked, boiled and fried all laid on platters down the centre of the table. There were sheep being roasted in the kitchen, and goose, game and pork in plenty. There were vegetable dishes, pies and puddings, and a profusion of French wines and October ale.

The puddings were decorated with crystallised rose petals, violets and marigolds. There were fruit jellies, herb and gooseberry sauces, cream fillings and preserves, also decorated with marzipan and candied fruit. A mouth-watering display, which Alice, with her culinary expertise, thoroughly appreciated. The centre-piece of the table was a white swan. On a large sideboard on the right of the room was the *piece de resistance*; a gleaming white edifice made from almond paste, decorated with icing and gold baubles, in the shape of a castle, pieces of which were handed out with wine at the end of the feast.

At this point, carol singers gathered in the room, and the whole company joined in.

Driving home in the carriage, Alice snuggled up to Dick, and remarked sleepily, 'That was a lovely feast.'

'I enjoyed it too.' Dick kissed her head pressed close against him.

Book Three

I

There was a christening feast at Towneley Hall in January 1603 to which the Nutters were invited. They arrived, by prior arrangement, the night before the official christening. After all the children were in bed, the adults gathered together in the small chapel where masses had been celebrated since 1395.

Mary Towneley held her seventh son in her arms. Anne Towneley of Carr Hall, and her husband Henry, stood godparents as the baby was christened Christopher, by his namesake Christopher Southworth, once more risking his life by holding a mass at Towneley Hall.

John Towneley was financially much oppressed by the fines he had to pay for recusancy, and much discourse was held on the subject as the close friends supped together after the ceremony. Christopher Southworth left the house during darkness, taking letters for Alice's children in Douai.

The following morning Alice took a walk round the wooded grounds of the Hall. It was peaceful, and though cold, birds could be heard singing. As she entered the hallway, a voice hailed her. 'You are here early, Mistress Nutter.' Roger Nowell approached her. Alice looked at this man who she felt would ever be her *bête noire*.

'What do you infer, Sir?' she asked.

'Why, my dear, we are formal today. I merely wondered if I had missed some important occasion.'

'I fear you would not be here enjoying John's hospitality if you truly felt you had failed in your duty,' she replied, before moving away, Christopher having run to hold her hand.

'Roger. Good to see you.' Dick held out his hand. Taking it, Roger replied, 'I would like a private word once the formalities are over.'

'You sound stern, Roger, what ails you?'

'Merely a matter of business we could do.'

'Such as?' Dick replied.

'Can I speak of it later?'

'Out with it, Roger. No time like the present.'

'I wish to make you an offer for the land and coal mine at Greystones.'

114

'That land, and what is on it, is not for sale, and will not be in my lifetime.' Dick, with a furious glint in his eye, strode away. Roger had the grace to look embarrassed. Nicholas Bannister joined him.

'Do I gather you broached the subject of the mine at Greystones? Dick looked mighty annoyed.'

'Damn him and his independence,' Roger drained his glass. 'He may not always be flying high, and I'll be waiting.'

The dinner party was merry. Friends and neighbours jostled together with many pleasantries, and partook of the lavish feast spread out on tables in the hall. The children ran along the corridors, laughing and playing. The new baby gurgled in his cradle. Roger Nowell, gazing down at the child, knew full well what sort of an occasion had been covered by the dinner party.

John Towneley had already spent three periods in prison for his refusal to attend the Church of England, and under the ruling of the Lord Chancellor, it was intended to suppress and destroy Catholics by means of fines and imprisonment. The death penalty would be imposed should it be proved a priest had been harboured in any home.

Roger gazed contemplatively on the guests. He knew them all, and had, in fact, grown up with them, but he was not a man prepared to pay fines or suffer the indignities of a faith he had readily set aside. He embraced the new faith from necessity, and the desire for comfort and a life without harassment, and he wished his neighbours would do the same.

He knew that news of this gathering would spread, and expected comment. He also knew that his presence, and that of fellow magistrate Nicholas Assheton, and their families, was to ward off suspicion of the true nature of the proceedings.

Roger Nowell was, in some respects, an indolent man, unless his personal finances were at risk. He enjoyed the social life, feastings and celebrations at homes he knew well to be Catholic, and put no pressure on these people to attend church. The Nutters were punctilious in their attendance at church. He could not fault them on that, but he was annoyed at Dick's refusal to negotiate in any way the land at Greystones. He pondered as to whether there would be a method to entice Dick to sell this land. He desired more land. His eyes met Dick's over the heads of the other guests. They were both over six feet tall, Dick stared back, but felt uneasy when he saw the venom in Roger's eyes.

'Come, dear,' he said to Alice, 'collect Christopher and we will ride home.'

'So early, Dick?' she looked surprised.

'Yes.' He made his way towards John Towneley. 'Alice has developed a headache. Will you excuse us?'

John clasped him by the hand. They were old friends.

'The important business was performed last night, Dick. I'm glad you were here. God go with you both.'

Riding home, Dick was pre-occupied and Alice was worried because she knew he was not sharing his thoughts.

'What has upset you, Dick,' she said at last.

Tersely, Dick replied, 'Roger Nowell asked me to sell the Greystone land.'

'How could he? He knows how we all feel about the coal mine. I knew he was at the bottom of your quietness. I hate him, he tried to upset me by insinuating we had foregathered for "another reason", as he put it.'

'Roger does not improve with age,' Dick replied. 'He is becoming greedy and covetous.'

'Your father always said he was like that,' Alice said. 'Don't let him persuade you.'

'You know nothing will persuade me to sell the land. It holds a good number of sheep, and the coal is best left alone. It will belong to Miles some day, and he may do as he chooses with it.'

'Oh, Dick, do not say such things, we have many years together yet.'

Alice's gaze was troubled as she looked into her husband's normally smiling face.

'I fear our friendship with the Nowells will not be the same in future, Alice. Will you mind?' Dick looked questioningly at Alice.

'I could not desert Ellen. She is not well,' she replied.

'By no means desert Ellen, but try to avoid family gatherings. I no longer trust Nowell. He does not react well to being thwarted of his object.'

Alice and Dick missed Charles and Margaret very much. They made light of the subject in public, but at home, round the table at mealtimes, young Miles and Christopher did their best to entertain their parents with tales of their everyday affairs. Christopher was driven to Towneley Hall five days a week for lessons with the many Towneley children, and others of local families. He was quick and proficient in learning.

Though just eleven years old, he had set his heart on the sea as soon as he was old enough. He talked excitedly of the New World, and his intentions to go there and see things for himself.

Alice looked ruefully at Dick one evening when Christopher was

116

particularly excited. He had been to Towneley Hall that day, where a sea-faring man had entertained the children with his stories of sunny islands, black people, exotic fruits and coloured birds.

'It seems we will lose another of our children,' she said.

'We have each other dear, and Miles and Ruth will present us with some grandchildren in due course,' and his eyes twinkled as he looked at Miles, who blushed a violent red.

'Oh Father, I am in no hurry to marry. I need to build a house first.'

'You know this house is large enough for us all,' Alice replied, looking hurt.

'Oh, Mother, we would like to be independent. You have taught us to be so, and Aunt Sybil has encouraged Ruth to be the same.'

'Well, I have,' agreed Alice, 'but I would like you to take over the Hall. Perhaps your father and I will move to a smaller house.'

Dick smiled warmly at Alice. 'Good idea, we'll pick a spot. What say you to that, Miles?'

'I'll speak to Ruth, I'm sure she would like to be the mistress of Roughlee Hall.'

'Yes, do that Miles,' Alice replied.

'Baldwin has nearly finished his new house at Wheathead,' Miles continued. 'Christopher says he will not live there, he plans to build a house for Maria not far from here.'

'You young people have so many plans,' Alice said. 'I hope they come to fruition and that you are as happy as your father and I have been.'

II

On the eve of Lady Day, 24 March 1603, the old Queen died, and her cousin, James, son of the Catholic Mary, Queen of Scots, rode into England and made his way, without hindrance to London, where his claim to the throne was not disputed. He was a staunch Protestant and the persecution of Catholics continued, and any hopes that religious freedom would come with the new reign were soon dashed.

Word filtered through into Lancashire of priests' martyrdom. The Nutters and their friends continued to pay lip service to the Church of England whilst celebrating mass whenever possible.

Alice, Dick, Christopher and Miles had spent four weeks at Douai with Margaret and Charles. On their return they were regaled with stories of whippings by Baldwin and fines meted out by Roger Nowell on any refusing to attend church.

Alice rode over to Read one crisp autumn morning, and found her friend Ellen very ill.

'Alice, how pleased I am to see you. I have not recovered from my last confinement, but you are a tonic to me.' Ellen lay in bed, her face white, enormous shadows surrounded her eyes and her fingers plucked nervously at the sheets. Her two younger daughters played with their dolls by the fire, and a wet-nurse held the new baby in her arms. The air was fetid, and Alice asked if she might open a window.

'Oh, Alice, how I long to ride with you again, but I fear those days are over for me.'

'Ellen, my dear, you are young. You will regain your strength. What does Doctor Gabriel say?'

'I fear he has given up to me Alice. I have tried to eat to strengthen myself, but I have no heart left. Roger never comes near me. She buried her face in her hands, sobbing. 'He wanted children, but now he has them he doesn't want me. My inheritance is within his grasp.'

Alice felt anger towards this man who seemed to haunt her every move and circumstance.

'Roger seemed happy with you at Christmas, dear,' she said, wishing to placate her friend. 'What has happened?'

'He cannot stand illness,' Ellen said.

'Come Ellen, let me change your bed linen and give you a glass of wine, it will be a tonic to you.'

Alice was furious at the neglect Ellen was suffering. She went down to the kitchens and demanded hot water and clean bed linen. The servants scowled, but reluctantly did her bidding.

When Ellen was comfortable, Alice entertained her with stories of France, and her sea journey. Ellen's eyes had begun to sparkle, and she drank a glass of wine with her friend and ate a little food. As Alice was preparing to leave, Roger Nowell appeared in the doorway.

'So, Mistress Nutter, you would take over Read Hall?' he said, his face like thunder.

'I merely asked for clean bed linen for your wife. Surely you do not begrudge her comfort?'

Roger Nowell swayed slightly, his once handsome face was becoming ruddy and bloated, his penchant for wine was becoming noticeable.

'I will say what my wife needs, if wife I still have. What a delicate creature she has become. She cannot stand up to child-bearing.'

Ellen began to whimper and Alice's eyes flashed.

'Your wife has done a great deal of child-bearing, and grows weak. Where is your compassion, Sir?'

Nowell had the grace to look ashamed.

Alice continued, 'You are cruel, Sir, your wife needs sympathy, not accusation. Where is Doctor Gabriel?'

'None of your business, Madam. Please leave,' said Nowell, regaining his composure.

'I shall leave,' said Alice, 'but Doctor Gabriel is a friend of mine also, and I will relate my concern to him. You do not intimidate me, Sir.' Kissing Ellen, Alice walked across the room, descended the stairs and left the house. James Wilsey was waiting with the horse. Alice mounted, and together they left Read.

'Ellen is ill, James,' Alice said.

'Oh, I know Mistress. Word has it that Nowell has no time for invalids and neglects his wife's needs.

Alice worried about Ellen, and a few days later, she set out to visit Doctor Gabriel, who was staying at Samlesbury Hall. She was accompanied, as always, by the faithful James, and they made good time, stopping only for a meal with James' sister at Mellor. Alice enjoyed the rest and refreshment offered.

Arriving at Samlesbury Hall, Alice was immediately welcomed by Thomas Southworth, whose sons had studied with her brothers in France. She told him of her wish to see Doctor Gabriel, and Alice was shown into a large room, which was always slightly chilly, despite the fire burning brightly in the hearth. Servants brought wine and biscuits.

Doctor Gabriel came into the room, hand outstretched. 'What is the purpose of your visit Madam. You are not ill, I hope?'

'No Sir, I come on behalf of Mistress Nowell. I fear she is very ill and her husband was so cold to me when I tried to cheer her.'

'I am afraid Mistress Nowell will not recover my dear. Her husband did send for me. He knows there is no hope and hides his true feelings by drinking too much. Her blood is poisoned and I cannot find the source of the affliction. She suffered badly in her last confinement. She has given birth to ten children. She is now worn out.'

'She seems to have lost the will to live,' Alice said.

'Yes, my dear, her husband is a hard man and does not return her love. She fades like a flower without sun.'

Alice was shocked by these revelations. Bidding good-bye to Sir Thomas and Doctor Gabriel, she returned with James towards Read Hall.

On arrival she was shown immediately into Ellen's bedroom and saw at once that her friend was sinking. Taking Ellen's hand in hers, she knelt at the side of her bed.

'Let us remember the happy times we have had together, Ellen,' she said.

'I remember your lovely garden, Alice. You have been my only true friend in Pendle. Remember the Christmas feasts when the children were young?'

Alice felt tears running down her cheeks as the wasted fingers clutched at her hand.

Roger Nowell walked into the room and quietly knelt down beside her, and the three prayed together.

Ellen died the next day. A messenger brought the news to Roughlee Hall, with an invitation to the funeral.

When Ellen had been laid to rest, friends and neighbours congregated at Read Hall.

Roger Nowell made his way over to Alice. 'Forgive my behaviour towards Ellen,' he said. 'I was beside myself with grief. I did not know what to say to her; I have my regrets to live with now.'

'We will not speak of it again Sir, there is nothing to gain. Ellen was my dear friend, and I grieve for her and for her lonely children.'

Roger's eldest son and daughter made their way over to Alice. 'We thank you for your kindness to our mother. She loved you dearly.'

'I am sorry I was away in France when she needed me,' Alice replied.

'There was nothing you could have done to save her,' Elizabeth Nowell continued. 'Now tell us how Margaret and Charles are faring, we miss them so.'

Alice gave them the news from Douai.

'I will ask my father if I may go to Douai to visit them,' William Nowell told Alice.

Roger, who had overheard, smiled at his son. 'You have great expectations, young Sir, but we will enquire into this,' he said.

Dick approached and asked Alice if they could return home. Alice was glad to depart. Her heart was sore as she and Dick rode back home.

'The first of my old friends to die,' Alice told Dick. 'Things will never be the same, not at Christmas, or any time, and we will lose touch with the Nowell children, I know it.'

'We have each other, and our own family,' Dick leaned over and pressed her hand, and they continued their journey in accord.

III

Christmas passed quietly. Alice and Dick were happy to receive messages from Charles and Margaret, and together with Miles and Christopher, spent Christmas Day at Bawle House with the Bannisters. Miles and Ruth were to be betrothed on Ruth's eighteenth birthday, and Alice and Dick offered to build a small house for themselves.

'Mother, Ruth and I want to start our married life together in a small house. Roughlee Hall would not be the same without you. We will build on Slipper Hill. We have chosen the spot, and Uncle William has given us the land. I did tell you we were considering this.' Miles looked hurt.

'Yes, dear,' Alice smiled at her son, 'if you insist. Will you take one of the servants?'

'Kathcrine Hewitt wants to come with us. She is a widow and devoted to Ruth,' Miles told his mother, who looked enquiringly at Sybil.

'I will be happy to spare Katherine,' Sybil smiled. 'Now, how long is the betrothal to be?'

The old friends discussed the plans for the wedding. A date was fixed in 1605. It was hoped that Charles and Margaret would be able to return for the occasion.

Alice nursed secret fears about Charles, wondering whether it was common knowledge he studied to be a priest. In February 1604, to add to her worries, came a proclamation from the King that all Roman Catholic priests were to leave England.

Late in 1604, Baldwin began a further harassment of the Demdikes. He used as a weapon a recent Act of Parliament, again instigated by King James, that any person who would 'use, practise or exercise any witchcraft, charm or sorcery, whereby any person shall be killed, destroyed, wasted, pined or lamed in his body' should receive the death penalty.

At supper one evening, when Maria had joined them, Alice noticed that the girl looked pale and drawn.

'Is something the matter, dear,' Alice asked?

'Christopher's father has forbidden him to marry me,' she replied sadly.

'Christopher is over twenty-one and may do as he wishes,' said Dick.

'He wants his father's blessing, but his father says my grandmother Whittle is a witch. Is it true Mistress Alice?'

'I do not believe in witchcraft, whatever proclamation our King may make. As for your grandmother, she is a sick old woman. Her mind has become unhinged because of hardship and poverty. Doctor Gabriel has visited her and prescribed remedies which calm her. That is not your fault and Baldwin should not blame you,' replied Alice.

'Christopher has been working on the cottage on the Bar Road at Blacko. I am sure he intends to marry you, no matter what his father says,' Miles added.

'Oh, yes, but his father makes it hard for the family,' said Maria.

'Christopher is renting some land from me,' Dick said. 'He has a way with rearing animals. His father needs Christopher at the mill, but Christopher does not need him. He can earn his own living with his livestock. When the cottage is finished I am sure Christopher will ask you to marry him, dear.'

'Mother and father say the same thing,' said Maria, brightening up, 'I hope we can get married whilst Margaret and Charles are here for Ruth and Miles' wedding.'

'Well, they will be if you make it next year,' Alice looked happy, 'then we will all be together again, if only for a short time.'

122

'Baldwin had Elizabeth Device in the pillory again. He caught her begging at Colne,' Maria told the family.

'Elizabeth has a licence to beg,' Alice retorted. 'If I see her in the pillory, I will have her set free. Her health is not good, and if she is begging she must need our help. I must go and visit her.'

'The villagers are calling her Squinting Lizzie, since her accident at the mine,' said Maria.

'The villagers are ignorant, and know no better,' said Alice sadly.

IV

The next day was cool, but dry, and Alice made up her mind to visit Malkin Tower. James drove a cart filled with wood and Alice carried panniers of food. Several of the Device children were playing outside.

The youngest, a little girl about eighteen months old, was tied by a rope to a tree stump. As Alice walked up to the door, it opened, and James Device stood there, smiling vacantly. Alice walked past him, peering through the smoke, she saw Elizabeth lying on a makeshift bed, and her mother, old Demdike, in her usual posture, crouched on a stool by the smoking embers of a fire.

'Elizabeth, why did you go begging? Why did you not send Jamie to me? You know I will always help you.'

'I wasn't begging, Mistress. I was just visiting a relation, and on my way home I met Baldwin. He arrested me, accused me of begging, and charged me. The magistrate at Colne believed him and had me put in the stocks. There is no justice for the poor, Mistress.'

'We starve because of your mine, he, he, he,' shrieked old Demdike.

'Shut your mouth, Mother. We do not starve, and Mistress Nutter is not to be blamed because of Baldwin's viciousness.'

123

'I'll pray for him, still and loud, I will,' the old woman shrieked again.

Alice turned her back on the old woman and spoke to Elizabeth, 'Why is the baby tied up?' she asked.

'She wanders, and the others get tired of her. She needs fresh air, and I cannot get out. Sellars had me released, but not before I had suffered injury at the hands of some ruffians who threw stones at me,' replied the woman bitterly.

'I shall see Roger Nowell and complain that Richard Baldwin is harassing you. There must be some action he can take.' Alice stated.

'He whipped Jamie again this week and he blames mother for cursing his daughter. I heaped curses on him in Colne that he will not forget,' she said menacingly. 'I would do him an injury if I knew how.'

'Elizabeth, do not speak so. It is dangerous. You must promise me you will ask for food, and you know I will give protection if you are in trouble. Now, I will take the little girl. What is her name?'

'Jennet, Mistress.'

'Well, I will take Jennet to Jane Bulcock. She is not working so much for me just now, and she will care for the child until you are recovered. I will pay her.'

Alice walked to the doorway and looked out, 'Alison,' she shouted. A girl of about ten years, ran towards her.

'Look after your mother, and send James to me with a message if Baldwin troubles you again. I know you are young to have this responsibility, but you must care for the other children. I am taking Jennet, she is too much for you.'

Alice untied the small, struggling baby girl. Screwing her face up at the unpleasant smell emanating from the raggy clothes, she set the child in front of her on her horse.

'Mistress Alice, you will catch some illness through tending the likes of the Devices',' said James. 'They have always been feckless.'

'Feckless or unfortunate, James?' asked Alice. 'They seemed reasonably respectable when I first knew them. Elizabeth was pretty and lively. They have gone downhill since the pedlar died. The final straw was Elizabeth's injury at the mine.'

'You always see good in people, Mistress Alice,' James smiled affectionately at her. 'I trust you are never called to account, because of it.'

James and Alice trotted their horses homewards, toward the Roughlee Road. As they reached the top of the hill and began the descent towards Roughlee, they became aware of a horseman

124

approaching. It was Richard Baldwin, dressed as usual in his puritan black.

'Good day, Madam. Good day, Sir,' he said, drawing closer. Then, peering closely at the squealing bundle in front of Alice, he said, 'What do you do with one of the witch's brood?'

'I resent your statement, Sir. There are no proven witches in Pendle. I take this child to relieve the burden on a family recently persecuted by yourself.'

'There will soon be more laws to rid the land of such families,' replied Baldwin.

Alice's eyes flashed. 'Let us hope there are laws to protect the poor against such as you.'

'You do yourself no good protecting them. They are a burden on our society.' Baldwin's face was like thunder.

'The Lord said, "suffer the little children to come unto Him,"' Alice replied, 'and I try to follow his Christian example.'

'The Bible says we should not suffer a witch to live,' Baldwin replied.

'You have not found a witch yet,' Alice coolly replied. 'I wish you good day,' and nodding to James, they urged their horses forward.

Baldwin was silenced. He wanted to shout after her, but knew that on this occasion she had the last word. He watched Alice go, with venom in his heart. He was tempted to ride to Malkin Tower to wreak vengeance there, but he knew Sellars had paid for Elizabeth's release from the stocks and was not prepared to quarrel openly with him. Instead, he turned down Wheathead Lane with an expression on his face which boded ill for his wife and family.

When Alice had arranged for Jennet to be bathed and fed, she called for Jane Bulock and asked her to foster the child for a while.

'I will pay all expenses, Jane.'

'I know you will, Mistress, but the child looks sadly neglected, and I will have a hard task ahead of me,' replied Jane, looking somewhat reluctantly at Jennet, who stared back solemnly, finger in mouth, little curly head full of tangles.

'I think we will start by cutting her hair, Jane,' said Alice. 'We will never get the tangles out otherwise, it will soon grow.' Together they took the struggling child aside, and an hour or so later, taking her into the kitchen, Anne gasped at the transformation. 'You wouldn't know it was the same child, Mistress Alice,' she said.

'Let us hope Jane can transform her character likewise, she is quite wild,' said Alice. 'It will not be easy.'

Jennet stayed with Jane Bulcock, only returning home for short periods when Elizabeth requested to see her. She was always neglected when she was returned to Jane, who would complain loudly to Alice that the child should not keep returning home.

'She belongs neither to her mother nor to me,' she told Alice, 'and shows no loyalty to either.'

'Maybe, as she grows older, her mother will see that she is better off with you,' Alice comforted her.

'I hope so. I have grown fond of her, although she is a wild little thing,' Jane replied.

V

Plans for the two weddings had been finalized. Ruth and Miles were to be married in June 1605 and Christopher and Maria in July. Both couples were busily preparing their respective homes. Miles and Ruth had help from both families, but Christopher Baldwin's father refused to accept his son's betrothal. Christopher had been forced to live in his cottage for his father made it impossible for him to remain at Wheathead. His mother had urged him to go saying, 'Your father is a hard man, he will not see that opposition will not change things. Go, be happy with Maria, you will be happier than I have been with your father.'

'Mother, come with me. You have stood father's tyranny long enough. You and Sarah should live with Maria and me.'

'That would not be fair to Maria. She wants you to herself when first you are married. I will see. If life becomes unbearable, then I will leave, but I feel my duty is to stay.' His mother's voice faltered.

'Mother, no one has to be so unhappy. Promise me that if he raises the whip to you again, you will come to me.'

'I promise,' she said.

Alice helped Maria and Anne to sew furnishings, and Dick helped

Tom and Christopher in making cupboards and doors. Soon the cottage was ready.

Alice and Anne walked arm in arm along the road from Christopher's cottage to Roughlee Hall. It was a fine summer evening, birds called drowsily.

'It doesn't seem five minutes since I came with you to Roughlee, about 22 years ago. So much has happened to us all, but I have Tom, and you have Dick,' Anne smiled at her friend and mistress, 'and we have each other.'

'Indeed we do have each other,' replied Alice. 'You have always been my sister substitute, ever since we were eight, Anne. I cannot imagine life without your cheerful presence.' The two friends walked slowly home, in tune with one another.

James and Dick had gone to Hull to meet Margaret and Charles, who were coming home for the wedding.

Several days later, a cavalcade of riders was seen approaching. Alice rushed towards the gate to greet Margaret and Charles. She threw her arms around them in turn and felt her heart would burst with happiness to have her family united once more.

Margaret and Charles looked well. They were brown and glowing with health. They spoke happily of their lives in Douai. Alice and Dick threw a banquet the week before Miles' wedding. Roughlee Hall rang with laughter as Dick handed out the glasses of rich Bordeaux wine brought from France by Margaret and Charles. Toasts were made to the future of the happy couple and an air of deep contentment surrounded the gathering.

As always, when they were entertaining, Dick and Alice stole a few minutes together to wander in the garden.

'This is the time of day I love best, dear,' Dick said.

'Yes, Dick, Daylight Gate,' Alice replied, holding his arm tightly. The roses scented the air, the cat purred softly, rubbing himself against them. The dogs wandered back and forwards as they strolled along the paths lined with parsley and other herbs.

'Come, we must not neglect our guests, Alice,' and Dick bent to kiss her as they turned towards the kitchen door.

The wedding at Newchurch brought crowds. It was a cloudless day, the villagers had not needed much persuading to make the day into a holiday. A maypole fluttered in the breeze as Ruth passed by in her father's carriage to Newchurch. All their friends were there to see them married. After the wedding ceremony they all returned to Bawle House, where they happily accepted the gifts and congratulations from their family and friends.

After the celebrations they were carried, by their friends, in the local tradition, to their new house, on Slipper Hill. In the usual way, Ruth threw her posy into the crowd, who, after cheering, headed back towards Roughlee Hall and the promise of more ale and food.

Alice and Dick had made their way back to Roughlee and were waiting as happy laughter announced the arrival of the young people, headed by Charles and Margaret. Sunlight filtered through the trees and danced on their faces. There was nothing to mar the happiness of all.

The weeks passed quickly, and the date for Maria and Christopher Baldwin's wedding approached. Alice and Anne were busy preparing food and sending out invitations. The whole village turned out, as they had done for Miles and Ruth, to watch the wedding party leave for the ceremony at Newchurch.

Alice and Dick had insisted that Maria be married from Roughlee Hall, which had been her home, far more so than the cottage where Tom and Anne snatched occasional days or nights.

When the wedding party returned from Newchurch, Christopher felt sadness momentarily sweep over him. He had not really expected his austere father to wish him well, but had hoped for some sign of paternal affection, although he knew in his heart that his father lacked any softness.

The couple were standing by the table receiving the handshakes and good wishes, when a sudden silence filled the room. Christopher followed Maria's eyes to the door. Standing on the threshold were his mother and his sister Sarah. He opened his arms wide as they came towards him and enfolded them in a great hug. With tears running down her lined cheeks, his mother turned to Maria.

'Make him happy, my dear,' she said.

'I will, I promise,' and Maria bent her head to kiss the older woman.

'Dear new Sister, I hope I can spend time with you in future,' Sarah hugged Maria and the two clung together. They had known each other all their lives, though Sarah had never been allowed to play with other children, and had not been allowed the freedom Christopher had been able to steal in his work around the farms.

'Christopher knew what a price his mother and sister would have to pay if his father discovered they had been to wish him well. He held his sister close for a moment and tears welled up in his eyes as she spoke.

'It is awful at home without you, Christopher,' her words ending in a sob.

'Trust me. If things become too bad for you I will find you a cottage. I am earning a good living now.'

'I will bring mother to you if things do not improve, I promise,' Sarah assured him.

'Will you stay and share the feast?' Alice asked.

'We would dearly love to, but I fear we dare not,' said Mistress Baldwin, 'If my husband should come and seek us out it would spoil the day for all. I do not wish that to happen, but I had to come to wish Christopher and Maria happiness.' Mother and daughter walked slowly from the scene of the celebrations.

'If ever I am lucky enough to meet a man who wants to marry me, I shall take you with me, Mother dear,' said Sarah as they walked slowly down the road.

'Yes dear, I fear the time is coming when we will have to find a sanctuary somewhere. We have no means of support, and your father would search us out if we do not have protection,' her mother replied.

When in sight of their home, they saw Richard Baldwin waiting for them. In his hands he held his whip.

VI

The persecution of Catholics continued, and insurrection flourished, culminating in 1605 with the Gunpowder Plot and the subsequent execution of Guy Fawkes and his friends.

At the same time the Ecclesiastical Commission, headed by Sir Richard Sherbourne, dealt with many individuals who had been accused of witchcraft. A general feeling of hysteria reached out from London, and insidiously began to spread through the land.

Alice and Dick were mourning the death of John Towneley, who, borne down by a total of twenty-five years in prison on different occasions for recusancy, and assisting priests to escape, eventually became ill and died. They gathered together with their Catholic friends to comfort his widow and children.

On their way home from Towneley Hall, Dick complained of sickness. Once at Roughlee he went straight to bed. He tossed and turned all night, shivering and burning alternately.

Alice sent James Wilsey with an urgent message to Read, where Doctor Gabriel often stayed. He came immediately and examined Dick. His expression was serious as he turned to Alice.

'I have tended other patients with the same symptoms. You must keep giving him drinks in order that he does not dehydrate, even when he is sleeping. You must raise his head and pour the liquid into his mouth as often as possible. I will leave some laudenum to calm him.'

Doctor Gabriel explained that only time, and Dick's own strength could fight the illness, and Alice must be patient and pray. Promising to return the following day the good doctor rode away, his heart heavy. He had seen so much of the sweating sickness, he knew Dick would have to be strong to recover.

Dick's fever continued. Alice bathed his forehead, stroking his face. Tears welled up in her eyes and dropped on to his face. She felt her heart was breaking. How could such a strong and healthy man be struck down? Day followed day. Doctor Gabriel paid regular visits, and implored Alice to rest. She could not. She lay beside Dick on the bed, praying and crying, 'Oh, God, if he dies make me die too.' And so the days passed.

Doctor Gabriel visited again and listened to Dick's breathing. He said gently to Alice, 'I must stay awhile. I am afraid he has contracted pneumonia now.'

Alice was incoherent with grief. She had not eaten or slept for days. Dick was now unconscious. Doctor Gabriel feared for her sanity when she knew Dick would not recover.

An hour later, he died in her arms. The doctor tried to extricate her from him, but she screamed, 'No, no, Dick, take me with you.'

Miles came and lifted his mother in his arms, she had shrunk in the last week. He held her to him whilst her body was racked with sobs.

'Hear me,' said Doctor Gabriel, 'you have children who need you. Drink this potion, you must sleep.'

Alice fell into a deep stupor. She was unable to move. Miles arranged the funeral. Dick was to be buried with his father at Newchurch.

The day of the funeral arrived, and Alice, helped by Anne came down the stairs and stood by the coffin in the parlour of the house.

'My life has ended Anne, I lived for him. I cannot see him buried.' Turning she walked back up the stairs. Miles and Christopher followed her.

'Mother, we love you and we need you,' Christopher said.

She gazed bleakly at him, 'I am no good without him, he was my life.'

She stumbled into the room she had shared with Dick for all the years since their marriage, and laid on the bed. Doctor Gabriel, ever at hand, and present for the funeral, came quietly into the room.

'Mistress Alice, I cannot keep putting you to sleep. You will have to learn to live again for the sake of your children,' but she drank deeply of the potion he had prepared for her.

After the funeral only Sybil stayed to share the meal with the family in the parlour, once the scene of happy feastings, now a house of grief. Alice lay asleep in her room.

Miles wrote a letter to Margaret and Charles to tell them of their sad loss. He urged them to return to help give their mother the will to live. Alice lay in bed, day after day, her mind ranging back over the years, the good times and the bad times, always with Dick to share them, but never again. Sybil Bannister visited, pleading with Alice not to reject her children.

'Dick would not have wanted you to ignore them like this, my dear. They love you, they fear for your sanity. Please try to respond to them, they have lost their father, you know.'

Miles and Christopher came to bid her good night when Sybil had gone. Alice held out her hands to them.

'Forgive me, my children, I love you dearly, but I grieve for your father too much.' They held her to them, whispering their love, telling her the pain would ease with time. They would try to help her bear the grief.

Two months later, Charles and Margaret arrived in Roughlee. Alice was still confined to her room. Miles and Christopher had been unable to revive even a spark of her former self. When she saw her two children who had been so long in France, she collapsed on the floor, her body racked with the sobs which had been so long withheld.

Charles and Margaret lifted her and held her to them, their tears mingling with hers. At last Alice calmed and her anguish returned as she realized Charles was on English soil whilst known to be training as a priest.

'Charles, Charles, you risk yourself by returning here.'

'Mother, Miles and Christopher feared you were in a fatal decline. We had to come; we love you. Father would not have wanted us to let you fade and die. We have lost him, we do not want to lose you also.'

'Charles, your father and I were so close, I fear I cannot carry on without him.'

'You must, Mother,' said Margaret, 'and Miles has some news for you.' Miles came forward.

'Ruth expects a baby in the autumn,' he said, looking hesitantly at his mother, giving her this news which, had Dick been alive, would have been the cause of much rejoicing.

'Am I to deny my child a grandmother?' he asked bitterly, hurt written all over his face.

'Oh, Miles,' Alice held out a thin, pale hand. She had lost weight in the months since Dick had died. Her once raven hair was streaked with grey. Her face seemed lined and old in comparison to when Margaret had last seen her. Alice rose to her feet, and leaning on Miles, she said, 'I will come downstairs and we will have a family meal.'

They all smiled with relief.

'I will try to become strong so that I will enjoy your visit,' she said, looking at Charles and Margaret, 'but Charles, we must not spread the word that you are here. It will be dangerous.'

'I know, Mother, Uncle Thomas has been here and he thinks I should stay at Firber awhile. Will you come and see me there?'

'Oh, yes, but you do not need to go today. Now Miles, bring Ruth to me. I am happy I will have a grandchild. I will try to live without my dear husband, but it will be hard.

Alice looked at Charles. He was so like Dick had been when he was young that her heart lurched. Dick is not dead whilst Charles lives, she thought, but that is not fair. He lives in them all. For the first time since he died, Alice smiled.

'God gave you a good husband, you have happy memories Mother, be grateful,' Charles pressed her hand.

Slowly, Alice took up the reins of household management again. Her garden, long overgrown, lay accusingly in the sunlight when Alice walked through the gate for the first time in months. The cat they had rescued from Whalley Fair rubbed his head affectionately against her as she took up a small trowel and was soon digging the weeds away from the damask roses. She felt strength returning to her as she inhaled the smell of the warm, damp earth.

Charles prayed with his mother each night. He rode down in the darkening evening from Firber House, dressed in the rustic garb of a farm worker, and it seemed that his presence went unnoticed; either that, or no one was prepared to stir up strong feelings at this time. Communications, always bad, kept Pendle reasonably isolated from the rest of the country.

Margaret spent all her time with her mother, helping in the kitchen and spending endless hours talking together.

Alice felt a peace within her, and an acceptance settle upon her. She threw herself once more into the life of the village, to the delight of all, teaching one or two of the village children whose parents were willing to let them learn to read. Anne, her servant and friend, who had indeed kept her alive these last months with dainty morsels to tempt her appetite, was able to relax and spend some time with her husband Tom, in their cottage. Life again took on some semblance of normality in the Nutter household.

James Wilsey and Henry Mitton helped Miles to run the farm, and organised the collections of coal for distribution amongst the local houses, the Devices were included in their round. Alice was grateful to Miles for his part in the work of the farm. At least one of our children is interested in following his father, Alice thought. Christopher still said he was going to be a sailor, and travel the world.

'Mother, I called at Reedley on my way back from Burnley this week. John Moore and his wife keep the house well. Why not go back for a few weeks, with Anne and Margaret, to collect your strength?' suggested Miles.

'I haven't been there since my marriage,' said Alice.

'All the more reason why you should go now,' he replied. 'It belongs to you and Uncle Christopher.'

Charles was to return to Douai alone. Margaret promised to join him when her mother was well again. 'Margaret, why not stay in England, don't you wish to marry and settle down?' her mother asked wistfully.

'I feel my home is in Douai now, Mother. I wish to serve our Lord also.'

Alice accepted what Margaret said, and made up her mind to enjoy her daughter's company as long as she could. They travelled to Reedley, and together they wandered through the fields and lanes. Sometimes they went on horseback, and rode through the forest as far as Whalley.

Alice was to remember with great pleasure these days spent with Margaret. Anne would welcome them home with a table spread with delicacies, and Alice relived her childhood in this house.

Charles left stealthily, under cover of darkness. He had been fearful of any reports which would force Roger Nowell to make an investigation, as the persecution of Catholics continued unabated. He was sure of many open doors as he travelled through Yorkshire to Hull, and a ship where he could start his journey to France.

VII

Richard Baldwin, mindful of the lack of opposition from Roughlee Hall, seized the opportunity to intensify his campaign of hatred towards the family at Malkin Tower.

Jennet now spent little or no time with her mother, preferring the stability and comfort of her foster mother, Jane Bulcock. Elizabeth Device and her elder daughter Alison, seemed able only to exist by begging, and had a licence from Roger Nowell to do so.

James Device still did occasional work on the farms in the area, but he was considered by all to be moonstruck, and was therefore excused a great deal of hard work. He was to be seen wandering in the woods, collecting the fruits of the seasons. He knew all about the haunts of badgers, the dens of foxes and the nests of birds, and the family fed well off rabbits he trapped, or wild ducks he stalked. He suffered the taunts of the village children with a lop-sided grin but they soon tired of chasing after him.

Grandmother Demdike, leaning heavily on her stick, and peering short-sightedly before her, oversaw the younger children, who ran wild, unkempt and dirty. Sellars, it seemed, had turned his back on Elizabeth, and no longer took any notice of the children she had borne him. Without Dick, and his father, to champion the family and exhort Sellars to do his duty, they were at the mercy of Baldwin and his fellow churchwardens.

Elizabeth and Alison often went to Colne to beg. If they set off early they could avoid Baldwin. Their main dread was in meeting him on their way home. During the time Alice had spent at Reedley, James had constantly searched for her, constantly asking when she would return. Then one day he saw her working in her rose garden. Alice looked up to see him peering over the wall and went up to him. She asked kindly about his family.

'Oh, Mistress, my mother is so distressed and near to starving. There is no work. We have no corn for the hens, and Baldwin has had her and Alison in the stocks again. Help us, help us.'

Alice was shocked. 'Poor James,' she said. 'You and I, we both miss Dick. We have no one to fight for us and must look to ourselves. Miles is young, but he will learn. I will speak to him about provisions for you.' She hurried from the garden, her cheeks pink, her eyes flashing. When Miles saw her he was pleased to see her emotions aroused in the old way, and listened intently as she explained the position. Miles looked embarrassed.

'Mother, I am experiencing difficulties with Baldwin myself. He has blocked the water supply down the middle field. James and Henry are reluctant to oppose him because they need the mill.'

Alice's heart sank. 'I have been grieving too long. I will call on Master Baldwin and sort this matter out. His mill is on our land. How can he do this?'

'Mother, he blames you for what he calls your encouragement of Christopher's marriage to Maria, and says you encourage Christopher in to popery.'

'Miles, why wasn't I informed before?'

'Mother, you would not listen to me,' Miles replied bitterly.

'You know we keep our religious beliefs firmly in the family,' she said.

'I know, but Mother, there are those in the village who are jealous of our good fortune, our obvious happiness and previous good health; our trips to France, and our education,' he paused,' also our ability to mix with what they consider to be the "gentry", and above us. Now they watch to see our fortune diminish with father's death.'

Alice looked at Miles. He has grown older, she thought, then she said, 'Pay no heed to them Miles, you are as good a man as your father.'

'He had his own father to lean on, Mother, remember.'

'I do, dear, it is hard for you, I know.'

'You have been asleep these months, Mother. I have had to see to the farm, the mine, the accounts, the markets, and the wages,' he looked defensive.

'I will take over the accounts. You have had too much on your shoulders. The rest at Reedley has given me strength. Dick would have wanted me to carry on.'

Speaking to James Wilsey later, Alice was horrified to find him worn and tired.

'Mistress, Henry is taken very bad with pains in the chest. He cannot breathe at times. He lies in bed and has not been able to help me during these last weeks.'

'Oh, dear, is there no end to the changes I find?' Alice said. She left the house and crossing the road, hurried towards Henry's cottage. She was hailed by a figure on horseback, and perceiving it to be Sybil, she ran towards her. Sybil dismounted her horse and embraced her friend.

'Alice, my dear. I did not believe I would ever see you running again. We thought we were going to lose you too.' Tears ran down her face, in relief, as she held Alice close.

'Come with me to see Henry Mitton. I only learned today that he is ill.'

Together they walked down the river path towards Henry's cottage, and opening the door, they stepped over the threshold into a small room, very clean, but sparsely furnished, then through in to a bedroom.

Henry was lying in bed. He smiled weakly at Alice. 'I'm mending Mistress, but it's taking time. I need to rest. When I walk about I cannot breathe well.'

'I will send for Doctor Gabriel,' Alice stated. 'It seems that everywhere I look there is need.'

'It is doing you good to realise there is work for you to do, Alice,' Sybil replied, smiling.

'Come Sybil, walk back with me and we will have some refreshment,' turning to Henry she asked, 'has Anne sent you food?'

'Oh, yes, Mistress, and James calls daily, I have not been neglected.'

'Only by me Henry, but that will not happen again,' she smiled as she looked at him.

'You were grieving, Mistress. I felt I was letting you down, not helping the young master. Things are not the same now, and I tire,' his kind old face was sad.

'We had good times, Henry, with Dick and his father. Now we have to help the young ones prosper.' She smiled as she left him.

Unhooking the horse's reins from the gatepost, Sybil linked arms with Alice and the two friends walked slowly back to the Hall. Sybil excitedly discussed their forthcoming grandchild.

'If it's a boy, Miles wants to call him Richard,' she said.

'Alice's smile faded, 'Oh, how Dick would have loved a grandchild.'

'Alice, you will love it, and we are all so pleased you have rallied. The stay at Reedley has done you good.'

'Well, I got a few things into perspective and I enjoyed having Margaret to myself for a while. We rediscovered each other,' Alice smiled. 'Of course, the responsibility for Reedley is with Miles and Christopher needs the revenue from the farm.'

'It won't be long before Charles is ordained, will it?'

'No, I only hope he stays in France when he becomes a priest. I hope he won't feel a need to be a missionary here.'

'You will miss Margaret when she goes back to France.'

'Yes, but she plans to return next summer, and I may visit Douai again when I am able.'

The two friends dined together and Alice was glad of Sybil's company. Margaret and Christopher were pleased to see their mother talking animatedly again, and all were able to relax together.

Next day, Alice sent a message to Doctor Gabriel, care of Read Hall, and a few days later the lean, grey-clad figure of the doctor arrived at the house. Alice accompanied her old friend to Henry's cottage, and as they walked, he commented on her changed appearance.

'You are a shadow of your former self, my dear,' he said.

'Oh, I am much better, I am fresh from a stay at our house at Reedley, where I ate large meals and enjoyed the open air. I miss my husband. There was a time when I wished to die too,' she said.

'That is natural when one has been so close to someone as you were, but you are needed by your family, and time will help your grief,' he replied.

Reaching Henry's cottage, they entered. Doctor Gabriel held Henry's arms, felt his pulse and listened to his chest. He asked him many questions, then retired to the outer room with Alice.

'He is suffering from a tired heart, I fear. His body carries too much weight for his heart to bear, it can only stand so much. He should eat less red meat and fat. More fowl, game or fish. You have fed your servants too well, I fear. And, I suspect, allowed them too much claret!' he smiled.

'Oh, I know,' Alice laughed. 'Henry has always been fond of his food. In the days when Dick's father was alive, Henry worked inside the house and was in charge of the wine cellar. Miles always teased him about his partiality to the Bordeaux!'

Doctor Gabriel had a few words to say to Henry before accompanying Alice back to the house. On the way he told her, 'I have given Henry a potion of juice extracted from foxglove leaves. I think I have mentioned it to you before. If he takes it sparingly, it should help him, providing he eats less,' and he laughed. 'He must try to lose some of the weight he carries, but he will not find it easy.'

Doctor Gabriel dined with Alice, Charles and Margaret. As the good doctor said grace, Alice felt a kinship to him and knew him to be a man of the same doctrines as herself, however well hidden. He discussed with Christopher his journeys to foreign lands, and Christopher talked eagerly of his plans to take ship to America as soon as he was old enough.

Alice smiled at Doctor Gabriel saying, 'I hope my older son and his wife will come to live with me with their children. If not, I will have a lonely old age.'

'Do not worry, Mother, I will return with treasures from the New World and exciting stories of my adventures.' Christopher smiled happily in anticipation.

The time came for Margaret to return to France. She was to travel with a group of people known to the Towneleys, who were going to visit friends in Douai. Alice accompanied her to Towneley to meet her fellow travellers. Margaret thought how well her mother looked in comparison to when she and Charles had arrived.

'See you next year, Mother dear.' She waved her hand as the carriage bore her away. She was happy to be returning to her friends in France.

VIII

With Alice's help, and Doctor Gabriel's medication, Henry recovered sufficiently to spend a few hours every day helping around the farm. Alice was aware, however, of hostility when she walked through the village. She asked Anne if she knew of any reason for this.

'They say, Mistress, that you are working Henry Mitton into the grave when he is ill, and that you give him potions and he is now wasting away.'

'Oh, Anne. It is for his own good that he is losing weight. Doctor Gabriel himself ordered it.'

'I know, Mistress, but I am telling you how the ignorant see his loss of weight.'

'I cannot please everyone, Anne, and Henry goes home as soon as he feels tired.'

As Alice reflected on these new revelations she saw a familiar horseman ride into the yard. She had not seen Roger Nowell since Ellen's funeral. She knew he had attended Dick's funeral, but she herself had been confined to her bed at the time. She experienced the sinking feeling he always brought upon her.

'Anne, please answer the door, look who is here.' She and Anne exchanged a grimace. Anne was aware of her mistress's feelings.

'Bring some refreshment for him,' Alice asked as Anne went to the door.

Roger strode into the kitchen, dwarfing them both. He looked at Alice. 'Mistress Alice, you are wasting away. You must try to bring the roses back into your cheeks.'

'I am sure I will, given time,' she replied. 'However, I miss Dick, and find if difficult to enjoy life these days. Pray take some refreshment.'

He followed her through into the parlour where they had shared so many family occasions. Ghosts of Miles senior, Dick and Ellen, flittered through their memories in a flash. Anne came in to the room with glasses of Bordeaux.

He smiled as he accepted a glass. 'I am reminded of Dick's father as I drink this,' he said.

'I brought the wine back with me when I last visited France. Dick and I seldom opened a bottle when we were alone.'

Sipping the wine together, Roger wondered whether this was a good opportunity to broach the subject of the mine. He was sure she would sell now. He decided however, to wait a little longer, and chatted at ease about the village gossip.

'I believe you have had your children home, Mistress. They are lucky that they encountered no hindrance. You, of course, know of King James' edict forbidding us to educate our children abroad?'

'We have good friends, Sir. I am grateful to you for not noticing. I will not encourage Charles to visit again. It grows more dangerous.'

'He is very like his father,' Nowell said, looking directly at Alice.

'You saw him?'

'Of course, I saw him. He stayed at Firber mostly, didn't he?'

'Yes. You prove to be a friend,' Alice said, looking faintly surprised.

'Did you not always know I was a friend?'

'We had our good times, of course,' she replied.

'I always had a duty to perform, Mistress Alice, as you know. I had to bear bad tidings to you. It was my duty. I try to do what I can, and I try to avoid certain instructions, but the Earl of Derby grows more relentless in his searches, and local puritans, such as Baldwin, hinder me. I am for an easy life, if possible.'

Alice looked at Roger Nowell. He had grown large in his middle age, and his face, once handsome, was coarse and ruddy. Too much over indulgence, she reflected, and her thoughts went again to Dick, who had been lean and strong. The years had not changed him, he had been moderate in his habits. Why, oh why was Dick taken from me when he was so healthy, she thought sadly?

'You have lost your exuberance, Mistress Alice,' Roger remarked.

'I miss Dick.'

'You have suffered personal tragedies before and recovered,' he said.

'I will never recover from Dick's death,' she replied, and continued, 'I just live from day to day until I join him.'

'I trust you will have many years before you, I believe you are soon to be blessed with a grandchild?'

'Yes, I look forward to that.'

'I have two already, and I take great joy in them,' he replied.

'Poor Ellen would have loved her grandchildren, said Alice. 'Life is so cruel.'

'Indeed, yes, we can comfort ourselves with happy memories, not given to everyone, Mistress.'

'Oh, I do not mean to complain. I did indeed enjoy a blessed family life for over twenty years.'

'Does Miles run the farm ably?' asked Roger.

'He is doing his best. I fear I neglected him in the first months following Dick's death, but I am picking up the threads again and James Wilsey is a good shoulder for him.'

'And Henry Mitton?' asked Roger, rather too carefully.

Alice's eyes flashed. 'I can tell by your expression, Sir, that you know Henry ails. I brought Doctor Gabriel to him.'

'The old Alice showed for a moment,' Roger smiled. 'Of course I know you sent for Doctor Gabriel. He was staying with me at the time. Mistress Alice, we live in strange times. All are not as educated as you and I, and some are bigots. One of these is Richard Baldwin, as well you know, and he constantly bombards me with complaints. He accuses the Demdike brood of witchcraft, which, as you must know, is King James' own particular bent, and calls for them to hang. What can a mere Justice of the Peace do when faced with evidence of a sort?'

'I understand your predicament,' Alice replied soberly.

'He accuses the Chattox of keeping images, and accuses you of protecting them all.' Roger leaned back, sipping from the glass and enjoying the mellow taste of the wine. Twirling his glass, he went on, 'I came to visit you as an old friend. I also came to warn you. King James is a superstitious man, and he looks for evil everywhere. I am bombarded with literature from him. The hysteria spreads among the ignorant.'

'Master Baldwin and I have been enemies for years,' Alice replied. 'For a God-fearing man he has little humility, and since the death of his daughter he is bitter. Add to that his son Christopher's marriage to Maria, the Chattox's granddaughter, for which his father does not forgive him, and you have the basis of the campaign against me. He stopped me teaching the village children again, you know.' Alice, too, sipped her wine, her hand trembled slightly.

'Have a care not to antagonise him further, Mistress,' Roger said slowly.

'Why? What can he do to me?'

'You are not popular, Mistress. It is known your son is training to be a Catholic priest.'

'Will there never be freedom to worship as we please?' asked Alice sadly.

'Not in our lifetime, it would seem,' he replied.

Roger rose to his feet. 'Thank you for the refreshment, Mistress. May I call again?'

'Certainly, you are most welcome,' she replied.

When he had ridden away, Anne came into the room.

'How did his visit go, Mistress?' she asked in the manner of an old friend.

'Anne, Nowell claims there is bad feeling against me. Why?'

'Mistress, you know Baldwin is at the root of it. He rants that you champion the Demdike and her brood, and bring disrepute on the neighbourhood with your papist leanings. Tom has heard it said in the alehouse in Barrowford.'

'The people need some real hardship, then they would forget me,' Alice remarked bitterly.

'Maria and Christopher are also slighted. They persecute my mother also if she ventures abroad, and she has been better of late.'

'When Miles and Dick were alive no one dare utter words against us,' Alice said sadly.

'Mistress, I must tell you that Christopher, your son, is being subjected to abuse as he rides home from his lessons at Towneley Hall. He was stoned one day. His face was bleeding and he would not let me tell you.'

'Oh, my God, is there no end to it all?' Alice put her hands to her face. 'Send Christopher to me the moment he arrives home.'

'Mistress, he bade me not to tell you.'

'Why did I not notice his face was bleeding? What sort of mother am I?' She rocked in sadness, and Anne, placing her arms around her, whispered words of comfort.

Alice did not wait for Christopher to arrive home. Instead, she saddled her horse and went to meet him. She passed a group of villagers and called, 'Good day,' watching for their response.

Christopher Howgate was there, Elizabeth Device's half-brother. He lifted his hand, but his eyes did not meet hers. She sensed some embarrassment in him, and for the first time in all the years she had lived at Roughlee she felt an unease.

She trotted her horse slowly alongside the river. As she reached the bottom of the hill which led to Fence, she saw Christopher in the distance, slowly picking his way down the stony slope.

'Mother,' he shouted, 'how good to see you out and about.' He joined her and together they turned for Roughlee. As they drew nearer to the collection of rough dwellings again she noticed he looked about him warily.

From the corner, a small boy aimed a stone, 'Papist, papist,' he shouted. His mother, coming to the door of the cottage, saw Alice and pulled the boy inside.

'What was all that about?' Alice asked as innocently as possible.

'Children who do not even know the meaning of the word, Mother. They have learned it from their elders,' he replied bitterly.

'Has this happened before?' Alice asked.

'Yes, sometimes worse. Because you are with me today they are less sure of themselves.'

'I will ask James to escort you in future.'

'No, Mother. I am not a child. I will not be intimidated. I have had my jerkin off to them before and will do so again. They have been less inclined to come to grips with me since then, I assure you.'

'Oh, Christopher, how I wish your father was here to protect us.'

'We all do, Mother. These ignorant, uneducated peasants are being bullied by Baldwin into expressing this hatred. I do not want to leave you but I have had enough of them. I intend to seek my fortune at sea in the next few years. I want to learn more of the world. All I see here is bigotry and hatred.'

'If you go away Christopher, I may return to live at Reedley. Roughlee is becoming an alien place to me. I am not sure Miles and Ruth will want to live in the Hall, but we shall see. Come, I have your favourite roast chicken with herb sauce, and fruit pastries. I will race you home.'

For a while they forgot their troubles in the exhilaration of a quick gallop. They arrived, laughing, in the yard as young Miles and James led a new bull through to the pen.

Alice did not have to ask Miles and Ruth to join her at the Hall. Later the same evening, when she and Christopher were relaxing by a glowing fire, Miles and Ruth arrived.

'Oh, Miles, Ruth. What a lovely surprise.'

Alice's face was pink with pleasure. She pulled the bell rope, and as Anne entered, she asked for wine and pastries.

'Mother, we feel the time has come for us to join you here. You are too much alone,' Miles said.

'Yes, Mother, I agree with Miles.' Ruth approached Alice and put her hands in hers. 'You will enjoy having the baby here.'

Tears began to well in her eyes and ran slowly down Alice's face.

'Surely you are glad, Mother?' asked Christopher anxiously.

'Oh, I am crying for joy,' she said. 'Let us have a party to celebrate. We will ask your family, Ruth, and the Firbers, and of course, Maria and Christopher.'

Eagerly they made their plans for the following Sunday.

It was a bright day, the sun shining out of a blue sky when Sybil and William arrived with their family for the party. Soon they were joined by Maria and Christopher, James Wilsey and his wife, the Firbers, servants and friends, all mixed together. Alice happily presided at the table, the first happy occasion since Dick's death.

Two small girls, Anne's assistants in the kitchen, ran in and out with the food, and even the dogs sensed a normality once more in the household at Roughlee Hall. Henry Mitton was welcomed when he arrived later in the afternoon. Alice pressed a glass of his favourite Bordeaux wine upon him.

'I am sure one glass will not harm you, Henry.' He smiled at her fondly. She had been like a daughter to him.

The following week, Miles and Ruth moved into Roughlee Hall.

IX

When Ruth had her first baby, Alice felt the Hall was home again. As she stood by the window, holding young Richard William, she looked back into the past when she had stood by this self same window holding Miles, watching for Dick and his father to ride into view. Quickly she pushed the thoughts from her mind, and turning she smiled at Ruth, who was lying back on the pillows.

'He reminds me so much of Miles,' she said, 'and he was a good baby.'

Margaret came home for the christening. Alice was relieved that Charles had stayed in France because of the general feeling against the family which still persisted. Margaret brought with her a French companion, Isobel, who excited great interest in the area. She spoke perfect English and Ruth's brother, Joseph, was obviously infatuated with her and spent more time at Roughlee than ever before.

The christening feast was held at Bawle House and Sybil welcomed all the old friends. She walked over to Alice who was standing by the window peering out sadly.

'Alice dear, pray do not be sad, it is a happy event, our grandchild has been christened.'

Alice turned to face Sybil, 'I was just remembering all my children's christenings, and the time when poor Anne lost little Jacob. We have all had so many ups and downs.' She walked over to the table and accepted a glass of wine from William.

'To Richard William Nutter,' she said. He also raised a glass.

'Yes, my dear, to our mutual grandchild,' and they smiled at each other.

Christopher and Maria Baldwin now had a baby, Katherine, and they were constant visitors to the family at Roughlee Hall. Christopher had taken over the duties of both Henry Mitton and James Wilsey, who also had the duties of a constable for a year.

Alice was happy to see the children growing up together, just as Maria had grown up with her children. Richard Baldwin still had not made any approach to his son, but his mother and sister sometimes called to see the babies.

Alice knew that this was always when Baldwin was at market, or at the court at Read, but at least the two women had the opportunity to watch little Katherine grow.

When the time came for Margaret and Isobel to leave Roughlee, William approached Alice and said, 'I am going to apply for permission for Joseph to travel abroad. He insists on accompanying the girls, he says he wants to marry Isobel.'

'I cannot imagine Isobel wanting to live in the cold north of England after living in Douai, even though it is not as hot as the south of France. It is much milder than here,' Alice replied.

'No, I am afraid Joseph is in for a broken heart,' his father replied, 'but I will let him go, if he is given the permission. The travel will educate him.'

Alice and Sybil chatted about the young people. 'I also think our ways will be too rustic for a girl from a seminary town like Douai,' Alice said.

'I agree. Joseph was more interested in horses than girls, or he was until Isobel came,' Sybil replied, as the young couple came into view. They were laughing as they wandered slowly down the garden path, Joseph so tall, Isobel diminutive in comparison, smiling up at him. In her hand she held a rose.

'So, you have been picking my roses, young Sir,' Alice laughed at Joseph.

'Oh, Aunt Alice, I knew you would not mind. I told Isobel you got the first bush from Padua when Uncle John visited Italy. She says her father travels to Italy regularly, and she will take me to Padua. We can travel, can't we Mama?' Joseph asked anxiously.

'If you are granted permission to go Joseph, I will make sure the trip is not wasted. It will be a once in a lifetime journey for you. You are lucky I have had some good years with my wool and horse breeding!' His father grinned at Alice. 'Our youngsters will beggar us yet.'

Roger Nowell duly arrived at Bawle House with permission to travel for Joseph. 'Just do not decide to study for the priesthood, or you will not be allowed back,' he said.

'No chance of that,' Joseph said, looking at Isobel, who blushed becomingly.

'Oh, so that is the way the wind blows,' Roger looked enquiringly at Sybil as the two young people left the room.

'Joseph is hoping Isobel will return with him,' she said.

'How is Mistress Alice these days,' he asked Sybil.

'Still fretting for Dick,' she replied.

'She is a handsome woman, and rich. She may marry again,' he remarked.

'Alice will never marry again. She is still obsessed with her memories of Dick. They were ideally happy together. No one could replace him.' Sybil glanced at Roger Nowell quizzically. He was

145

standing with his arm leaning on the fireplace, in his hand a glass of their finest wine.

I wonder if he thinks Alice would have him? Little chance of that, thought Sybil. She smiled to herself. The clock ticked the minutes away, and William, sensing some tension, refilled his own glass.

'Baldwin still harbours ill will towards the Nutters,' he said to Nowell.

'I am tired of Baldwin's accusations,' Roger replied, 'He rants against the Demdike, and Chattox, accusing them of witchcraft. I am for a quiet life, but he goes above me sometimes and actually sends messages to Lord Derby himself.'

'He is a dangerous man,' William replied.

Roger finished his wine and turned towards the door, nodding to Sybil, who quietly smiled back. William went outside with him, 'Thank you for your help in this Roger, Joseph is pleased.'

'You are welcome, William. Anything for an old friend.'

William watched him mount his horse. With his servant in attendance he quickly disappeared into the distance.

Although he had not mentioned it to William and Sybil, Roger intended to call at Roughlee on his way home. He held permission for Christopher to travel abroad also.

He was shown into Alice's parlour. She rose as he entered, 'Why, Master Nowell, I have been expecting you. Christopher asks each day if you have brought his permission to travel.'

'He does not intend to stay with his brother, I hope?' Roger asked Alice.

'Oh, no. One studying for the priesthood is enough, don't you think?' she said. 'Christopher wants to go to sea, this is a taste of adventure for him.'

'I could not promise him a safe return if he had been. You know that if Charles comes again he will be in grave danger? I will not be allowed to look the other way.'

'I understand, Sir.'

Alice and James Wilsey accompanied the party to Hull. Whilst there, Alice had conversations with sea captains. There was no doubt of a place for Christopher, when Alice offered to invest money in a voyage the following year.

'Life is hard at sea, young man,' one captain said, looking at Christopher.

'I know Sir, I am strong,' he replied.

Alice smiled at her youngest son. 'Your heart is set, then?' she asked.

146

'Quite set, Mother. I wish to find out more about the world. I feel too obstructed here, there is no freedom.'

'You may find there is less freedom in other parts of the world, young Sir,' the captain replied, and looking at Alice, 'but he will learn the hard way, as they all do.'

The good-byes all said, Alice and James waved at the young people, smiling excitedly together. The ship slipped anchor, the sails billowed in the strong wind and she sailed smoothly away.

The time moved inexorably forward. Alice knew the only member of her family to remain at Roughlee would be Miles. She was grateful he had married Ruth, and united the two families, and she was happy watching young Richard growing all the time.

Book Four

I

Alice was in her rose garden one afternoon in late summer. The berries on the rowan trees were bright orange in the rays of the sun, horse chestnut and sycamore leaves were starting to show their autumn colours, a few roses still bloomed, and blackberries grew in profusion alongside the wall.

A clatter of hooves announced the arrival of a horseman, and looking up, Alice saw Roger Nowell.

Assuming a smile, she walked towards him. 'Good day to you, Mistress Alice, you look in fine humour. The roses are back in your cheeks.'

'The weather has been kind to me,' she replied.

'How is your grandson?' he asked.

'He is growing and thriving, and how are your grandchildren?' she asked.

'Very well, thriving also. I understand your son and his family have moved to live with you here.'

'Yes, it makes me very happy. I am not so lonely. Please come inside and take some refreshment,' Alice replied.

Roger Nowell followed her into the house, a sardonic glint in his eye. His hair now receded from his florid face. He looks old, thought Alice. He was soon reclining in the familiar parlour, visited by him so often in the past, and then a lull after his offer for the mine had been turned down, by Dick.

'How are your stocks of coal?' he asked.

'We have sufficient for the village and the local houses such as Sybil and William at Bawle House. We also supply some further afield, in Burnley. Just small amounts. I have one or two men working, mainly to give them employment. It was against my wishes really, but a deputation of village men asked if I would open it. Miles oversees it, of course.'

'I have a mind to invest further this way,' he said. 'I would take it off your hands, if you were so inclined?'

'No, I do not need to sell it. Dick wanted to leave the estate whole for our children,' she said. 'That land has been in the family for two

148

generations now, and I will keep it that way,' she looked sad, 'and Miles lost his life in it.' They were silent, remembering Miles senior, and his love of life.

'Maybe the memories are too sad?' he asked.

'Master Nowell, I know that you do not need this land. You desire to extend your boundaries, that is all. I fear you covet what is not yours.'

'I resent your implications, Mistress.'

'Do not harbour resentment, Sir'

'Well, I would prefer to deal with a man. You have too much to say,' he replied dourly.

'Dick and I had an equal say in everything. I am not a shrinking violet, Sir, but an educated woman, and I manage this family's finances as well as any man, better than many. I fear this conversation is at an end.' She rose, 'Please take some refreshment, let there be no animosity between us,' and she pulled the bell rope.

Roger Nowell accepted the refreshment with good grace. He had not really expected her to sell, but delighted in arousing the spark in her, and was rarely disappointed. He took a bite of a pastry and a look of appreciation came over his face.

'I must compliment you, Mistress. Did you make these, or your servant?'

'I made them, Sir, I enjoy cooking. It takes my mind off my loneliness.' The atmosphere became more relaxed and they chatted amicably about village affairs.

II

In the late afternoon, Alice sat down in the parlour to read a letter recently arrived from France, giving her much news. Charles had been ordained a priest and Margaret was still in Douai. Alice missed her very much. The King had instigated new laws stopping people from travelling abroad, especially to France, and it was not as easy to travel as it had been in the past.

Isobel had at last agreed to travel to England to marry Joseph. Alice and Sybil had agreed together that the two must be sure, as they had endured a long separation since Joseph's return from France. He had been moody and depressed until the news came.

Anne brought Alice some refreshment, and Alice sighed.

'Sit awhile with me, dear. Let us remember the old days when the family was complete.'

Anne put her arms around Alice. 'Dear Mistress, we will always be together.'

'You are closer than a sister to me, Anne', Alice replied.

'And you to me, dear.'

'It is lonely without Miles and Ruth and the baby,' Alice remarked. They were spending a few days at the house at Reedley.

'They will soon be back, and then you will long for peace,' Anne laughed.

'I have had a letter from France.'

'Good news?'

'Charles has been ordained, but I hope he stays in France.'

'You must be proud, Mistress.'

'I am, but worried. I fear we could not hide his presence long if he comes. Henry is ill, and the villagers are hostile to us. Roger Nowell ostracises me since I refused to sell him the mine.'

'You have Miles and Ruth,' Anne replied. 'Soon, maybe Christopher will return with exciting news of his first voyage.'

'I hope he is safe. He was always determined to go to sea, away from the restrictions of life here, he used to say.'

The two women sat together on the oak settle, content in their established familiarity. Happy laughter was heard and Maria came into the room with her two children. They ran up to Alice and Anne, climbing all over them. Alice, laughing, reached for the marzipan she always kept for the children.

'You two looked sad as I walked in,' Maria exclaimed. 'Not bad news I hope?'

'No, dear, just sad memories. Your mother and I have been through much sorrow together,' Alice smiled at Maria.

'Oh, you must not be sad. I have good news, I am to have another baby. This time I hope for a girl. I shall call her after you, dear Aunt Alice,' and Maria gave Alice a fond hug.

'I am happy for you, dear. Have you been able to tell Christopher's mother yet?'

'Not yet. You are the first to know, after Christopher, of course.'

'Baldwin does not relent. He is said to be so proud of his new house at Wheathead. You would think he would want his grandchildren there.' Anne looked at Alice.

'You would think so, but he seems to be more bitter than ever. I suspect he plots against us secretly. The villagers look askance whenever I go out.' Alice looked sad. 'I am happier at Reedley these days. I will go again when Miles comes back. It is necessary for one of us to be here.'

'You are right about him plotting, Mistress,' said Maria grimly.

'Do you know something, dear?' Alice asked.

'He was standing on a large stone at Downham, with Elizabeth Device in the stocks, ranting and raving about recusants and witches. He does not seem able to tell the difference. He was accusing Elizabeth of killing by witchcraft a cow belonging to John Nutter of Bull Hole.'

'Oh, no, he isn't still on about that, is he?' Alice asked.

'Yes. Apparently, she offered to cure the cow of some ill, and it died.'

'Poor woman,' Alice looked hurt.

'Her children were running all over Downham whilst she was in the stocks. Christopher tried to get her released. He went for Nicholas Assheton. In the end he got her out, but it took hours.'

'I expect Christopher had to pay for her release, did he not?' Alice asked drily.

'Yes,' Maria admitted, 'and he brought her home in the cart with the children. Alison is pretty. She deserves better than to live in that dirty place, she would make a good maid.'

'I've asked her before,' Alice replied, 'but she refuses to be housebound. She prefers to beg round Colne.

'She prefers to be with her mother,' said Anne. 'Blood is thicker than water.'

'I have tried to help that family, and I still send them fuel, but they are independent. Malkin Tower was a decent house when the pedlar was alive, but that is so long ago.' Alice's mind again drifted back through the years to when Will Device would bring her the letters from France, and of his untimely death. Baldwin had something to do with that, too, she thought.

'Malkin Tower becomes more decrepit all the time,' Maria said.

'They do not care, or they care too much to ask. Who can tell?' Alice remarked.

'They always have coal, Christopher sees to that,' Maria said.

'They are welcome to the coal. Elizabeth was badly hurt in the accident at the mine when father was killed. I do not begrudge them fuel.'

'Christopher has shored up the passage. He says it's secure for years, and there is plenty of coal.'

'Miles always said there was coal in it for years,' Alice said.

'Christopher said Roger Nowell was up there last time he rode that way and asked him whether he had permission to be there.'

'How dare he,' Alice bristled. 'That man! He is the bane of my life. Why, Christopher is like my own son. I would trust him with anything. The nerve of the man!'

'So, you are not alone, my dear.'

A head poked round the door. 'I knew Ruth and Miles had taken the children to Reedley, and so thought to keep you company,' said Sybil.

'How lovely to see you, Sybil. Please stay for dinner.'

'Oh, I am definitely going to stay. William has had to go to Preston on business and will stay overnight. Is there a bed for me here?'

'Oh yes,' Alice gave a delighted laugh. 'To think how sad I was an hour ago, and only had Anne to console me. Then Maria and the boys came, and now your dear self. Oh, how lucky I am in my friends,' and she clapped her hands. 'Let us have something special for dinner and we will open a bottle of Bordeaux.'

When the evening meal was over the two friends walked slowly down to the riverside.

'Dick always called this part of the day Daylight Gate,' Alice said.

'What a lovely description of evening,' Sybil replied. 'From the daylight to darkness is indeed like passing through a gateway.'

'My life feels like a gateway, Sybil,' Alice said. 'I sometimes want to pass through it to Dick. I am tired, I have no fight left in me. The children are independent now, and have their own lives.'

'Alice, do not talk like that. Your children still rely on you very much.'

'You still have William, Sybil. I am bereft without Dick, we were so close.' Tears sprang to her eyes and ran down her cheeks.

152

'Now, now, my dear. I came to cheer you up. Do not cry.'

'Oh, Sybil, you are an old friend. Who else can I cry with?'

'Always on my shoulder, dear.'

'I must go to mass at Towneley soon. I need the comfort, and I feel a hostility in the village when I pass by.'

'I will contact Mistress Towneley, my dear. I ride to Burnley tomorrow. She will welcome us.'

Alice brightened up at the words and the two friends walked slowly back to the welcoming lights of the Hall.

III

When the lights were at last extinguished and shadows from the dying embers of the fire flickered against the walls and hangings, Alice stood quietly behind her bedroom door. The great clock at the bottom of the stairs ticked the minutes away, and at last came the time she was waiting for, the ding-dong, ding-dong, signifying the quarter hour. When the last notes had died away she slowly opened the door, and emerging into the passageway, she listened intently. Nothing stirred. The only sound was the murmur of the wind through the trees outside, and the only light was from the waning moon as it peered through the windows.

Alice walked stealthily along the passageway and descended the stairs. Pausing at the bottom, she again listened intently. No sound reached her ears and she turned the well-oiled handle of the door. She opened it just wide enough for her to enter, and quickly closed it behind her. Walking decisively towards the fireplace she pressed the panelling on the right-hand side and an aperture appeared, growing rapidly wider. As soon as it was wide enough for her to pass through she stepped inside, quickly closing the opening behind her.

Alice reached into a cavity in the wall. Removing a candle and tinder box, she quickly lit the candle. In its light a flight of stairs was shown and she hurried down. At the bottom, a man's figure rose from a pallet to embrace her.

'My dear Sister, the hours have been long this day. I thought you would be unable to come, and I decided to try and get some sleep.'

'Christopher, I will always come to hear your prayers, no matter how late,' and kneeling together, the priest and Alice prayed.

Rising, Alice asked, 'How are your provisions?'

Christopher replied, 'I have enough for the next couple of days, but I am short of water and I need to clear the cess pipe.'

'I will see to that whilst the servants sleep,' Alice said. 'Now come to the top of the stairs for some fresh air.'

The priest looked down at this foot, which was bandaged. 'It feels easier today. I will try to climb the stairs for some fresh air.'

Slowly, leaning heavily on his sister, he dragged himself up the stairs. At the top he leaned, gasping against the wall.

Alice opened the panelling and he took deep breaths of the fresh air. They stayed like that for at least five minutes, Christopher drinking in the air and letting the fetid smell out of the hiding place. Then Alice helped him down the stairs. She returned to the opening, closed it behind her once more, and hurried towards the kitchen. Filling a container with water, she returned and passed through the panel again.

He took the can from her and drank greedily. She splashed a tankard full down the cess hole.

'I will clear the outer pipe in the morning early,' she said. 'Do not fear.'

'I have arranged with James to ride with you as soon as the moon is gone.'

'Thank you, dear sister. Once I reach Yorkshire I can find shelter, then I will return to France to recover my strength.'

'God willing,' she replied.

Later that week, James Wilsey and another man, cowled, rode out of the yard in the darkness. Rapidly they reached the brow of the hill and turned left towards Gisburn, not noticing the shadowy figure emerging from the clump of trees on their right. Richard Baldwin, always abroad scenting out trouble for others, was pleased with himself this night. He recognised James Wilsey, but would not approach him alone. His face was grim as he turned in the direction of Read.

Later, as he mounted his horse outside Read Hall, he spoke to the man beside him.

'If you continue to turn a blind eye to the papists who flout the law at Roughlee Hall, then I will be forced to inform the Earl of Derby. I have warned you to watch the Nutters, and you ignored my warnings.'

'You have no proof that Wilsey was with one of the Nutters. You did not see them leave Roughlee Hall.'

Oh, God, I am tired of this man, thought Roger Nowell.

'Then where did they come from?' demanded Baldwin.

'I do not know. Mayhap you imagine things, Sir,' Nowell replied.

'I imagine nothing. It was Christopher Nutter, or else his nephew Charles. They were harboured in the Hall, and you would not let me search.'

'Baldwin, you tire me. The Nutters are friends. Their religion pains me, but I am sure Mistress Nutter would not have admitted his presence to me.'

'You are a Justice of the Peace, Sir. Use your power of search.'

'Do not tell me my duties.' Nowell was becoming angry.

'I will inform Lord Derby directly of my suspicions next time.'

'You over-step yourself. Why are you not at home with your family?'

'I wish to see the Catholic scum wiped out in Lancashire.'

'You are an unhappy man, Sir.' Roger Nowell walked back into his house, with a frown on his face. He poured himself a glass of claret and leaned against the fireside. One priest had perhaps got away again. So be it.

He had studied at Towneley with the Nutters, the Bannisters, and the Towneleys themselves. But Baldwin will go above me, straight to Derby, he thought. He had no wish to incriminate himself. It was one thing turning a blind eye to a priest escaping, but if it could be proved he had taken no action following reports . . .

'Confound Baldwin!' he exclaimed, and smashed his glass against the hearth.

IV

In mid-March Alison Device was on her way to Colne. She had a licence to beg and on market day there was money to be had. Men would get drunk and throw pennies her way, and she would bring back food. They ate well at Malkin Tower on market day. She hummed a tune as she walked along and lifted her face to the sun, which seldom had the warmth it had today. A rabbit ran out in front of her and she jumped. Then, looking ahead she saw the pedlar, John Law. She hurried a little, and reaching him, asked to see his pack.

'Only if you are going to spend a penny, young Miss,' he replied. 'It is a lot of trouble to open my pack and close it up again. You could see it at the market at Colne.'

'Oh, please show it to me. I may get a penny at Colne, then I will know what to buy.'

'Well, I was just about to have my pie, so you may share it,' he said, and sitting down they ate companionably. He asked her about her family. He knew them of old, had watched her grow up, and had always been sorry for the family since their father drowned. Alison walked beside him, wishing she already had a penny because there was a decorated pin she would have liked, fearing it would sell quickly.

'Can I have the pin, and I will pay you at Colne when I get some money?' she asked.

'I've already told you, you must wait until you get the penny.'

They were approaching the incline to Colne as the sun continued to beat down. The pedlar started to pant, and wiped his brow with his kerchief.

'I will help you carry the pack,' said Alsion, 'then you can reward me.'

'Look, Miss, I've already told you to wait until you get a penny.'

Alison looked at the man. 'Please let me have the pin and I'll give you the penny, I promise.' Reaching over, she took the pin and started to run.

'I'll pay you, I promise,' she shouted.

'Stop, you are a thief.!'

'No, I'm not! I will pay you at Colne. You are a mean man. I have nothing, and you have all that is in your pack. You should be struck down for your lack of charity. You know me, I cannot get away.' She started to run and he ran after her.

156

'You cheeky young Madam. Don't say I should be struck down. I'll whip you when I catch you.'

Suddenly, he gave a cry, and as Alison looked back, he seemed to sway, clutching at his chest. He fell, his hands holding out towards her. Frightened, Alsion ran back.

John's face was ashen and he foamed slightly at the lips. He was conscious and said, 'You have struck me down. You said I should be struck down.'

'Oh, no, no, I was but jesting.'

She looked at him, her superstitious mind running riot. Had she struck him down? Maybe she had the powers? He was on the ground, wasn't he, and she had the pin? Two men approached. Alison ran up to them.

'The pedlar is ill, he fell on the ground.'

They ran towards the pedlar and carried him into a nearby alehouse. 'What happened?' one of the men asked when the pedlar's eyes opened. John pointed a finger at Alison, who had followed them into the alehouse.

'I am bewitched,' he said, and lost consciousness. The men looked at Alison, who stared back in fear. Then, sensing she should make herself scarce, she ran back to Malkin Tower and told her mother the story.

Eleven days later, horsemen headed by John Law's son, Abraham, arrived at Malkin Tower. Alison walked out with her head high, and she was taken to see John Law, who was still ill at Colne. Her mother stood sobbing at the door. Why did these things happen, one after the other, to members of her family? First Will, then the accident at the mine, the years of hardship and poverty, and now her child accused of bewitching a man? Elizabeth sank to the floor, overcome.

The next day, Abraham Law returned with Alison. His father had again accused her of bewitching him and she had begged forgiveness. But Abraham was not satisfied, so he had come for Elizabeth and James as well. He would bring them all before Roger Nowell that very day, following questioning Elizabeth and James returned home.

V

Sybil rode into the yard at Roughlee with a tall, handsome youth. Alice, walking out of the house, looked, stared, and rushed towards him arms outstretched.

'Oh, Charles, how lovely. But were you seen?'

'We came straight from Bawle House, and only passed Malkin Tower. Elizabeth won't say anything.'

Elizabeth would not, but little eight-year-old Jennet was on her way to Jane Bulcock's, at Whitehough, when Richard Baldwin stopped her.

'Ah, the youngest of the Device whelps. Where are you going?'

'I live mostly with Jane, Sir, I do not beg.'

'So, perhaps you can tell me who rode by your house an hour ago?'

'Why, Sir, Mistress Sybil, Sir.'

'And who else?'

'One of her sons.'

'Which one?'

'I dunno, Sir. I wasn't close enough to see.'

'Well, go to Roughlee Hall and find out, and I will give you a shilling to buy your grandmother food. But say nothing.'

Jennet ran off, her childish mind thinking of the food she could buy for her grandmother. In the farmyard she saw Alice with her arm linked in that of a young man. They were admiring the horses.

'Hello, Jennet. Go in and Anne will give you a pie.'

Jennet ran into the kitchen. Anne saw her, and laughing, said, 'Hello, Jennet. What, hungry again? Second time today,' and handed the child a pie. She reached out her hands and, bright teeth biting into the pie, she looked round.

'That doesn't look like Mistress Sybil's son with Mistress Alice?' she said.

'You are a bright one, too bright for your own good.' Anne looked at Jennet with an affectionate gaze. 'That is Master Charles, but say nothing.'

Jennet's eyes filled with cunning. 'If I am to keep a secret I want a shilling.'

'Get out, you little rascal. You get no payment here. Mistress Alice keeps you alive. She pays Jane Bulcock for your keep, and think of all the food we give you for your mother and grandmother.'

Anne picked up a broom and caught it sharply across Jennet's legs. She screamed and darted out, across the yard and towards the fence. She climbed quickly over the gate and was off.

'What ails Jennet?' asked Alice.

'Wanted a shilling to keep quiet about Charles.'

Alice looked startled. 'That is unusual. Where did she get that idea? Charles had better stay out of sight,' and she hurried in to tell Sybil the strange tale.

In the distance, the figure of a man on horseback could be seen leaning down and listening to a young girl.

Jennet scurried homeward, pausing only to retrieve the luscious meat pie she had secreted earlier that day in the wall behind the rowan tree. She quickly removed the stones exposing a space carefully lined with smooth stones, safe from predators. Grandmother Demdike would eat well this night.

Crossing the river on the large stepping stones she emerged at last to Malkin Tower. It was now no more than four walls and a leaking roof. Slats of tree branches were laid across the roof and flat stones were piled on top of these, but smoke curled from a rude chimney. Opening the door, she stepped back as more smoke belched outwards. Coughing and spluttering from the constrast to the cool evening air, Jennet hurried towards the fireside with her offering for her grandmother.

Old Demdike was rocking in a rickety chair, long-scrawny fingers outstretched towards the pie. She was dressed in a variety of ill-fitting garments, dragged on, one on top of the other, all mildewed and grimy, a black bonnet, a cast off of Mistress Nutter's, pulled so far over her face that it was difficult to see the beady-dark eyes and long-pointed nose.

'What have you brought your grandmother today. Crumbs from the Nutter table?'

'Don't be ungrateful, Mother,' said a voice from the corner. Rising swiftly from the fireside where she was stirring the contents of a cauldron-like cooking pan, hanging from a tripod over the fire, a younger version of the old Demdike, similarly clad, walked over to the girl. Taking the pie she broke it in half and, placing each piece on a wooden trencher, she spooned the broth-like substance over the pie. Giving one portion to her mother, she sat down with the other and soon there was no sound in the derelict cottage but the satisfied gulping of the two women.

Since the accident at the mine, Elizabeth Device had eked out a precarious living, begging, doing odd jobs on the farms, receiving help from Alice whenever she asked, always coal and clothing. She was grateful to Jane Bulcock for caring for Jennet but it made the child more precocious.

'I have a shilling, I have a shilling,' chanted the child.

'Show it, show it,' cackled her grandmother.

Jennet showed the shilling. 'Where did you get it?' Elizabeth stepped forward as the old crone reached for the shilling. 'Wait, Mother, I want to know where she got it.'

'Doesn't matter. Give it here, child.'

'It does matter. Now, I ask again, where did you get it?' She gave the child a resounding smack across the face, then gripping her tight, she asked again, 'Where did you get it?'

'From Richard Baldwin,' she whimpered.

'What!' her mother screamed. 'That bastard, who makes our lives daily more miserable? That man who has caused me to spend long hours in the stocks, who has whipped me, whipped my sons, and persecuted me. The man who left Will to die?'

'He paid me, he paid me,' Jennet whimpered.

'For what? For what?' screamed her mother, holding on to the child.

'He wanted to know who came with Mistress Sybil to Roughlee Hall. He sent me to find out. It was Master Charles.'

'You told him that? I'll kill you!' She hit out at the screaming child. 'The Nutters are our friends. Mistress Nutter has helped me for years. She has kept us alive, you scum, you.' She took her broom and began to beat the child, screaming obscenities all the time. The door opened and James lumbered in.

'Leave her, Mother, you'll kill her!'

'I don't mind if I do,' she answered. 'She has sold Mistress Nutter to Baldwin.'

Her grip relaxed. Jennet slipped from her and ran through the doorway. Terrified, and with hatred in her heart towards her mother, she ran until she reached Jane Bulcock's house, and fell, sobbing, into that woman's arms.

'What is it, child? Who has hurt you.'

Jane looked at the weals on her arms and legs.

'My mother, my mother.'

'Whatever for?'

'She hit me because I took a shilling from Master Baldwin. She always wants a shilling. Why did she hit me?'

'Because none of us would take a shilling from Baldwin. Throw it away.' She prised the shilling, still clutched in the child's fingers, out of the grimy hand, and threw it, spinning, into the river. Jennet continued to sob. I'll get another off him. I want a shilling. I've never had one, she thought.

At the same time, James Device was running towards Roughlee

Hall, where he blabbed his story to Alice and Sybil. They acted quickly, and soon James Wilsey was riding away with Sybil, dressed in Charles's clothes. Alice quickly opened the door of the hiding place once more. Charles went quickly inside.

An hour later, Roger Nowell rode into the yard with Richard Baldwin and several other horsemen.

'I must search your house, Mistress. Baldwin has made a complaint that you harbour a known priest.'

'Search where you will, Sir. The only visitor today was Sybil Bannister, who rode in with James Wilsey. They left not an hour ago. Your information is false, Baldwin,' Alice coldly addressed the other man. 'From whom did you obtain your information?'

'Do not question me, Mistress. My informant saw your son, Charles, with you in the yard,' Baldwin replied sourly.

'Your informant saw me with James Wilsey. You should make sure of your facts. The only person outside this household who has been to the house today was just eight years old. I can only assume that is where you received your information. Hardly reliable.' Alice turned to Roger Nowell, 'Please search.'

Nowell strode through the door, Baldwin following. Quick as lightning, Alice ran and stood in front of Baldwin.

'You are not a magistrate, Sir, and I forbid you to enter my home.'

Baldwin fell back, his face blazing with anger.

Nowell returned five minutes later. 'You have been misinformed, Sir, get more reliable witnesses in future.'

Baldwin stared at Alice, 'You win this one, Mistress, but the time is near when you will lose. I give you my word on that.'

Alice felt chilled. Turning to Nowell, she said, 'This man threatens me, Sir.'

Nowell looked at Baldwin. 'The lady is right. You threaten her. I must warn you that if you act against the law I will have to take action.' He turned to Alice. 'As a magistrate I had to take action when the complaint was laid before me. As your friend, I will say be careful not to cause this man to make further complaints.'

Turning his horse, he rode away, his servant following.

Baldwin rode off in the direction of Wheathead, hatred in his heart. Alice's pleasure in Charles' arrival was all but dispersed. Oh, how I wish Dick were here, she thought, but her mind was already working on plans for Charles' departure.

James Device lumbered up. 'Mother says to tell you she has beaten Jennet, and please to share a meal with us on Good Friday, just to show you do not blame us, Mistress.'

'Well, I'll tell you what I will do, we are all to go to Sybil's on Good Friday for a meal, so I will call on my way and sup with you,' she smiled. 'Will that suffice?'

'Yes, Mistress.' He lumbered away in his own ungainly fashion. Mistress Alice had always been his friend.

On Friday, Miles and Ruth, and Christopher and Maria departed for Bawle House. 'I will join you later, dears. I have promised to stop at Malkin Tower first,' said Alice.

'Oh, Mother, why do you act so friendly to that rough crowd?'

'Miles, I have known the family from my childhood. Remember, Elizabeth lost her health in our mine.'

Miles had the grace to look chastened, and he and Ruth and the children rode out of the yard.

Alice arrived at Malkin Tower. A warm sun shone down on the gathering, and the main conversation was Alison's predicament. Alice looked down from her horse and accepted the tankard of ale offered to her.

'Thank you, Jamie.'

Looking up, she saw Katherine Hewitt walking towards the gathering. 'Mistress Sybil sent me to meet you, Mistress.'

'Please have a tankard of ale.'

Elizabeth offered the drink to Katherine, who smiled at Elizabeth and took it.

'It is a strange affair, Mistress, that Alison is arrested, and old Demdike and Chattox have been questioned by Master Nowell. Even your Anne has been questioned,' she said to Alice.

'We live in superstitious times, Katherine. If people, including the King, believe in witches, it is a sad time for us all. Maybe Alison and the others will be found to be innocent and they will come home.'

Elizabeth was standing near to Alice. 'Oh, Mistress Alice, she has said she is guilty. She admitted before Master Nowell and me that she had struck the pedlar down.'

'That is impossible, Elizabeth.'

'There are those who believe it.'

The gathering was becoming more aggressive as each tankard of ale was swallowed. Wild suggestions, such as helping Alison to break out of the prison were aired. Alice looked at Katherine.

'I think we can go now, dear. I have shared their celebrations with them.'

They left and cantered on the trail down to Bawle House, unknowing that, hidden behind a wall just inside the wood, a malevolent face peered out. Jennet, still smarting from her beatings, took notice of Alice's presence at the feast.

With several friends, and a priest from Towneley, Alice and Sybil and their families took part in the Easter mass, as they had done for years. The problem of Charles' escape was in all their minds. How was he to be helped out of the area when Baldwin's spies abounded?

EPILOGUE

Miles' Story

Now I am an old man, I can look back over the years with more understanding of my mother's sacrifice. Ruth and I remember together the pleasant days when her parents and my mother and father, and my grandfather Miles were great friends and shared many happy hours together, both at her home, Bawle House, and my home, Roughlee Hall.

Ruth and I never returned to Roughlee after the dreadful events of 1612. We have made our home at Reedley, and Margaret, my sister, lives here with us. Christopher Baldwin and Maria have looked after the Hall, although their hearts were also broken, as ours were, when we lost our dear mothers so tragically.

I try to explain to my grandchildren, when they ask, 'Was great-grandmother a witch?' how a dear and lovely lady came to be hanged as such. Children at church and school are sometimes cruel, and chant and tease. I must write down the events of those days before I grow confused, and the memories come and go, both Ruth and Margaret may remember where I forget.

After my father died so tragically young, things were never the same at home. My mother grieved for him, and even my children could not bring a smile to her face for long. Where once she had fought unceasingly for justice for the oppressed, and poor illiterate villagers, particularly against Richard Baldwin, she seemed to shrink before him. He became more vicious, and I remember the Demdikes were usually his victims.

James Device, old Demdike's grandson, was of very low intellect. He worked for my mother, around the farmyard, and he would take the cart for coal to Greystones every week. After my grandfather was killed in the mine, and Elizabeth Device badly disfigured, my father would not re-open the mine commercially, but again and again refused offers to buy it, mostly from Roger Nowell. He got it eventually though, through a foul deal, but it never did him any good as no one would work in it.

I clearly remember Roger Nowell. I used to call him 'Uncle' when our families exchanged visits. I remember my brother Charles'

164

christening, when all my world was happy, and all the important people of the neighbourhood celebrated with us. I did not understand then the sadness in my mother's heart for the premature deaths of her mother and brother and the way Catholics were persecuted. As a child, who knows no differences of faith, I prayed at my mother's knee to a good God. It is man who perpetrates evil in the name of God, but I did not know of that in the halcyon days of my childhood. It seems to me, looking back, that my parents were always laughing.

I remember when my mother and I took ship for France to visit my uncles at Douai, and the wonderful time we had, but how happy my mother was to rush into my father's arms on our return, my little sister Margaret dancing on the quayside. It did not seem possible to me that the same uncle who had walked and talked with me in France should later die cruelly for his faith in England. I think it was my first taste of sorrow when Uncle Robert died, although others followed hard on the heels of that one; the death of grandfather Miles, then my father, and most terrible of all my mother and her dear friend, Maria's mother, Anne Redfern, and the poor unfortunates who died with them.

Still, I digress. I must set down, before it is too late, the true reasons for my mother's sacrifice, so that my children and grand-children can tell the world that their great-grandmother was not a witch, but a brave woman who died to save others, others who did not know, until it was too late, of her sacrifice.

Roger Nowell is long gone himself now, but I hope he never had a day free of the guilt he shared with Baldwin for perpetrating those evil deeds, on his part for personal greed and covetousness, and on Baldwin's for jealousy, bigotry and hatred.

Those olden times, when King James, first came to the throne, were fraught with danger for any man or woman who had the courage to flout the conventions of the day. The King had published his book, *Daemonology*, before he came to the throne, and he looked for witches when he was not searching for Catholics. I sometimes wonder whether he indeed had parcelled the two together in his mind as one, yet his own mother met her death on the block as a Roman Catholic.

We are what we are born. We do not realise as children, that according to our religion we may be acclaimed or persecuted. Maybe, in centuries to follow, my descendants will not be called upon to answer with their lives for the faiths they have rarely chosen for themselves, but inherited from their parents.

As my dear wife, Ruth, leans over to read what I have written, she smiles and tells me gently that I digress again.

'Set down what happened, Miles, to bear witness for your mother,' she says.

After my father died, my mother seemed to enjoy living more at Reedley, where she had spent her childhood, and Ruth and I, and the children, often joined her there, particularly at Christmas, when Anne and Tom Redfern, their daughter Maria and her husband Christopher Baldwin, and their children would join us. Ruth's parents, Aunt Sybil and Uncle William, dear friends of my mother, and their other children, would share the festivities also.

Christmas of 1610 springs to my mind as the last time we were truly happy. Mother seemed her old, vivacious self, and she organised the Three Wise Men to bring gifts for the children, as of old; it was James Wilsey, Tom Redfern and myself, dressed up, and our faces painted, yellow, black and brown, and the house rang with children's laughter as they received their gifts.

Our faithful servant Henry Mitton used to be one of the Three Wise Men, but he had died some years before, mother had always treated him as one of the family, but that did not stop Roger Nowell arresting my mother and accusing her of causing his death. But I race ahead, I am confused, someone else was accused of bewitching a person, before mother.'

'It was Alison Device, dear,' said Ruth gently. 'She was accused of bewitching the pedlar, John Law.'

Oh yes, now I remember. The Device family had become real beggars. I remember the family. When I was young, their father, Will Device, a Welshman, who was always whistling merrily, called to sell my mother his wares.

He used to bring her letters from her brothers, I discovered in later years, he delivered to all the Catholic houses in the area. But he died tragically, drowned in the river at Roughlee. Indeed, I ask myself, who has not died tragically in Pendle Forest in my lifetime?

Yes, yes, Alison stopped the pedlar on the road to Colne and asked him for some pins. He refused to give them to her and she is said to have cursed him so that he dropped down in a fit. He later accused her of bewitching him. My mother was an enlightened woman. I remember at the time, not knowing that she herself was soon to be accused, said to me that John Law was a big man, and on a hot day, chasing Alison, it would have been too much for his heart and might have failed him temporarily. Alison, who was a simple girl, had stared in horror at the man on the ground, and truly believed she was responsible.

John's son, Abraham, took her to his sick bed and she asked for his forgiveness. Poor girl! That was her own death warrant. Abraham Law had her, her mother, and her brother James, stand before Roger Nowell, and Alison repeated her confession. There is only I to chronicle her innocence. There is no grandfather to write the Device story for their descendants.

Tom had left the area before his mother's trial and Beth had gone into service somewhere in Yorkshire, it is not surprising that they did not return to Roughlee. Young Jennet, who was only nine years old at the time of the trial, and whose word was believed above my mother's, was herself accused of being a witch in later years.

How much bitterness was in Jennet's heart as she grew to womanhood and realised the part she was forced to play when she was but a child? Or did she truly believe the things she was tutored to say? Who knows?

Shortly after Alison was arrested, Roger Nowell came knocking on the door of Roughlee Hall, together with Nicholas Bannister of Altham, and accompanied by many of the villagers, all carrying torches. My mother faced them most regally. She ordered me to stand aside and demanded to know his business.

'I have a warrant for the arrest of Anne Redfern on a charge of causing the death of one Robert Nutter of Greenhead,' he said.

'But he died years ago. What ails you, Roger Nowell?' my mother asked. 'He raped Anne, more than once. The last time he stole a potion meant for her mother to drink in small quantities, and drank it all, but he drank heavily of ale, who is to say the potion killed him?'

'If you have proof of this, bring it to me.' Roger swung down from his horse. 'Is Redfern here?'

Anne came slowly forward, but my mother stood in front of her.

'You know we have no proof. It was all settled with Robert's father at the time, between the families.' My mother's voice rose and she wrung her hands.

'Robert's father is dead. Methinks she may have caused his death also,' Roger's face was set and hard, Anne's a picture of bewilderment.

'This cannot be true, Sir,' she said. 'Who makes these charges against me?'

'Robert Nutter's mother and sister have signed statements.'

'They did not know of the rape, their father wished to spare them,' Anne replied.

'Again I say, he is dead.'

'Dick and Miles dealt with the matter at the time,' Alice pleaded.

167

'They were foolish then, as they too are gone and cannot give evidence. Redfern, you will join Alison Device and her mother at Lancaster, and your mother, the Chattox, will accompany you.'

'Oh no, not mother. She is ill, moonstruck.' Anne struggled as two men grabbed her. Tom was pushing his way through the crowd towards his wife, but was felled by a blow from I know not who. Anne was dragged screaming to the cart.

I held my mother tight, Maria was screaming hysterically and pleading for her mother. She rushed to Tom as he rose slowly to his feet, but the cart was moving now and the constables pushed him away.

Behind us, in the house, in the hiding place made long ago by grandfather Miles, lay my brother Charles, an ordained priest, in England as a missionary. Anne knew. She always helped my mother with everything, and together they had cared for Charles. Anne was to go to her death with her lips sealed.

I remember my mother turned to me, 'The world has gone mad Miles, what can I do to help Anne? Baldwin will question Anne to see if we have a hiding place in the Hall. He has had the house watched since before Charles arrived. We were lucky to hide him as we did.'

'We will have to arrange his escape, Mother,' I said.

'Miles, we must not tell him what has happened to Anne, or he would be reluctant to go. Promise me you will get him away. There are the safe houses in Yorkshire, you must ride to Towneley for an address,' she told me, 'He must sail from Hull, we must try to send word to Christopher to warn him Charles is on his way.'

'It would be a good time now mother. All the villagers are following the cart to Read', I said.

'I fear for Anne, she is not strong,' my mother said.

'You cannot help Anne at the moment. Let me speak to Charles.' I went into the dining-room and entered the hiding place. Charles was looking anxiously up the flight of stairs, 'I heard the commotion outside, Miles what has happened?' he asked.

I remember the quandary I was in. Yet mother had told me not to tell him of Anne's arrest. 'Constables looking for members of the Device family, mother soon got rid of them,' I told him.

'I thought they had come for me,' he replied, relief on his face.

I told him we were hoping to arrange his escape and also to be prepared.

I returned to my mother, who told me James Wilsey had been in to say Nowell had left two men outside the Hall. It did not bode well.

'We must arrange a diversion to lure the men away. I fear for

Anne. I must go to her, and then you must help Charles escape', she said.

That conversation is as fresh in my mind as if it were yesterday.

Baldwin soon had grandmother Demdike, James and Elizabeth indicted for witchcraft, accusing Elizabeth of killing Henry Mitton. My mother had tended Henry, but his heart gave out one hot day when he tried to hurry home to his cottage to avoid a thunder storm. He begged my mother on his death bed to find a priest to give him the last rites, and my mother had not let him down. She also arranged for his burial at Newchurch.

The Demdikes and Anne Redfern were taken by cart through the Trough of Bowland, and Tom Redfern followed them to Lancaster to try to arrange some comfort in their prison.

As my mother rode through the village following Anne's arrest, she was shocked to hear villagers chanting, 'Who killed Henry Mitton?'

When Baldwin passed the Hall one day, with Jennet Device held in front of him on his horse, my heart lurched. What trickery is afoot, I wondered? I learned later that she was housed at Read Hall and was clothed and fed in real style, Roger Nowell having received a directive from the Earl of Derby, informing him that further failure to act on information received would render him liable to question himself.

Baldwin had done his groundwork well, and had sent a direct message to Derby. He knew that Christopher and Maria were living at Roughlee Hall and was beside himself with rage. He had never forgiven Christopher for marrying Maria Redfern.

Accusations were coming thick and fast. William Bannister called to tell us of a meeting at Read Hall when Richard Baldwin made his accusations of witchcraft, and Roger Nowell quoted from King James' book *Daemonology*. William said it was as if Nowell were caught up in a web from which, unable to escape, he must become a ringleader.

William asked my mother if she had been at a feast at Malkin Tower on Good Friday.

'I called on my way to your house, William, to ask about Alison, and if they knew how she fared in Lancaster. I offered them money. Katherine Hewitt came to meet me, and we rode to your house together, after we had drunk a measure of ale with the family and their friends, just to be friendly.'

'Oh no, Alice, not you and Katherine?' I still hear his cry in my dreams. 'All those at Malkin Tower on Good Friday are to be indicted for witchcraft.'

'Rubbish, William, I merely took ale with them to be friendly. Then we made our way to you.'

'Alice, young Jennet has said those who were there were taking part in a witches' coven. Now, besides the Devices, who else was there? Think carefully.'

'Well, I remember the Bulcocks were there, Jennet's own foster mother,' I vividly remember my mother saying, 'and a few I did not know. They were all discussing Alison's imprisonment, but Katherine and I did not stay long. She had come to meet me as Sybil was busy preparing the food, as you know.'

'Alice, the feeling was high at that meeting. They are determined to prove Anne killed Robert Nutter and that Alison maimed the pedlar. Also, Richard Baldwin accuses Elizabeth of killing his daughter by witchcraft. Roger Nowell must listen to all this and act on it. I smelt hysteria. The child Jennet is being schooled from the *Daemonology*, and says her mother and grandmother are witches. I suspect Nowell seeks for notoriety in this, and also perhaps financial recompense. King James gives rewards for witch catchers, you know, and people burn in Scotland. Beware of false accusations, Alice. Baldwin has always hated the Nutters, as well you know. If he realises there is a chance of charging you, he will take it.' William stared hard at Alice.

'Charge me? With what? It's utter nonsense, William. You know it is.'

'I know, dear, we all know. We also know that Anne did not kill Robert Nutter of Greenhead, but she is in prison and charged. We know that Alison did not maim the pedlar. She also is in prison and charged. Face facts, flee while you can. Take Charles and go with him to France.'

'Oh, William, if I did that it would seem I was afraid of being found guilty. Oh, how I wish Dick were here. It would not have happened if Dick were here,' my mother's voice broke.

'We know that also, Alice, but he isn't here, and Baldwin is out to destroy you.'

'I have an idea,' said my mother, her dark eyes suddenly gleaming, 'I can help Charles to leave through this. I can create a diversion. I must go. Give my love to Sybil and tell her I will send Miles and Ruth and the children to her soon.'

Shaking his head, Uncle William left the house. Calling for his horse, he rode along the track in the direction of Bawle House. He passed Malkin Tower, it was deserted. He later told me that it was the first time in his life he saw no smoke curling from that chimney.

He had felt a foreboding of doom and urged his horse forwards towards the warmth of his own fireside where Sybil waited.

That night my mother called me to her room. Placing her arms around me, she said, 'I want you, Ruth and the children to go to Bawle House tomorrow, Miles. You will be safer there, just in case I have to answer any questions about my presence at Malkin Tower on Good Friday.

'I cannot leave you, Mother,' I said.

'You will. What good will you do here? I will ride with you to allay suspicion. Christopher and Maria, who do not know of Charles's presence in the secret room, can stay here after you have helped him escape. If I am asked to go before Roger Nowell, Baldwin will have to be there as our churchwarden.' She smiled reflectively.

'I think I may turn this situation to our advantage. You will be able to help Charles to escape.'

'Mother,' I said, 'you play with fire.'

'Nonsense,' her reply rings in my ears. 'I am rich. I can pay for my release. After all, I have done nothing and they cannot prove anything against me. My mind is made up. I shall, in fact, go to see Roger Nowell first, and demand Baldwin's presence. Then you must seize the chance to move Charles. The Towneleys will have an address of a safe house where Charles can be taken. Give him money and take money yourself to pay for my defence, if necessary, against Nowell. We must help Charles to make his escape. He cannot stay in that room much longer. I am unable to let fresh air in and the cess pipe is becoming blocked. I dare not be seen attending to anything in the yard.'

I remember feeling anger against my brother, whom I had always thought had chosen an easy life as a priest, rather than a hard one as a farmer. Then I remembered how my uncles had died so cruelly, and so young. I did not want that fate for Charles, but I wished he had not put us all at risk.

The following morning my mother was up very early, rousing us we made haste. James Wilsey saddled the horses, and Ruth and I, with the children and my mother, rode out of Roughlee together. We passed Malkin Tower, now desolate, a few hens still picking round the empty doorway, and avoiding the track to White Moor, we descended Slipper Hill. Towards the bottom, by a stream, my mother reined in her horse.

When I think of my mother that is how I remember her. In her russet cloak and a high hat with a feather, she looked in every way a carefree country lady out for a ride. The big black horse pawed the ground and shook his head. Mother patted him and spoke soothingly, then she looked at me.

'Miles, I will leave you now. When you have seen Ruth and the children settled, you must return to Roughlee and tell Charles to prepare to leave. Then go to Towneley Hall. Find out the name of the safe house. You and Charles must ride hard. The house will be in Yorkshire and Christopher's ship should be at Hull, to take Charles to France. Not a word of Anne's plight to Charles or Christopher, remember?'

'Mother, I do not want you to ride to Read Hall alone,' I said.

'I must. I intend to demand an explanation from Roger Nowell. I will tell him I was at Malkin Tower, and ask what of it?'

'Be careful, dear.' My heart was full of foreboding.

She leaned down and kissed my cheek. 'When you return, I am sure Anne and I will be back at Roughlee and all this anxiety will be a memory, a great mistake. We will have a feast,' and, urging her horse forward, she was off, back up Slipper Hill, the trees merging in behind her until I saw her no more.

So I said goodbye to my mother, not realising I would never see her again under normal circumstances, and I remember her on her black horse, her hair streaked with grey, yet her face young and bright, her cheeks rosy and her eyes flashing as she planned her diversion for Charles.

I rode to Towneley Hall later that day and learned an address. I returned to Roughlee where Christopher was in the yard, much agitated.

'My father has been here asking for your mother,' he said.

'In what connection?' I asked.

'He did not say, he just looked grim. I fear for his sanity. I heard him say he would ride to Read for a warrant. What does this mean Miles?'

'Christopher, take Maria and the children to Bawle House. Aunt Sybil expects you. Tomorrow I will come and explain everything. You must stay for a few days. Then it is my mother's wish that if she is delayed, you and Maria will take care of this house for her.'

Looking bewildered, Christopher went into the house and shortly afterwards, he, Maria and the children, all mounted on ponies, left for the short journey to Bawle House.

'I will return and see to the animals tonight, Miles, if you are unable to attend to them,' he said, waving.

'Thank you, Christopher,' I responded gratefully, knowing not what was in store for me.

172

James was in the yard. 'I have the horses ready, Master Miles. I am going with you.'

James, our rock and help, he had never let us down. He had helped my mother and father in all their past adventures with her brothers. He was ageing now, but his devotion was unquestionable.

'What of my mother, James?' I asked.

He gripped my arm gently. 'She has gone to Read. Do not let her down by following her. We have to help Charles now. We will wait until Daylight Gate before we make our move. I have brought Tom Moore from Reedley to help with the stock. The servants at Reedley are not involved in this travesty of witch hunting which prevails here.'

There was hardly a soul stirring later, when we opened the gate of the Hall and turned left towards the Gisburn road. Charles was dressed in russet homespun, and looked for all the world like a farmer leaving after a visit. He had no idea of the turmoil in Pendle Forest, and said gravely, 'I am sorry mother was not there when I left. I wanted to say good-bye to her.'

'She had to go to Read on business. She thought it would be a good time for you to make your escape, she made sure Baldwin would follow her.'

'She seems intimidated by Baldwin these days,' reflected Charles. 'It is not like her.'

'Mother is losing her confidence, she misses father, and seems to have no anchor now,' I replied. 'She will be happy to know you are safely away.'

'Baldwin was always looking for trouble, even when father and grandfather were alive, I remember,' Charles said.

'She will stand up to Baldwin when she knows you are safe,' I told him.

'I did not like putting you at risk, Miles, you do know that?'

'I know,' and we smiled at one another, as in the old days.

We stayed at the address I had been given at Towneley, and having memorised another address, we left the following morning, again in possession of a safe address for the next night, we eventually arrived in Hull three days later. On the water front we immediately saw Christopher's ship, the Black Falcon. Charles raised his hat and whooped for joy. I had to be merry with these brothers of mine, who had no idea of the peril our mother faced.

Christopher talked eagerly of Christmas, and his return to Roughlee. I had promised my mother I would remain silent, and I know now, that in any case, any other course of action on our part could not have prevented the inexorable movements of the law of those times, and could well have caused Charles to be captured, and Christopher and I to have become accomplices in shielding a priest, so making mother's sacrifice a vain one.

We saw Charles and Christopher safely away the following day, watching as the sails unfurled and the ship slipped anchor, sea birds screeching overhead.

'Come now, my lad,' said James, 'there is work to be done on your mother's behalf at Roughlee.'

We hurried back, only staying two nights but changing the horses several times. Worn and tired we rode to Bawle House. Sybil and William had received no word from my mother who had apparently not returned to Roughlee. She was held at Read for questioning, so they had been told. William said there were many men at Read. The Shuttleworths, Assheton, and their retainers, and Richard Baldwin. Nowell was holding a magistrates' court.

William would not allow me to ride to Read straight away. 'You must rest,' he said. 'Your duty is to Ruth and the children. Your mother has chosen the path she walks, and she wanted you and Charles to be safe. Do not jeopardise your safety now.'

'I must go when I have rested.'

'Of course you must. I will go with you,' said William. 'Your mother was sure of Roger's honesty, but I am not. He seeks notoriety and power. But Charles is saved, so do not place yourself in danger now, Miles.'

I remember Ruth holding me in her arms as I cried like a baby. Where was my mother? What were they doing to her?'

The following morning Sybil took my hand and I looked at her kindly familiar face, my mother's best friend.

'Whatever happens, remember this, Miles, your mother has never been completely happy since your father died. She will martyr herself for her children, if need be.'

The next day, Christopher Baldwin rode in from checking stock at Roughlee. His face was streaked with dirt and sweat.

'I came immediately, Miles. Your mother has been committed for trial at Lancaster. My father sought me out to tell me. He says she will hang. What for? Oh, why has my father so much hatred in him? I am sorry, so sorry,' he broke down, crying. 'She has always been so good to Maria and me.'

'Calm yourself, Christopher,' I said, 'all is not lost yet.' Turning to Uncle William, I told him I intended to ride to Read. He implored me to wait for him, but I could not. I jumped on my horse, and with

Christopher Baldwin following close behind, I set out.

Read Hall, the scene of happy family gatherings, Uncle Roger, as I used to call him, and Aunt Ellen, had welcomed us to their home many times. Scenes with my father, and my grandfather Miles, at Read and at Roughlee, went through my head. Roger Nowell quaffing my grandfather's best Bordeaux wine, Roger Nowell with his little son at his heels, smiling as he carried the rocking horse my father had made, out to the carriage. What had happened? What had gone wrong?

It seemed to me that it had all started after my grandfather's death. The Nowells were never so friendly afterwards, although poor Ellen was ever my mother's friend. But she died young, and Roger became sullen and unsociable.

I remembered my father, returning from a visit to the Towneleys, pacing up and down in the parlour, saying over and over, 'He shall not have the Greystone land,' and my mother trying to placate him.

All these thoughts passed through my mind as I rode the familiar trail from Roughlee to Read, not knowing what I would find at the end of it. Christopher rode silently beside me, full of despair because of his father's part in all this.

I jumped down from my horse outside Read Hall, tied it to a ring, and banged on the door. As it was opened, I strode in, pushing the servant to one side. Roger Nowell came slowly into the hallway, a glass of wine in his hand, his face red and bloated. He stared at me through bleary, red-rimmed eyes.

'The Nutter whelp, I see. And what brings you here?'

'I wish to see my mother.'

'You have left it a few days. What reason do you have for not coming before?'

'I expected my mother to return. I have duties to the farm, my wife and children,' I replied, following him into a large parlour.

'Oh? I have been informed you were not in Roughlee during the past few days. In fact, I have it on good information that you were indeed in Yorkshire,' and he swayed slightly, as he turned towards me.

'Why do you spy on me, Sir? It is not against the law to travel to Yorkshire, and I had business there.'

'And was your business satisfactorily concluded?' he asked sternly.

'Indeed it was, Sir.'

'It seems the business was more important than your mother,' he stated.

'I was on my mother's business,' I replied.

'What, may I ask?'

'You may ask, Sir, but I refuse to tell you. It was a private matter. Surely we are still allowed a private matter? Or am I to be accused of some ridiculous offence also?'

'Witchcraft is not considered to be a ridiculous offence, young man, but a blot on civilisation. King James has ordered that it be stamped out, and he says witches must not go free.'

'My mother is not a witch, Sir, and you know it,' I retorted angrily.

Roger Nowell drained his glass. His hands trembled, he was ill at ease. Striding towards a long rope he pulled it. A servant ran into the room.

'Fetch more wine, and be quick about it.'

He gave the fellow a kick, and turned to me. I stared at him. Kicking his servants! What has happened to the gentleman I once knew?

Roger turned to me. 'I only know what I have been told. I have been instructed by the Earl of Derby to act on information given. The evidence was not only heard by me but by three other magistrates. Your mother attended a witches' coven on Good Friday. Elizabeth Device says your mother was responsible for causing Henry Mitton's death.'

'My mother helped Henry. He was our servant and our friend, all his life. Elizabeth must have been made to say those things,' I screamed out.

The servant returned with wine and Roger drank deeply. He was not sober.

'So, now you accuse me of torture?' he said.

'Why else would Elizabeth confess to such things? My mother was her friend also,' I replied. 'I wish to see my mother now.'

'You may, she is being well treated.'

'I should think so. I wish her to have the best defence, I can pay for the best.'

'There is no defence – that is the law. Witchcraft is proved, and the facts are to be heard before Judge Altham at Lancaster Assizes.'

'No defence?' I was struck with horror, and could only stare like one mesmerized. He rang the bell again and ordered the servant to take me to see Mistress Nutter. I was led into a dressing-room where my mother sat, pale and composed. She stood up and came to me, I took her hands in mine.

'Miles, dear son, I am charged with killing Henry Mitton, and with consorting with witches at Malkin Tower,' and, aside, 'Did Charles escape?'

I nodded, and putting her hands to her face, she wept, and I knew they were tears of joy.

'Miles, I am innocent, as you know, and it is only a matter of time before I come home,' she said. 'Do not look so shattered dear, we will have a family gathering at Christmas,' and she smiled.

I was, however, near demented, and I demanded to see Nowell again. The servant refused and went to show me the door. I pushed past him. I knew Read Hall, I had known it all my life. I knew every room from playing hide-and-seek as a child. I walked into the dining-room. Roger Nowell sat at a large table, I thought how bloated he looked, he was breathing heavily as he tried to drag his heavy body to his feet.

'I have said all I have to say to you. Do not force your way in here again, you whelp. Your mother is a prisoner and goes to Lancaster tomorrow. Take care you do not accompany her, in chains.'

'My father and my grandfather would kill you for this, Nowell,' I gasped as two of his servants gripped my arms.

'They are dead, and you, young sir, are the only one left. A fine set of sons Dick Nutter left, a farmer, a priest, and a seafaring man. Not much use to their mother now. I have evidence of your mother's other interests in Roughlee. You would do well to hold your tongue.'

'I demand to accompany my mother to Lancaster, and I ask that she may ride her own horse. She is not found guilty yet, she is not a felon.'

'We ride tomorrow at dawn. She may ride her own horse. It pains me to send her for trial, young Sir. We were friends in the past, but I have no alternative. I am pressed by others. Now leave.'

I stumbled out and made for the stable. Christopher saw me and came quickly towards me.

'What is happening, Miles?'

'Mother goes to Lancaster tomorrow to be tried as a witch.'

'Oh, no! What has my father done?' Christopher looked ashen.

I pulled myself together. Gripping Christopher's hands in mine, I looked him in the face. Here was my childhood friend. We had always been close. His wife, Maria, was like another sister to me. Maria. I thought of Maria. Her mother was also at Lancaster. I knew I must reassure Christopher of my feelings for him. My mother would not want any blame to be attached to him. After all, no words had passed between him and his father since he married Maria and his father had disinherited him.

'Christopher, go home now, to Roughlee. Look after the Hall and farm for us. You must. I have to go to Lancaster with mother. Pledge me your word you will do that for me, and tell Ruth what is happening.'

'I will. I make you my solemn promise. I will look after the Hall and farm.' We shook hands, and he left.

I informed the ostler my mother needed her horse for the following day.

He had a shifty look. 'I think your mother's horse has gone to pay for her keep.'

I took his neck in my hands. 'I will kill you with my bare hands unless you bring the horse to me.'

I let him go and he fell to the floor. Rising, and casting a terrified glance in my direction he rushed away. It seemed hours, maybe it was not, before he returned, leading the horse.

'The master says you are to have him for your mother.'

'I told you so.'

'I had to ask, Sir.'

'You thought to sell it yourself, you common cur,' I said, giving him a hard kick.

I felt the horse all over. He nuzzled me familiarly and I buried my head in his mane. I lay down beside the horse and slept, exhausted.

The following day I rose and immediately went in search of my mother. I found her pale and composed. I bent to kiss her.

She whispered. 'Be of good faith, Miles, do not despair. I am prepared for whatever is to come. I am innocent as you know, and I can only pray that justice will prevail, although as we both know, that is not always the case in these desperate times.' She turned to take the hand held out to help her on to her horse.

A crowd of villagers, many of them from Roughlee, Goldshaw Booth and other surrounding areas, stood silently as the cavalcade passed by. These were mainly illiterate peasants who did not understand what was happening. They were ignorant and willing to believe whatever stories they were told. Most of them were too young to remember the true faith. The stories of papists mingled with the stories of witchcraft until they seemed as one.

We passed through Whalley and rode on towards the Trough of Bowland, the scene of many happy hours for me when my father took me and my brothers fishing in the old days. As we passed the gates of Browsholme Hall, I knew my mother would be remembering, as I was, the happy times we had spent there when the Nutters were welcomed with the Nowells, Asshetons and Towneleys on feast days, and so on we rode.

178

When at last, after two overnight stays when my mother and I shared those last precious hours together, we arrived at the castle in Lancaster. We were met by Thomas Covell, the keeper. He was a powerful man, grown rich on the payments made to him by families prepared to pay for better treatment for their relatives. I knew I would have to approach him on mother's behalf. I was going to ask for Anne to be with my mother. Surely they would allow this?

The preliminaries over, I approached Covell. He agreed to house mother comfortably. I also mentioned the other unfortunates from Pendle. The Devices in particular. He said Roger Nowell was to see my mother with regard to their treatment. I found this curious, but did not prolong the conversation. I wandered blindly around the streets of Lancaster.

My mother's fortitude amazed me. Light shone from her eyes. I knew she was prepared for whatever came. Her crucifix hung quite openly round her neck and she fingered it constantly. I reflected on this. I was sure my mother was persuaded she was dying for her faith, and in a way, it was true, I thought. Charles was saved to continue the missionary work.

I remained in Lancaster for several days, and when I had done all I could to make life easier for her I asked to see her. I was shown into a room, bare but clean, Anne was with her. Mother was pale and composed. She bade me return to Roughlee, to my wife and children.

'Return for the trial,' she said, 'and I must have your promise you will not inform Charles, Christopher or Margaret of my plight. They can do nothing by rushing back here, and will only be in danger themselves.' I nodded mutely. Remembering that dreadful day, I feel the tears springing to my eyes and running down my cheeks, as they did then.

'Miles, dear, calm yourself. It is nearly over now, you are telling your mother's story,' said Ruth gently.

Margaret came over and pressed my hand. We are both grey haired, and lines of sadness show on our faces. 'We could have done nothing Miles, do not reproach yourself,' she said.

I find the writing of this chronicle harder as the days go by, but I force myself to finish. There is only I to tell. I was there, none of the others were. It is hard to bring back the agony of those days in Lancaster, but I will try.

On the 17th August 1612, I sat in the public gallery in the court room at Lancaster Castle, and heard the charges against the people standing there. I thought I was dreaming and that I would awaken and find it would not be true.

As well as my mother, the people in the dock had been known to me all of my life; dear Anne Redfern, my second mother, Jane Bulcock and Katherine Hewitt. The old crone Demdike, who had frightened me as a child as I passed her on the road, we children had called her a witch, little knowing the realities of the future, and we had hidden from her, and as children do, calling out names after her as she passed. She had died in the prison weeks before.

Elizabeth and Alison Device were standing there and James, poor Jamie, head lolling and his tongue, as usual, hanging out, he was simple, but harmless, however had Baldwin framed him, I thought.

Anne's mother, Mistress Whittle, known as Chattox, was also there, looking very frail, teeth chattering as always.

I could not understand, and still cannot, how these people came to be on trial at Lancaster. Even Jane Bulcock's son was there accused. I could not believe my ears when the charges were read out. I listened to the ridiculous allegations of witchcraft, and I watched as young Jennet, only nine years old, was lifted on to a table. I listened as she chanted, as if reciting nursery rhymes, what she could only have been taught. She was quite ignorant, unable to read or write. It must have taken many hours to school her, I thought wearily.

Judge Bromley heard the evidence against them. First Mistress Whittle was accused of killing Robert Nutter of Greenhead, many years ago. She cried, begging for mercy, saying she had wished him dead because he raped her daughter. She was told to be quiet, but rocked, crying still. Elizabeth Device was accused of killing Henry Mitton, helped by my mother. Young Jennet smirked as she stood on the large table, enjoying the attention. She cannot have known what she was doing, it was all a game to her. Elizabeth started to shriek and scream at her daughter and was led away.

Poor James. He was accused of killing Mistress Anne Towneley, of Carr Hall. This was news to me. I remember Mistress Towneley died young. Roger Nowell must have worked hard to find the names of those who had died young in Pendle Forest in the last twenty years.

I listened as James was accused of causing the deaths of John and Blaize Hargreaves, whom I vaguely remembered. There had been no suspicion attached to any of these deaths at the time, I knew. A great many people died young, aye and still do, I thought. Indeed my poor father had died young. There was disease aplenty in the district, and poverty which bred disease, and none were immortal.

I watched Anne as she was accused of killing Robert Nutter of Greenhead. She cried, saying he stole her mother's potion and drank it, and that he raped her. She was ordered to be silent.

Then my mother was brought to the front. Her whole demeanour haughty and her face unflinching, as she replied, 'Not guilty' to the charges against her.

I looked round wildly for some sign of defence for her. There was none. I stood up and demanded justice.

'They are all innocent,' I cried.

My mother turned her face towards me, and smiled, but I felt strong arms grip me and I was marched out of the court room. I must have fallen in a faint, as I remember someone leaning over me, wiping my brow and holding a cup of water to my lips. I tried to re-enter the castle, but the crowd was surging out, in a vast, sweaty, ugly pack. Words such as, 'when will they hang?' met my ears.

I fought my way through the crowd to the house of Thomas Covell. Giving my name at the door, I was shown into a large room where I had previously arranged my mother's comfort when she was first brought to Lancaster.

'What can I do for you now, Sir?' asked the portly, red-faced man.

'I could not stay in the court room, Sir, what has happened? What is the verdict?'

'Master Nutter, I am sorry to be the one to inform you that your mother has been found guilty and is sentenced to death by hanging.'

I must have swooned again. I recovered consciousness to find myself lying on a bench, Thomas Covell was holding a glass of water to my lips.

'Guilty? But how, why?' I whispered. 'She is not guilty of anything.'

'She has been found guilty of witchcraft,' he said.

'You know it isn't true,' I said weakly.

'I do not make the laws of the land, Sir, and I do not enforce them. I merely look after those who have fallen foul of the law, and I have seen to the comfort of your mother and her friends.'

'My mother is not a witch,' I screamed.

'Calm yourself, Sir. You do your mother no good by acting in a hysterical manner. Take my advice, keep calm, or you yourself may be indicted for some offence.'

I lay back and allowed him to place the glass to my lips again.

'Young man, have you a family?'

'Yes.'

'Then take my advice. Go home, see to your family. You can do nothing for your mother. She has told me she is prepared to die. Do not cause her distress by placing yourself in danger. These are difficult times. There is fear of the unknown, of the Spanish, of

Catholics, of everything, and your mother is a victim. She is not on her own. People die all the time for their beliefs, for their faith, whilst shielding others. She believes in God. She believes she will be reunited with your father. Let it be, young man, go home.'

I realised the truth of his words. 'Thank you Sir. You have been good to my mother and to the others.'

'I have made sure they have been dry and warm and that they have been well fed. Roger Nowell ordered things so.'

'Why should he trouble himself, he brought the charges. He could have stopped the case.' I said bitterly.

'He could not,' Covell replied. 'He was pressed by the Earl of Derby, who believes his own father died by witchcraft. If such a man believes, what chance have we?'

'Roger Nowell could have saved my mother,' I said bleakly.

'I doubt it. Hasn't your mother had brothers executed as priests?'

'She has, but what fault is that of hers?'

'Maybe it is thought she harbours Catholics.?'

'She was charged with witchcraft, not with harbouring priests.'

Covell looked at me sadly. 'Maybe there is no proof that she harboured priests, but that it is known she has done so in the past?'

'What are you suggesting Sir?' I asked.

'That there are reasons. Further than that I cannot say, but there are ways of dealing with people, and it is easy to prove a case of witchcraft under King James.'

I understood. It was as if a light suddenly shone bright. I turned to him.

'Are you of the true faith, Sir?'

'I was once, young Sir, but I cannot admit to it now. I have chosen my path, God forgive me. Do you understand?'

I understood, and he had been kind to my mother. I thanked him.

'Now, we will visit your mother, and you may say farewell.'

I followed him, again the long walk. Down a long passage, a flight of stairs. He opened a door and I rushed into my mother's arms. She held me close.

'Mother, how can you bear what is to be?' I cried.

'Miles dear, I do not have to bear the drawing and quartering such as my brothers bore. I feel in my heart I die for the cause also. After all Mary, Queen of Scots, in another way, was beheaded, for the cause. Do not be sad. I will be with your father Miles. I have not enjoyed life since he was taken from me. Although I love my children and grandchildren.

'I did not choose this end, it was chosen for me. I accept it. You must also. Take care of Ruth and the children. Take them to Reedley, away from wagging tongues. Christopher and Maria will stay at the Hall and care for it until a better time.'

'Yes, Mother, Christopher has always loved the Hall, but it will hold sad memories for him also, and for Maria,' I replied.

'Christopher will want to stay, Miles, to stand up to his father on his own ground. Let him take up the tenancy, Miles.'

'The mine, Mother! Shall I sell the mine to Christopher?'

There was a pause, a long silence. My mother looked at me, and I returned her gaze. A premonition came to me.

'What of the mine, Mother?'

'I have sold it to Roger Nowell.'

'How could you? When? When was the deed executed?'

'Oh, Roger saw to the matter. I assure you. He had an attorney in the prison before I could turn around. Suddenly it did not seem to matter, Miles. He promised better treatment for us all. He kept the promise. All these months my friends from Pendle have received good treatment also. Indeed Thomas Covell is not a bad man. Let Roger have the mine, I thought, much good may it do him. I will not discuss it further Miles. Now, how is the child Elizabeth had to Sellars?'

'Sellars has taken him to his home. He is well cared for,' I replied.

'What of Jennet?' she asked.

'She can starve,' I said grimly.

'No, Miles, do not let her starve. She is a child. She knows not what she has done. She was but an instrument. Promise me you will not let her starve.'

'I promise.'

The door opened, Anne came in. They clasped each other and Anne stared at me, unable to speak.

Mother spoke again, 'Please ask Thomas Covell to send for Doctor Gabriel again. He has been very kind.'

'I will.'

'He has promised me a potion for the morning of the execution. I shall be calm, but I fear for Anne. You must go now. Leave Lancaster. Try and persuade Tom to go with you, he can do no more for Anne. He is here somewhere, please take him with you.' My mother said with a sense of urgency, 'he was so happy when Anne was found not guilty of killing Robert Nutter and then when they found her guilty of killing Robert's father I thought he would collapse, please care for him Miles.'

'I did not hear the verdicts Mother, I was taken out of court. I did not know.'

'I saw you dear, you are too headstrong. Thank God you were not arrested. Now promise me you will not send word to Charles and Christopher until it is over.'

'I promise, but they will not forgive me.'

'They will, dear. Here is a letter I have written to them.'

Taking the letter, I turned blindly towards the door. The gaoler stood waiting. Turning again I held out my arms to my mother. We clung together and I kissed her for the last time.

The door clanged behind me and in the passage I met Tom. Not the Tom I knew. He was unkempt, his face ravaged with grief.

'You must come with me Tom, you can do no more. Do not distress yourself by staying for the execution.'

'I must,' he said, 'I must know where they lay the bodies.'

'You may not be told, Tom. Please come with me and have some food.' Suddenly, my thoughts were for someone else and I found strength.

Tom walked back to my lodgings with me, and inside, waiting, we saw the dear familiar figure of my godfather, Thomas Firber, waiting for us.

'I had to come, Miles, I had to be here when the verdict was given,' he said.

'Thank you, Sir,' I said. 'Tom insists on staying for the execution.'

'Unwise, Tom. Have you the strength, do you think?'

'Yes, I have the strength,'

'When did either of you eat?' Uncle Thomas asked.

'Long ago, it seems. I want Tom to have a meal before we leave him,' I said.

Tom and I forced ourselves to eat. Tom became more calm and I was relieved, as I had feared for his sanity.

'How is your mother?' Thomas asked.

'She is calm, Thomas, she feels she dies for her faith. They will hang her, you know.' I felt the tears coming again.

'And Anne, and Anne,' Tom Redfern sobbed.

'Maria and Christopher and their children are waiting for you in Roughlee, Tom, please return with us. Thomas Covell will send us word of the burial place, I promise you. Doctor Gabriel is to attend my mother and Anne before the execution. They would not want you to stay, please come with us.'

We persuaded Tom he could do no good by remaining at Lancaster and the three of us rode back to Roughlee. Leaving Tom at the Hall with Christopher, Maria and the children, I rode on to Bawle House. Aunt Sybil and Uncle William were there to welcome us. I was secure but wretched. We all prayed for my mother and the others. What else could we do? Life had to go on. I had a family who needed me.

On Thursday, 20 August 1612, those accused, known as the Pendle Witches, were taken from Lancaster Castle and publicly hanged. The fickle crowd, unknowing and uncaring, turned the day into a holiday.

Thomas Covell sent us word secretly of my mother's grave, and when my brothers and sister returned to Pendle Forest, we were able to say a mass over her resting place.

Charles lives in France and Christopher has settled in the Americas. He has a family we have never met. Perhaps some day, they or their descendants, will come to Pendle Forest, and will read my story, and know my mother was not a witch.

Bibliography

Catlow, Richard *The Pendle Witches*
Peel, Edgar and Southern, Pat *The Trials of the Lancashire Witches*
Neill, Robert *Mist over Pendle*
McGrath, P. *Papists and Puritans under Elizabeth I*
Haigh, C. *Reformation and Resistance in Tudor Lancashire*
Hibbert, Christopher *The English – A Social History*
Carman, Philip and Walsh, James *Martyrs of England and Wales*